"So, when this c
back to our regu
lives? Forget ab

Stefan leaned in then. Slowly, giving her a chance to pull away, to dodge.

Daria did neither.

And when his mouth, that mouth that could create that smile that melted her, came down on hers, the heat that had been building in her exploded, sending fire along every nerve.

She felt a moment of stunned shock. She'd lived forty-two years, some of it hard, some of it wonderful, but she had never in her life felt anything like this. Faint echoes of it, yes, and she'd thought that was all there was to it. But this...this was as if those prior feelings had been tiny candles leading to this impossibly deep, impossibly rich explosion of sensation.

And it was just a kiss...

* * *

The Coltons of Roaring Springs:
Family and true love are under siege

* * *

If you're on Twitter, tell us what you think of Harlequin Romantic Suspense!
#harlequinromsuspense

Dear Reader,

Some people love the ocean, some love lakes, some prefer wide-open spaces. Me, I love mountains. I don't have to be on them, but I'm happiest when I can see them. Perhaps it comes from having been born in a very flat place. But I was delighted to be asked to take part in the latest Coltons continuity series, especially when I learned it was set in a fictional Colorado mountain community.

It's always challenging, as a writer, to take characters and a story someone else has brainstormed and make them somehow my own. This one was especially so given that my heroine, Daria, is instrumental not just in her own story but in the entire series, and that she also had an already established history in the Colton annals. But as I thought about that history, and her current stressful job and situation, I realized that her home, what she chose to surround herself with, would give me the key. And so, even though it isn't shown until well into the story, Daria's home with a view of the mountains was my kick start. It makes her as happy as it would make me, and I was glad to give it to her. She needed that peace while dealing with this case that threatens to destroy the place she loves. And of course, adding sexy Stefan Roberts to her life was the best part!

I hope you enjoy her story, the penultimate book in the Coltons of Roaring Springs saga.

Justine

COLTON'S SECRET INVESTIGATION

Justine Davis

HARLEQUIN® ROMANTIC SUSPENSE

Special thanks and acknowledgment are given to Justine Davis for her contribution to the Coltons of Roaring Springs miniseries.

Recycling programs for this product may not exist in your area.

ISBN-13: 978-1-335-66221-7

Colton's Secret Investigation

This edition published by arrangement with Harlequin Books S.A.

For questions and comments about the quality of this book, please contact us at CustomerService@Harlequin.com.

Printed in U.S.A.

Justine Davis lives on Puget Sound in Washington State, watching big ships and the occasional submarine go by and sharing the neighborhood with assorted wildlife, including a pair of bald eagles, deer, a bear or two and a tailless raccoon. In the few hours when she's not planning, plotting or writing her next book, her favorite things are photography, knitting her way through a huge yarn stash and driving her restored 1967 Corvette roadster—top down, of course.

Connect with Justine on her website, justinedavis.com, at Twitter.com/justine_d_davis or on Facebook at Facebook.com/justinedaredavis.

Books by Justine Davis

Harlequin Romantic Suspense

The Coltons of Roaring Springs

Colton's Secret Investigation

Cutter's Code

Operation Midnight
Operation Reunion
Operation Blind Date
Operation Unleashed
Operation Power Play
Operation Homecoming
Operation Soldier Next Door
Operation Alpha
Operation Notorious
Operation Hero's Watch

The Coltons of Red Ridge

Colton's Twin Secrets

The Coltons of Texas

Colton Family Rescue

Visit the Author Profile page at Harlequin.com, or justinedavis.com, for more titles.

Chapter 1

She'd only capped off a few rounds, but Deputy Daria Bloom already knew her range score was going to suck. But she kept firing.

Fire.

A new missing girl.

Fire.

Bodies. Too many.

Fire.

Idiot media nicknames for monsters.

Fire.

Blue Eyes.

Fire.

Deputy Gates.

Fire.

Her mother.

Fire.

Stefan.

Fire. Fire. Fire.

She set down the Glock 19, still undecided whether the purchase had been worth it. She preferred her Springfield XD(M) because it fit her hands better. Her boss cut her some slack and let her carry the XD(M), since with it she was the best shot in the department. But the Glock was the official weapon of the sheriff's office, and so she had to qualify with it, as well.

At the thought of her boss, she would have fired another round if she hadn't already emptied the magazine. What if Trey Colton lost the election that was less than a week away now? She couldn't imagine working for someone else. Not to mention that if he didn't win, it would be so egregiously unfair. He was the best sheriff this county had ever had. But there was a serial killer still on the loose nearly ten months after the first body had been found, and the outcry was mounting. And while it was hardly Trey's fault, he was the public face of the department, so all the blowback hit him.

Daria pushed the button that brought the target silhouette back to her. She studied the pattern of holes. It wasn't as bad as she'd feared, but it wasn't pretty. She'd visited the ten ring a time or two, but otherwise she'd been wide and high. She smothered a sigh.

For a moment she went through the postshooting routine, focusing on every step as if she'd never done it before. She knew she was trying to stop thinking about everything that had crowded into her mind, throwing off her concentration. Her frustration about this case was uppermost, but a certain FBI agent was nearing the top of the list, as well.

And to think she'd been pleased when Trey had selected her to be the local liaison with the Bureau. But that was before she'd laid eyes on Stefan Roberts. In all his tall, broad-shouldered, hard-muscled glory. She'd never really thought of herself as a woman who would go for a younger man, but that guy would give any breathing woman pause. In a twisted sort of way that made her not particularly happy with herself, she was glad his domestic situation was a mess, because it had enabled her to get over the initial shock of this gorgeous creature and put him where he belonged.

In the "not interested in" category.

And yet in the three months they had been collaborating together, the man had turned her carefully controlled life upside down. He was as fiercely dedicated to this case as she was, and that made working with him easier than it could have been. He had also done what she'd been trying unsuccessfully to do for years—he'd unraveled the sad conclusion to her mother's story. She now had the history of Ava Bloom and knew the bravery her mother had shown. Thanks to Stefan.

He had done it as a favor to her. Without hesitation. And she couldn't describe how that had made her feel.

"Well, you qualified, but barely."

"I'm not done yet," Daria told the range master, who had appeared behind her. The man smiled at her. For a rather crusty old guy, Ray Ingersol could be nice sometimes.

"And with those words, wars are won," he said.

She smiled back at that. "I feel as if I'm in a war," she admitted.

"Awful stuff going on. Awful stuff."

She couldn't argue that. With a fresh target and a new magazine, she shut everything else out of her mind and imagined having this ruthless Avalanche Killer in her sights. And this time when the target came back, there were four holes in the ten ring—three small individual holes, and one big ragged one.

Ray gave a low whistle. "Eight through the same hole? That's some fine shooting, Deputy Bloom. I'm guessing you'll be wanting that one turned in as your qualifying score?"

"Turn them both in," she said as she gathered up her brass.

Ray's smile widened, and he gave her an approving nod. "Honesty. I like that. It's in short supply these days."

"Sadly true."

"Any closer on finding that maniac?"

"I think the official phrase is 'the investigation is ongoing.'"

Ray snorted inelegantly.

"My sentiments exactly," she agreed.

And she meant it. This case was beyond frustrating, for so many reasons. The obvious, of course—a deranged serial killer was destroying a town, both emotionally and economically, and here she was nearly a year later with no resolution—but also she felt as if she was letting Trey down. The sheriff had trusted her to get the job done when he'd had to recuse himself because the first suspect's body had been found on his cousin Wyatt's ranch, and there'd been an uproar about the Coltons getting preferential treatment. Which only made the load heavier, given her own personal history—which she had kept secret.

And then there was her gut certainty that Sabrina Gilford had not been a victim of their serial killer, which was just the cherry on top of this swirling mix. It was enough to give her nightmares, and in fact on occasion had.

Straighten up, girl—you didn't get to where you are

by quitting. Whoever, wherever this killer is, he's going down, and you're going to do it.

If he hadn't gone for the shaved head look some time ago, Stefan Roberts figured he'd be tearing his hair out about now.

"I won't go! I don't like it here. I don't like *you*!"

He stared at the five-year-old who was his son, standing there glaring at him with his arms crossed firmly across his small chest. He weighed his options. He could spend some more time trying to talk the child into going to school without a fuss. Except he was already running late for work. He could leave it for Mrs. Crane, the sitter he'd hired, to handle. But that seemed…cowardly somehow. He could pick the kid up and carry him out to the car. *And maybe stuff him in the trunk? That'd go over well.*

He sucked in a deep breath and fought for calm. Blowing up at his son would do no good at all, he was sure. He'd snapped at him a few times when he'd hit the end of his patience, and the boy had just closed off further.

"Look, Samuel, I know this wasn't your idea. You didn't want this. But we're here—we're stuck with each other. Can't you make the best of it?"

The glare only intensified. So once more, he'd apparently said the wrong thing. And his already frayed temper lost another thread. When he spoke it was with the rigidness of an anger barely held at bay.

"That's enough. You're going to school, Samuel. How you go is up to you."

Something shifted in the boy's dark eyes, so like his mother's. Something that was there and gone so quickly it was hard to pin a name on it. Had he been at work, he would have immediately registered it as fear, but he didn't want to believe his son was afraid of him. The massive changes in his life, sure. But him? He didn't like that idea at all.

But right now, he just had to get the boy out the door and to school. Mrs. Crane would see to him when school was out. He would have to talk to her, see if she had any ideas on how to deal with the rotten attitude Samuel seemed to have arrived with. But he didn't have time now. He had to get to work. Daria would be wondering where the hell he was. And he didn't want Daria Bloom mad at him.

Might be safer if she was.

He barely acknowledged the wayward thought. He was used to them by now. That day three months ago when he'd first walked into the sheriff's office and seen the deputy assigned to the case, he'd known this wasn't going to be routine. Working every day, in close proximity, to *that*? He'd known the first moment she turned those wide, beautiful, golden-brown eyes on him assessingly that this woman could be trouble. There wasn't a damned thing about her he didn't like, from the way that short, sleek haircut of hers bared the nape of her neck when she bent her head, to the way she moved, like a dancer he'd seen once back in Chicago.

Then again, he'd learned his lesson well; he'd been hot for Leah, too, and look how that had turned out. She hadn't had whatever it took to be married to an FBI agent, if that even existed. She'd been excited at first, but then the reality of long hours away and the stringent dedication that the job necessitated had settled in. When she'd gotten pregnant with Samuel, things had improved a little, but it hadn't lasted. By then she had bigger, grander plans for her future than being married to him.

And then it had fallen apart, and the son he loved so much had become a part-time presence in his life. He hated the fact, but between his work hours, Leah's lack of cooperation, and then his transfer, that's what had happened.

He shook off the thoughts; he needed to focus on the immediate issue, which was getting Samuel to school. In the end it took bribery—the promise of an extra bit of video-game time—but Stefan counted it as a win. At least the kid's favorite game was a fantasy instead of just blowing stuff up or shooting people. And as he finally headed off to work, he found himself smiling wryly that that was the most optimistic thing he could think of just now.

He called the field office to check in. It was a formality, since he'd been allocated to this case full-time until it was resolved. When he got to the sheriff's office and found Daria had not yet arrived, he felt a tiny bit of annoyance mixed with relief.

"She's at the range," the perky secretary they'd been assigned told him. Then, in a tone of confidentiality, she added, "She's the best shot in the department, you know. Some of the guys won't admit that, but she's outscored all of them at one time or another."

"Good to know," Stefan said drolly. "I'll try not to make her shooting mad at me." He was only half kidding. There was something about Daria Bloom that made him think she was not a woman to be crossed.

"Oh, she'd never shoot at *you*. That'd be like shooting at one of the local scenic wonders."

Stefan blinked. Was she flirting with him? She was, what, maybe twenty? He suddenly felt old.

"Now you're a scenic wonder?"

He nearly groaned aloud as the voice came from behind him. A voice he recognized too well, since the husky timbre of it sent the craziest tingle over his skin. But he put on his best unaffected grin as he turned to see the woman in question approaching.

"So's Denver International," he said, referring to the jaw-dropping airport structure voted the ugliest building in the state by half the population, the most beautiful by the other half. And to his inward delight, she laughed. It was rare enough with all the pressure on her right now that she even smiled, so he counted this as a win.

"Sorry I'm late. I needed to clean both weapons, so it took longer."

"Gotta keep the tools clean," he agreed. "I was running behind myself."

"Problem?"

"Only personal," he said with a slight grimace. She let it go without asking, and he appreciated that. He appreciated a *lot* about Daria.

She confirmed with the secretary, who was watching them with a little too much interest, that there were no messages she hadn't already gotten. They were turning to go to the office assigned solely to this case when the door behind them opened and Sheriff Trey Colton stepped through.

Trey was about Stefan's own height and had a no-nonsense air about him that Stefan liked. He was also, as far as Stefan could see, a fine sheriff. By the book and honorable and, up until this Avalanche Killer mess, nothing had happened to mar his stellar record. As the first African American to be elected sheriff, not to mention one of the youngest people ever to hold the office, he was clearly determined to keep it that way. And Stefan was glad to help. He'd had his own dragons to slay on his way to where he was now, so he could relate.

They gave him an update, not that there was much to report. Trey restated his complete faith in them, which made Stefan even more determined, and with a barely concealed grimace the sheriff went off to deal with today's round of media chaos.

Better him than me.

"He's actually much happier lately," Daria murmured as they said goodbye and headed down the hall.

"No thanks to us," Stefan muttered.

"I know. Or the election campaign," she added.

"I registered just so I could vote for him." He'd only been in Colorado for a couple of years, so there hadn't been a major election since his arrival.

"That's good of you," she said, sounding like she meant it.

"He's a good guy. I admire and respect him and the job he's done. And I'm glad if he's happier."

"Thank Aisha for that," Daria confided as they went into what they'd begun to call the Avalanche office. "Now that's a true love match."

"Not something I'd know much about," he grumbled, then regretted letting the words out.

"It's pretty obvious with them, isn't it? Besides, I happen to know she's loved him for years."

"She has?"

"Since they were kids in grade school."

Stefan's brow furrowed. "But they're only getting together now?" The couple had become engaged about the time he and Daria had begun to work together on this case.

"She didn't think he loved her, and she wasn't going to settle for less. So she made him prove he meant it. He had to make the first move."

She said it so approvingly even he couldn't miss it. "Obviously you agree with that."

"Yes. Completely. She had to be sure he felt the same."

He studied her for a moment. Told himself it not only wasn't his business, he didn't want to know. Because knowing more about this woman had so far only drawn him in deeper, and that spelled trouble. But the next thing he knew he was asking, anyway.

"Personal experience?" She gave him a sharp look. He put up his hands and remembered his earlier thought that this was not a woman to be crossed. "You just sounded so…positive."

Her expression changed to something more…he wasn't sure what. Damn, Daria was hard to figure out. "You really want to open those doors, mine and yours?"

Well, that was plain enough; if she talked about her past, she was going to ask about his. Fine with him—the bare bones of his situation were common enough, and he had it down to a sound bite. "Mine's easy. Married, she couldn't handle my job, divorced."

"I notice you left out the most important part."

He grimaced, wishing he'd never started this. "Love? I thought so. Not sure about her."

She studied him for a long moment before she said softly, "I meant your son."

He was glad his skin was dark enough she couldn't see what would be, judging from the heat he felt, a flaming blush. He couldn't remember the last time he'd blushed.

Maybe in the academy over a decade ago, when he'd missed a clue so obvious he'd felt humiliated.

"Yeah," he muttered. "Never mind. You're right. Don't open those doors."

Chapter 2

Unlike at the shooting range, there was only one reason Daria was having trouble focusing on the matter at hand right now, and his name was Stefan Roberts. He'd clammed up completely the moment she'd mentioned his son. And that bothered her.

She knew Stefan's son had just recently come to live with him full-time, but other than that he never spoke of young Samuel other than to say they'd had very little contact since the divorce and what there had been hadn't gone well. Most parents she knew were happy to talk endlessly about their kids. Her friend Fiona, with three boys, could go on forever. Yet Stefan never mentioned doing anything with the boy, or his interests, or even his existence. So she sensed things were not going well on that front.

As if this case isn't enough of a distraction, imagine trying to deal with it with a five-year-old at home.

She resolved to cut him some slack as they dived back into the case.

"This room," he said rather sourly as they closed the door on the office, "is starting to look like the lair of a lunatic."

She looked around at the whiteboards they'd wheeled in, covered now with photographs and names and locations and details, with a single, long timeline spanning them all. Those had been Stefan's idea—he said he'd always been able to work better with as much of the case as possible right in front of him all the time. She'd found it worked well for her, too.

"I can't argue that," she agreed. Nor could she argue the fact that his deep, rumbly voice did crazy things to her insides. Which made no sense at all.

"Worked a serial killer case in Rockford once. He had a room in his house that looked a lot like this. Only thing missing is the spiderweb of string he had pinned up, making up his elaborate conspiracy connections."

"Hmm," she said, looking from board to board.

"What?"

"Just wondering if a ball of yarn might help."

He laughed. He really did have a nice laugh to go with that deep, rumbly, sexy voice. And the rare grin that flashed with it was…well, breathtaking. "You got one around?"

"Not here," she said. "I have a stash at home."

He lifted a brow at her. "You hoard yarn?"

She put on her best snooty voice. "It's not hoarding, Agent Roberts. It's therapy."

He gave another chuckle. "What do you do with it?"

"Knit." He blinked. "And before you say anything

derogatory, keep in mind knitting involves two very pointy tools."

"I just...never pictured you as the knitting type."

"What you don't want to picture is me without it. Other people count to ten to hold on to their temper. I count stitches."

"Point taken. Er, no pun intended."

"Too bad," she retorted. "It would have been a good one."

And suddenly they were both laughing. And it was the most amazing feeling she'd had in a long time. That they could laugh amid what was going on was probably a bit macabre, but she couldn't deny it felt good.

"Thanks," he said. "I needed that."

"Me, too. So, shall we get back on the merry-go-round?"

As had become habit now, they went through it all again. They'd done it so often they both had every step of the investigation practically committed to memory. But this was her first case anywhere near this magnitude, and Daria was determined to justify Trey's faith in her.

They went over what little they had on the newest missing girl. They knew little except that she was from Denver, had been gone a week longer than expected and resembled the other victims. It wasn't even certain yet that she was a victim of their quarry. But the resemblance was there, so they factored her in, although as of now she was in the category of "possible."

Others were searching for her as an active missing person, and Daria sent up an earnest hope that she was found alive—and not simply because another victim would ratchet up the pressure on them.

"Blue Eyes," Stefan muttered when they finally reached the newest bit of information they had.

"Helpful, huh?" Daria deadpanned.

"More than we had before," he said. He turned to the laptop that was now booted up on the table in the center of the room. He tapped a couple of keys, and the recording she'd heard at least a dozen times played again. She listened to Lucy Reese, aka Bianca Rouge, tell her friend Candace—who had unexpectedly turned out to be the mother of the baby left on Fox Colton's doorstep—that her date had passed out drunk, so she was down in the hotel bar and had connected with an older guy who was "still hot." She had cheerfully referred to him as Blue Eyes and ended with a promise to see Candace later.

A promise she had been unable to keep.

It still gave her chills to listen to that rather ordinary message, given in such normal, even happy tones, by a woman who would soon be dead.

"I don't think I'll ever get used to that," she said.

"Used to what?"

Sighing, she looked at Stefan. "Hearing her sound so happy and chipper. It's still distressing to listen to, knowing what happened to her."

"Don't ever get used to it," Stefan said quietly. "If you ever get to the point where you can hear that, knowing, and not be distressed, it's time to walk away."

She hadn't expected that. Sometimes this man surprised her. There were depths to Stefan Roberts that he kept hidden. It occurred to her to wonder if that might be part of the problem with his son, if he kept his feelings so masked the boy didn't know how he felt, but she quickly pushed the thought away. It was, she reminded herself again, not her business.

An hour later they exchanged a glance, and both sighed at the same moment. He gave a low chuckle. "No sense putting it off any longer."

"Agreed. Frame by frame this time?"

He nodded. He adjusted the settings on the video player on the laptop while she grabbed the remote and turned on the flat screen. This was going to take hours upon hours, she knew, going through all relevant feeds and angles of the security video from the hotel one frame at a time, but they'd so far been unable to find anything at all, even in slow motion, and this was their last shot.

"What do you want to start with?" he asked.

"The elevator lobby," she said. "We know Bianca at least was upstairs first."

He nodded and called up the video. It was already at the point where they had spotted Bianca coming out of elevator two. The timing coordinated with the message she'd left Candace, which was how they'd located this moment when she had come out of the elevator after leaving her drunken, passed-out client up on the third floor.

It was slow work. By utilizing some facial recognition software Stefan had access to, they had managed to track Bianca from the elevator across the lobby. Daria felt like calling her Lucy, because that's who she really wanted to get justice for, the girl she'd once been who had found her way into this life for reasons they hadn't yet uncovered.

Bianca had been headed in the general direction of the bar off the main lobby, but as far as they had been able to tell, she had not appeared in any video of the bar itself. So they now set themselves to going second by second, looking at every figure in the busy lobby, as far into the background of the video as they could see. They made notes of clothing to compare with other shots, anything that looked even vaguely similar to what Bianca had been wearing.

They studied any exchanges between men and women, taking notes again on clothing and any other distinguishing characteristics, on the theory that any man in the lobby could have been the one she connected with, and that he might have tried to pick up another woman before Bianca. And just because her message to Candace had mentioned the bar didn't necessarily mean she'd met him in there.

She and Stefan had spoken little, but she'd found it interesting. Since they couldn't see eye color on the videos, they'd given up trying to eliminate on that basis. Especially after, when she wearily suggested they just look at blonds for a while, Stefan smiled wryly and said, "I've got a cousin who's darker than I am and has the bluest eyes you've ever seen."

"I was kidding," Daria said. "But I'll bet your cousin is striking."

"She's gorgeous."

Well, that doesn't seem fair. Two of them in the same family? She yanked herself back to the matter at hand, although her next thought grew right out of that.

"That brings up the other issue," she said.

"You mean her description of the guy?"

Daria nodded. Bianca had referred to the man she was meeting as handsome. They'd each pointed out men in videos to look more closely at, but after a couple of startled looks at each other over their selections, they laughed again.

"I defer to your female judgment," Stefan said with a grimace. "Obviously I have no clue."

"Different things are attractive to different women," she replied. "But I'm not sure that applies in Bianca's case. For her...job, she'd be looking for the ones who perhaps couldn't get any woman in the room with a look."

"You mean not the glamour guys, the movie-star types?"

"I mean," she said, risking a grin at him, "guys who don't look like you."

He looked taken aback. She knew it couldn't be at her assessment of his looks—after all, the guy had to look in a mirror now and then. He had to know he was way beyond handsome. Was it that she dared to tease him?

She shrugged. "I figured we'd been working together long enough now I could rib you a little. Sorry if I was out of line."

"I...no. I just didn't think you...thought that."

It was her turn to blink. "What, you didn't think I noticed? I'm not blind, Roberts."

He looked at her for a long, silent moment. Let his gaze slide from her head to her toes. "Neither am I," he said softly.

And that quickly he turned it around on her. Daria's breath jammed up in her throat. She knew she could clean up nice, and when she took the time and trouble in, say, formal wear, she was attractive enough. But on duty she was all business. She'd set her course when she'd first been hired on here four years ago, and any guy who tried to flirt with her on the job was quickly chilled by her lack of response.

She had, with some nudging from Trey, gone out a few times with one of his closest friends, fellow deputy

Keith Parker. Dates that were perfectly nice but utterly lacking in chemistry. And they had both quickly agreed they were much better off as friends, especially since they had to work together.

Which did not explain why she'd said what she'd did just now. It couldn't be simply that Stefan was from outside the department. Or that he was quite possibly the most luscious male she'd encountered in a long time, let alone spent any appreciable time with. Could it?

Since she had no answers, and couldn't think of anything to say that wouldn't get her in deeper, she simply went back to work.

On and on they went. Finding nothing. Only when her back began to ache—a rare occurrence for her, since she was determinedly in tip-top shape—did Daria finally glance at the time.

"Whoa," she said, startled.

Stefan, who had been as intent on the task as she, looked up from the screen. She guessed, by the way he blinked, then rubbed at his eyes, that they were as dry and weary as hers were.

"It's after eight," she said.

He blinked again, and apparently as disbelieving as she had been, glanced at his watch.

"Damn. I've got to make a call."

"And I've got to answer a call," she said. "I'll be in the ladies'."

Her way of putting it earned her another brief flash of that grin. But when she came back, there was no sign of the amused man she'd left.

"Problem?" she asked.

"Yeah. Look, I know we've got a long way to go yet

on this stuff, but…my sitter has to leave. And I can't leave Samuel alone."

"I should think not," Daria said, imagining all the trouble a five-year-old could get into left to his own devices. "So…you want to call it a night?"

"No, I don't, not when we've got so much more to get through. But…look, I know it's a lot to ask, but I've got a setup like this in my home office. It wouldn't take much to pick up right where we left off there."

Warning bells went off in Daria's head. No way did she want to be in a nice, homey environment with this man. But as she looked at him—once she managed to stop dwelling on his strong jaw, broad shoulders and narrow hips—she realized he was more than a little frazzled. He would likely be so worried about his boy that he wouldn't be thinking about…what she was thinking about. And couldn't seem to stop thinking about.

Just because you think he's the hottest thing that's ever walked these mountains doesn't mean he feels the same about you, idiot. And even if he did, it would not only be inappropriate, it would be downright stupid. For you, anyway.

"Fine," she said abruptly. "I'd like to finish this tonight."

"Thanks," he said, and it sounded so heartfelt she felt even sillier for her own thoughts.

And she shoved them back into that "not interested" box.

Chapter 3

Mrs. Crane couldn't leave fast enough. After a quick report that Samuel had refused to eat dinner or quit playing his video game or go to bed, she was gone. Stefan noticed Daria looking around the house with interest, but he couldn't read her reaction to his place in her expression. He wasn't sure if maybe he should be glad of that.

But right now he shouldn't be thinking about that. He shouldn't be thinking about Daria at all, but about the rebellious kid who had landed on him. He walked over to where the boy was indeed glued to his video controller, his eyes on the screen. He didn't even look up when Stefan came in. And not for the first time, Stefan thought he should never have hooked the system up to the big TV. He'd foolishly thought of it as a peace offering.

He walked over to the couch. "Way past your bedtime."

The boy didn't even look up from his game.

"Come on, Samuel. Shut it down."

Again the boy ignored him.

"He's almost to the big castle. He can't stop now." Stefan turned to stare at Daria. Even Samuel looked up, startled. "Watch out, there's a zombie!" she warned the boy, who quickly went back to the game, and with a couple of button presses, the stiffly walking, sickly-green creature was gone.

"Nicely done," Daria said. "Now, when you get to the castle wall, it's time to come have something to eat before bed. Got it?"

"Yeah," Samuel said, focused on the game but still responding.

And to Stefan's shock, when the game seemed to pause at the foot of a soaring stone wall, Samuel closed it and put down the controller.

"Have you encountered the dragon yet?" Daria asked the boy conversationally as they walked toward the kitchen. Stefan followed, suddenly feeling like a bystander in his own house.

"Not yet," Samuel said.

"Ohhhh, you wiiill," she said in an over-the-top creepy voice that made Samuel laugh. Stefan was gaping now; he hadn't seen his son laugh since he'd been here.

Then the boy looked at her curiously. "Who are you?"

"My name is Daria. I'm working with your dad for a while."

The boy's expression changed, became something wary. "Oh."

"You don't like that," Daria said. "Why?"

"My mom worked with someone. An' he doesn't like me. So she sent me away. Now I'm stuck here."

Daria glanced at Stefan, and he felt his jaw tighten involuntarily.

"Well, I like you, so no problem," she said to Samuel cheerfully. "What do you want to eat?"

The wariness faded from the boy's expression. And Stefan had the niggling thought that he should be paying attention.

"I don't know," Samuel said. "There's never anything good here."

"Really? Nothing?"

"It's all this fancy stuff."

"Not even a good burger, huh?" Daria sympathized.

"No."

"Maybe we should just look and see if there's anything we can make edible."

"What's edi—ed…what you said?"

"It means you can eat it without gagging," she said in a loud whisper.

And again the boy laughed. Stefan gave a slow, wondering shake of his head. *I should definitely be paying attention here. How does she* do *that?*

Daria was looking at him questioningly. He realized she was seeking some reaction from him, probably to her taking over. "Don't stop now," he muttered.

And then she was in his kitchen. Looking in the refrigerator. She ignored the leftover Szechuan takeout he'd had last night and figured they would eat later while working, and if she noticed the six-pack of beer—well, five-pack, now—on the top shelf, she ignored it. She poked into the deli drawer, then looked over her shoulder at him.

"Bread?" she asked.

Afraid to say anything for fear of setting Samuel off

again, he walked over to the small pantry and got out the half loaf that was in there.

"Good," she said. "Samuel, do you know where a skillet is?"

Stefan blinked, since it was hanging on a rack practically in front of her, opened his mouth to answer, then shut it again.

"Silly, it's right there," Samuel said, grinning and pointing.

"Why, so it is. Good eyes, my friend."

She'd done it on purpose, Stefan realized. She was bringing Samuel into the conversation in a way he never would have thought of. And the boy was responding, right before his eyes.

"Now if only we had some butter, we could have a mega grilled cheese sandwich."

Looking intrigued, Samuel trotted into the kitchen and pointed at a covered dish on the counter. He was tall for his age, but not quite tall enough to reach it. "It's in there."

"Then we're a go." She reached up for the skillet, unhooked it and handed it to the boy, who looked beyond startled. "Go set that on a front burner for me, will you? Don't turn it on yet, though. I have to get the stuff ready."

"'Kay."

With exquisite care, Samuel carried the skillet over and set it down as she'd instructed. Stefan was leaning against the opposite kitchen counter now, watching in complete fascination.

"Good job," Daria said. "But do you see a problem?"

"No."

"Back up a little." The boy did so. "Now walk toward me."

He started to do as she'd said. Then, suddenly, just before his face would have collided with the protruding skillet handle, he yelped, "Oh!" Samuel reached and moved the skillet so the handle wasn't sticking out.

"Wow, you figured that out quick," Daria said. And Stefan felt the strangest sensation somewhere in his chest as his son beamed at her. He'd been wrestling with the boy for a month now, and she had charmed him in fifteen minutes flat.

Not only that, but when she'd finished preparing the thick, melted cheese sandwich, the boy gobbled it down, along with a big glass of the milk Samuel had looked at scornfully when Stefan had offered it to him.

"Now, let's get you to bed, so you can be all rested up to attack tomorrow."

The boy seemed to like the way she put it and happily headed into the bathroom next to his bedroom to brush his teeth. Daria stood in the doorway, saying, "Look at you—you don't even need a step stool, you're so tall. Are you sure you're not six or seven?"

Samuel gave her a toothpaste-laden grin. And just to further emphasize the difference, he jumped into bed happily. Daria pulled the covers up over him as she said, "Kind of a big bed, huh?"

"Too big," Samuel muttered, so low Stefan almost couldn't hear it. He frowned. A bed was a bed, wasn't it? If you fit in it, what did it matter how big it was?

Well, unless you had someone like Daria in it with you.

He could feel the pressure on his teeth telling him just how hard he was clenching his jaw to make sure he didn't say anything even vaguely like what he had just thought.

"I see you've got some fun books there," she said,

sitting on the edge of the bed as she gestured at the two colorful books on the nightstand.

"They're dumb," Samuel pronounced. "For babies. Teacher reads it to us. 'The cat chased the mouse.' What kind of story is that?"

"I see. I guess you'd better learn to read yourself in a hurry so you can get into the good stuff."

For the first time, Samuel glanced at his father. "You mean like the boring stuff he reads?"

Daria didn't look at Stefan. She was fixated on his son as if he were the most interesting person in her life. "Boring, huh? What doesn't it have that it should?"

Samuel thought, his brow furrowed. "Dragons. Maybe spaceships. Or a cool dog, not a silly cat."

"Hmm," Daria said, and she pulled out her phone. "I might just be able to help you there."

Stefan couldn't see what she was doing from here, but he was afraid to move from the doorway and shatter the mood. Plus, he was feeling decidedly extraneous, unnecessary. Add to that the realization that was dawning that he'd never quite thought of his son as a person with opinions and ideas of his own, and he was feeling like a complete failure. *Again.*

He watched as Daria held out her phone for Samuel to see. "Maybe a dog like that?"

"Yeah!"

"Well, I just happen to have his story right here. Want to hear how it starts?" The boy nodded excitedly. "Okay," Daria said. "But you have to listen with your eyes closed, so you can imagine the story in your mind better."

Obediently, Samuel's dark eyes closed.

She swiped a finger across the screen, obviously opening what was a reading app. And then she began to read in a low, pleasant voice. But when she got to dialogue, her voice took on a different tone for each character, making it come even more alive.

Stefan found even he was caught up in the story of a lost dog looking for home. And when she stopped what seemed like a very short time later, he realized he was waiting for Daria to begin again. But instead she brushed her fingers gently over Samuel's cheek, stood up and stuffed her phone back into her pocket. Only then did Stefan realize his son was fast asleep.

"You're a miracle worker," he said softly when she had crossed the room to the doorway.

"It didn't take that much."

More than I've got, apparently.

He backed out into the hallway and stood there, still a little in shock, as Daria pulled the door closed behind her. Well, almost closed; she left it open about an inch. When he reached for the knob to close it the rest of the way, she looked at him curiously.

"Don't you leave it open a little so you can hear him in the night, if he needs anything?"

In fact, he had not. It had never occurred to him. He had looked upon the closing of that door as a sign they had survived another day, and usually felt a sense of relief that made him also feel guilty.

"I...didn't think of it. We used to, when he was a baby, but I didn't think— Damn, I suck at this," he muttered.

Turning away, he headed down the hall, embarrassed that she'd seen him at his most...ineffective. She followed him into the den, where he powered up the laptop and began to set it up to mirror onto the flat screen that was actually bigger than the one at the office.

"The first time you shot for a score, was it perfect?"

He stopped, wondering where that had come from. Looked over his shoulder at her. "Of course not. I'd never shot at a target before."

"Exactly."

"What?"

"You didn't expect to be a crack shot the first time, so why expect to be dad of the year when you've only just jumped back into the parenting pool?"

He blinked. "I…never thought of it like that. I mean, he's five, and…"

"You said you hadn't had much contact since the divorce?"

"No. And what we had was…strained."

"And you've been on your own for a couple of years now, so in essence, you're starting over. Building from scratch, and that takes time."

Stefan looked at his watch, not realizing why until the thought formed in his head. In the space of less than half an hour, Daria Bloom had both charmed his son and made Stefan himself feel so much better in the process.

"Miracle worker," he said, "doesn't even begin to describe it."

Chapter 4

Daria tried to focus on the screen as they laboriously went through the security video as promised, frame by frame, but her mind kept drifting back down the hall to where a little boy slept. He was a sweet kid who was just feeling helpless right now, ripped out of the life he knew and plunged into another world. A world that clearly hadn't ever had him in mind. No wonder he was snarly. It was self-preservation. Especially if what he'd said was true—that some man in his mother's life didn't like him and so he was discarded. At least her own mother had had no choice. She couldn't imagine what it would have felt like to know she just hadn't wanted her child.

And even more disconcerting, she kept looking up and finding Stefan watching her. Something in his eyes unsettled her.

"Problem?" she finally asked.

"Sorry," he said with a slight shake of his head. "I just

can't get over how you handled Sam. Samuel." He said it in the tone of a self-correction. When she gave him a curious look, he shrugged. "His mother insists on Samuel."

"What does *he* want to be called?"

Stefan glanced toward the hallway, then said rather sheepishly, "I don't know. I never asked him." He gave another, more definite shake of his head. "I never thought to talk to him the way you did."

"I gathered. Talk to him, Stefan, not at him. And more important, listen to what he says. He needs to know he's got your full attention, and not only when you're correcting him. He needs to believe he matters to you."

"Of course he matters." He ran a hand over his head. And let out a long, weary breath. "I remember when he was born. I was going to be the greatest dad ever. I'd had my own father for an example, you know?"

She smiled at him. "Siblings?" she asked.

"Three." His mouth quirked. "All sisters, after me."

"Oh, lucky them," she teased, but also meaning it. "A strapping big brother to look out for them."

He gave her an odd look. "That's exactly what my dad said when I hit about twelve. That it was my job, too, to watch out for them."

"You're close, you and your dad?"

He looked sad again. "We were. But… I couldn't…" Another long breath. "My folks have been married for thirty-five years. And they're still crazy about each other. They live in Florida now. My dad still treats my mom like a queen, and she thinks he hung the moon. But I couldn't even keep that going for five years, let alone thirty-five."

The moment he finished, she could tell he regretted saying all that. Essentially admitting that he felt like a failure for the destruction of his marriage. In the weeks they'd worked together, he'd rarely spoken of anything personal, so this was a switch. She wondered if he shared those feelings with anyone. And if, as she guessed, he didn't, what it must feel like to keep all that bottled up inside.

Asks the woman who has plenty of secrets of her own to keep?

"What about Sam? Does he have any contact with them?"

"Not much." He grimaced. "My ex saw to that."

"Well, I guess you can fix that now, can't you?" He gave her a startled look, as if he hadn't thought of that. "Your mom sounds like the kind of grandmother any boy would love. They'd probably both welcome the chance to help if you sent up a flare."

"I…you're right. Two of my sisters have kids, and they're really close to them."

"So there's some help." She frowned. "Who's the guy who didn't like him?"

Stefan's expression hardened. "His mother's fiancé."

"Oh. Ouch."

"And he doesn't just not like him, he hates him. Gave her an ultimatum. Get rid of him or the wedding's off."

Daria's eyes widened as she looked at him in utter astonishment. "His mother is marrying someone who would make an outrageous demand like that, and who feels that way about her own child?"

"Yeah, well, Leah's always had a…calculating streak."

"What is he, rich?" Daria asked.

"And connected. She's an event organizer, and he moves in all the right circles."

"No wonder your son is angry. He has every right to be."

He stared at her for a moment. And then he closed his eyes and shook his head. "I never thought of it like that, either. From his point of view."

"You probably haven't had time," she said, trying to be understanding. "Just trying to organize childcare is a pain, with this case ongoing. And you had to get him into school in a rush, so it's no wonder you haven't had a chance to fix up his room or connect with other parents."

He blinked. "What? What's wrong with his room?"

"It's fine…for a grown-up. But a kid needs his own stuff, needs things he likes around him, so he feels at home. And," she added, "a smaller bed."

Something flashed in those striking light brown eyes, something that made her wonder what he was thinking. But he only said, "I heard you say that. What difference does it make?"

"The difference between feeling lost in a place too big for you and safe in your own little shelter."

It was a moment before he leaned back in the desk chair he sat in. She'd noticed early on he had the seat set a good three inches higher than a normal seat, to accommodate his height. Her feet probably wouldn't even touch the floor.

"How do you know all this? You said you'd never had kids."

She felt the old, painful pang. "No. Nor will I ever, biologically. Doctors told me that long ago." She'd had years to get used to the idea, but that didn't stop her from feeling sad about it now and then.

"I'm sorry. You're obviously great with them," he said, and there was a note of genuineness in his voice that she appreciated.

"I have friends with kids," she answered evenly. "In

fact, my best friend has three boys, including twins about Sam's age." She purposely chose the name the boy's mother didn't like, felt a small pleasure in doing it and didn't care at the moment if it was petty. "I've been around them and babysat them since they were born."

"So…tell me what all I need to do. Besides a smaller bed."

"You might not like it."

"I just want *him* to like it."

She heard the undertone of desperation in his voice. He did truly love his son—he just didn't know him. And she doubted she or anyone could have done much better under the circumstances.

"All right," she said. "You want my opinion? There's no place for a kid here, not even a yard, and it's obvious. It looks like the proverbial bachelor pad."

His gaze darted away, and he said uncomfortably, "Yeah, I was kind of going for that, after the divorce."

"Do you still like it?"

"Actually… I never really did. I was kind of reeling, and it was just…"

"A declaration?"

His mouth quirked. "I guess."

"You need furniture a kid can get on, even climb on, without being afraid of hurting it or getting it dirty. He needs books, toys, maybe a stuffed animal to hug at night, although he'd probably deny it. And more playing room—another reason for the smaller bed—and pictures of what he likes."

Again he ran a hand over his head. "I don't even know what he likes."

"He likes that video game. Find some stuff about it—it's everywhere. He likes grilled cheese sandwiches, like most kids, and I'm sure your Szechuan is way too spicy for him. Kids have simple tastes at that age. Peanut butter and jelly isn't just a cliché. And," she added with a grin, "he likes dogs better than cats."

"Well, we're in agreement there," Stefan said with a wry laugh.

"Think about that, then."

"What?"

"A dog."

Stefan blinked. "You mean…get one? I don't even have time to take care of Samuel, and you want to add a dog into the mix?"

"I didn't mean tomorrow," she said with a laugh. "But maybe take a trip over to Max Hollick's place. The K-9 Cadets program. He's got a bunch of puppies there for training. And since they're all already spoken for, you won't be confronted with Sam insisting on taking one home. But you can see how he is with them, see if you think it would be worth it."

"That…makes sense," he admitted. "As long as he knows we can't do it now."

"Maybe when this case is over." She grimaced. "If it *ever* is."

"It will be," he promised. "But not if we don't get back to work."

"Yeah. Right."

They went back to the frame-by-frame analysis of the security videos. They enlarged each frame in quarters to get a closer look at people in the background, looking for even a slight resemblance to Bianca. Daria had begun this by looking for the dress she'd been wearing, but Stefan had pointed out she could have changed at any time. He'd rather offhandedly mentioned a witness he'd once had, also a "working girl," who'd told him she always carried a change of clothes with her in case something happened to what she was wearing. Like an extra-energetic client.

Daria had turned away as heat rose in her cheeks at his words. Unlike Stefan, if she blushed it would show beneath her lighter brown skin. Not, she thought, that he likely ever blushed. He'd probably seen too much, and he'd said that so casually. She didn't want him thinking she was so green that such things embarrassed her, but in fact her county was usually a calm, quiet place, and she'd never encountered a case like this one before. Thank goodness.

It was nearly midnight and Daria's eyes were burning when Stefan finally leaned back and rubbed at his own eyes, then shook his head. "I've had it," he muttered.

"Me, too," she agreed.

"I could be looking right at Bianca or our killer and it wouldn't register."

"Fresh start tomorrow?" she suggested, and he nodded. "I'll mark the spot where we left off."

"Maybe back it up to a half hour ago," he said wryly. "I think that's when my brain checked out."

"Done," Daria replied. She shut down the laptop; it was technically sheriff's department property, so she'd take it with her. As they left the den, she glanced toward the hallway. "You'll work it out with him, Stefan," she said quietly. "Give it time."

"Time? Took you less then half an hour to get more out of him than I have since he got here."

"I have more practice," she said with a smile.

He walked her out to her car, and she guessed from the way her breath made vapor that it was at or below freezing.

"Welcome to November," she muttered. "Why aren't

you shivering?" He'd come outside in just his long-sleeved shirt, whereas she had on her jacket and was still cold.

"This is nothing. Add a little northeast wind off the lake for some lake-effect snow, and you'd have a mild Chicago winter," he said.

"Humph. I'm from California. I'll never get totally used to this."

"There are ways to stay warm."

She was sure he didn't mean that as a double entendre, so she quashed her instinctive reaction. And he looked as if he regretted saying it anyway, so she turned back to what she knew was his biggest concern.

"Look, I know with work, and especially right now, it's impossible, but Sam's going to need kids to play with. Not to be critical, but Mrs. Crane doesn't seem the type to bend and get down on his level."

"No, she's not," he admitted. "But she was the only one available on such short notice." He grimaced. "Leah called me on a Friday and said he'd be flying in on Sunday."

Daria blinked. "Two days' notice?" He nodded. And her already low opinion of his ex dropped another notch. "I won't ask why on earth you got married in the first place, but..."

"She thought the job was glamorous, I guess. Exciting. Didn't realize it's mostly grunt work. And I..." He frowned. "Let's just say she's gorgeous. And can be quite charming, when it suits her purposes. We eloped after three weeks."

Daria managed not to comment on that. Instead she asked, "Do you have legal custody now?"

He sighed. "No. She just sent him."

Her mouth curled. "I'd want to make it all legal so

she can't yank him back if she changes her mind. I can't imagine anything worse for a five-year-old than being tugged in two like that."

"I would, if I was at all sure this was going to work."

At first she winced inwardly. Would he really send the boy back under these circumstances? But he sounded so exhausted she thought she understood; it was all just too much right now.

"Why don't I call my friend Fiona? She lives less than a mile from here. You could set up a playdate with her boys, see how they all get along. And if it works, make it a regular thing."

Stefan stared at her. "I…you'd do that?"

She gave him a puzzled look. "Of course I would. And Fiona is always looking for kids for her boys to hang out with. She's also big on them playing outside whenever they can. They've got a huge backyard with a sandpit and an amazing play set her husband built, with ladders and a slide and a fort up top, and all kinds of things for the boys to wear themselves out on."

"Sounds like five-year-old heaven."

"It is," she said with a laugh. "It's a built-in babysitter and gets them away from screens. She never leaves them alone, mind you, but she can be out there and read or garden or do other things at the same time. Until winter—then she's out there building snow things with them. She and the boys made a dragon once that was amazing. Shall I call her?"

"Please," he said.

"First thing tomorrow," she promised.

"Thank you," he said, with such relief in his voice it made her smile up at him. And in the next instant, before she even realized what was happening, his arms came around her in a fierce hug.

It was a thank-you, she told herself. That's all. Just thank you for help with a situation he was having trouble with. But repeating it didn't help much when her heart was hammering and her skin sizzled at the contact with that broad, strong chest. And there she was, the woman who had been cold enough to shiver mere moments ago, suddenly overheating as if it were midday LA in the summer. All because this man had hugged her? She must be—

Her self-accusatory thoughts broke off suddenly as something else registered.

Hers wasn't the only heart that had suddenly started racing.

Chapter 5

Uh-oh.

Stefan heard the warning in his head quite clearly. Crazily, his first thought was a memory from so long ago he couldn't be sure exactly when it was, except that he'd been a kid, at his grandparents' home, working on one of the endless jigsaw puzzles that were his grandmother's passion. He'd always figured the urge to put the pieces of a crime together had come from her, since often it was the same sort of puzzle, with a ton of tiny pieces that all had to fit together.

It wasn't any of his grandmother's puzzles he was remembering now, however. It was the burst of satisfaction when a piece he'd tried fit. When it turned out to be right. When it slid into place perfectly.

Daria Bloom in his arms felt that way.

And that scared the hell out of him.

So why wasn't he letting go? Why wasn't he backing off? Why was he still standing here, holding her tight against him, letting his body wake up in a way he hadn't felt since…he couldn't remember when?

Because it feels good. Too damned good.

With more effort than it ever should have taken, he released her and stepped back.

"Drive carefully," he said, as if that hug had never gotten out of hand. As if he hadn't been standing there savoring the scent of her, the feel of her luscious curves against him. As if he hadn't barely been able to resist the urge to tilt her head back and claim those lips with his own.

For a moment she just stood there, looking a little stunned.

"I…will," she said, sounding like someone who had momentarily forgotten how to speak.

He watched her drive off. Reminded himself that she was tough, smart, careful and highly trained, so there was no reason for him to feel like he should be seeing her home. Not that he had any choice in the matter. Not with Samuel—Sam—asleep inside.

He realized he was standing out here in near-freezing air, staring after a car that was long out of sight. He went back in the house and made his way down the hall, careful to walk quietly. He peeked in the door of his son's room. Or, rather, the guest room his son was using.

Guest room. And the truth of what Daria had said swept over him. Samuel felt like a guest—in other words, temporary. And that was his fault, for not thinking about this from the boy's point of view.

Stefan eased the door open and went into the room. The light from the hallway cast just enough light to see his way to the bed. He sat down on the edge and looked at the child curled up there. Realized the truth of what Daria had said—he looked tiny and helpless in the big expanse of the king-size bed he'd bought on the chance that someday his folks might come to visit.

He reached out and gently cupped his son's face, taking the time for the first time since he'd arrived to really look at him, to acknowledge that this little boy was the same baby he'd held in such wonder, the same miracle that had filled his heart near to bursting. His, a part of him, yet a unique individual.

When he got up, even though it was late, he settled in with his tablet and started a search for kid's furniture.

Daria was proud of herself. She'd gotten up and ready and all the way to the station without letting the memory of that hug last night invade her mind. True, it had been a battle, but by the time she'd settled in with the videos to pick up where they'd left off, she thought she'd beaten it back. Of course, the moment she'd thought that, the man himself arrived, and just looking at him blew up any idea that she'd permanently shelved the memory of what had transpired between them.

He'd stopped in the doorway to the office they were using when Melody Hughes, passing by with an armful of mail, had paused to talk to him.

Or flirt with him.

Daria fought the urge to get up and interrupt that conversation. Melody had a right to flirt with whomever she pleased, and Stefan was far too polite to shut her down.

Assuming he'd want to...

Melody was a cute little blonde whom some of the deputies secretly called Barbie because of her resemblance to the doll. Once one of them had accidentally done it to her face, and to his shock she had laughed. He was, she'd told the deputy, hardly the first person to do so. That reaction had earned her a lot of respect, including from Daria herself.

She watched them for a moment, assessingly. Not so much gauging their feelings, or lingering on the contrast of Melody's petite blondness and Stefan's tall, dark, powerful presence, but her own response. A response that was sharp, prodding and felt annoyingly like jealousy.

That thought roiled her even more, and she did not like it. She had no time for such nonsense, especially now, and especially with him. Not only was she working this case with him, but he was eight years younger than her, and his personal life was in chaos with Sam's arrival. That was a trifecta of stop signs, and she'd darned well better obey them.

Shc thought she had managed to quash her unwanted reaction by the time he actually came into the office.

"Morning," he said with that megawatt smile that could light up a room. He hadn't given *that* to Melody. "I see you're set up. I'll just get some coffee and we can dig in."

She gestured at the desk beside the seat he usually took, where a ceramic mug he'd brought in, telling her he hated drinking out of Styrofoam or paper, was already full of steaming coffee. "I poured you a cup when I got mine. Straight, right?" she asked as she sipped her own sugar- and cream-laced brew.

"I…thanks." He picked up the mug and took a sip. Then another. "I may live," he said wryly.

"We were up late." She studied him for a moment, trying not to think about him and Melody in the doorway, or the hug from last night. Truth be told, she was acquiring an annoyingly long list of things she was trying not to think about with this man. "How was Sam this morning?"

"Not bad," Stefan said, sitting down and swiveling the chair so he was facing her. "And he is Sam, by the way. I asked him. And it's a relief not to have to keep correcting myself."

"Good," she murmured with a nod.

"He asked about you."

She quirked a brow. "Did he?"

"He wanted to know if you were coming back."

"That's sweet. Unless he was hoping I wouldn't," she added.

"Hardly." He took another drink of coffee, bigger this time, then set the mug down. "He liked you. A lot. He asked if you could go with us this afternoon."

She blinked. "Where are you going?"

He held her gaze as he said, "Furniture shopping. For his room."

"I'm glad."

"So am I. He was so wary when I suggested it, it made me feel worse, but so excited when I said he could pick out whatever he wanted that it…it was like… I don't know how to describe it."

"You don't have to," she said softly.

"So will you? He really wanted you to come."

"And you?" The moment the words were out, she regretted saying them.

"I never would have thought of it if not for you, Daria. And this is the first time he's ever actually asked for something. So yeah, please. Unless you've got…a date or something tonight."

She didn't think she'd mistaken that hesitation. Which was odd, since they'd established early on, in that casual, getting-to-know-someone-you-were-working-with kind of way, that neither one of them was seeing anyone seriously. Or in her case, even nonseriously.

"All right," she said. "It would be a nice break from this for a couple of hours."

There. She'd put a time limit on it. That would make it…easier. Wouldn't it?

"Thanks," Stefan said, and he sounded relieved. "I just hope we can find something local. I'd as soon not drive all the way to Denver for this."

"There's a place over on Pine Peak Drive, where Fiona got some furniture for the twins. Maybe there?"

"Sounds like a good place to start."

They left it at that and started back in on the videos. Unfortunately, they had as little success as last night in finding any sign of Bianca, or any man that could clearly be her Blue Eyes. She'd lost track of how many times they'd watched the woman come out of the elevator, walk across the lobby toward the hotel bar, but never appear in the video from inside the bar. And the only people who visibly left the bar during the next hour they scanned were a group of three giggling women and the bartender who had gotten off duty and who they had verified had gone straight home to his very pregnant wife.

Finally, Daria got up out of the chair; she simply couldn't sit any longer, staring at that screen. "The phrase *beating a dead horse* comes to mind," she muttered. "I think it's time to focus on something else for while. Maybe then something new will bubble up."

"Agreed. Time to back-burner this."

She smiled at the phrase, since it was what she called

it as well when she put something out of the forefront of her mind and let it percolate. Often the answer she'd been hunting for popped up after she'd ignored the problem for a while.

Has ignoring the fact that he makes you twitchy stopped the feelings?

"When does Sam get out of school?" she asked abruptly.

He glanced at his watch. "In about twenty minutes."

"Why don't we go pick him up, feed him lunch and go shopping early?"

The smile he gave her then was well worth the gamble that a five-year-old boy would serve as a sufficient distraction—and keep her mind off pathways it most certainly should not be following.

Chapter 6

Stefan could almost see his son's thought process even from this distance. Sam had come out of class with a small cluster of other boys who looked about the same age, although he was a bit taller than all but one of them. Sam had been talking animatedly with the other tall classmate, gesturing with the hand that wasn't holding what looked like a drawing, but when that boy had apparently spotted a parent and headed that way, Sam's entire body language changed. He slumped slightly and trudged toward the parking lot, where he was apparently used to finding Mrs. Crane waiting.

But then Sam spotted him, and Stefan's jaw tightened a little at the boy's sudden wariness. Things had been better between them this morning, but apparently that had been forgotten. But then Sam spotted Daria and instantly perked up. A smile forming on his face, he picked up speed.

"Hi, Daria," he called out.

"Sam!" She waved at the boy, and a quick glance told Stefan she was smiling widely back at him. Sam broke into a run then and skidded to a stop in front of them. "What have you got there?"

Daria's voice was full of an interest that made the boy practically shine. "We had to draw today."

"Was it fun?"

"Kinda."

"May I see?"

The boy hesitated, then held out the page of rough-textured paper. Stefan looked at it over Daria's shoulder. It was recognizably a person in black, and a brown… creature of some sort, standing atop a long, wobbly green line he presumed was supposed to be grass. In the background was a gray scribble that went up and down across the page.

"Sam," Daria said with a wide smile, "I was expecting stick figures, but this is so much better!"

Again the boy lit up. Was it really that simple? Was genuine praise that important? He tried to remember himself at that age. Remembered the first time he'd brought home a perfect spelling test and his mom had cooed over it and made him cookies. Maybe it *was* that simple.

Daria pointed to the gray scribble. "Are those the mountains?"

"Yes," Sam said, clearly excited that she'd realized this.

"You're not used to those, are you?"

"No. Just buildings."

"Well, you did a good job showing them. And let's see here…" She pointed at the brown creature. "Let me guess. A dog?"

Sam was practically dancing. "Yes! Like the one I want. We watched a movie about a dog."

Stefan looked at the picture again. Okay, mountains he could buy. And the dog. The person…it definitely wasn't completely a stick figure—the person was a long oval with stick arms and legs. And short, straight lines of dark hair applied to the slightly crooked head, almost like a cap.

Hair that resembled, in a five-year-old way, Daria's.

"Well, I think it's wonderful," she said. "It should be on display at home."

"What does that mean?" Sam asked.

"It means put up where everyone can see it."

"Oh."

Sam cast a doubtful eye at Stefan. That doubt stabbed at him, and it was an effort to say casually, "I think the refrigerator is the requisite location? We'll have to pick up some magnets while we're shopping this afternoon."

"Shopping?" Sam asked.

"To find you some new bedroom furniture, remember?"

The boy's eyes widened. "Really? All of us? Today?"

"Right now, if you're ready."

Sam let out an excited yelp. He was even more animated when Daria suggested a local burger joint, and it was a toss-up over whether he talked or ate more. She was so good for him.

And stop thinking she's good for you, too.

And then Stefan found himself somewhere he'd never expected to be—a kids' furnishings store at the south end of the shopping district downtown. They had sections labeled with signs overhead, divided by age, and they headed toward the 5–7 sign.

"Look at everything first," Daria suggested, and Sam nodded eagerly.

The boy darted from piece to piece, first piqued by the bed designed like a race car, then to one painted like an Old West stagecoach. He reached out to touch a comforter printed with famous movie characters, then stood looking up in awe at a wall painted like space, with stars and planets over a bed that looked like a spaceship.

"I had no idea," Stefan muttered.

Daria smiled. "I think it's all about feeding their imagination."

"Kind of feels like I'm trying to buy his affection."

"No," she said quickly. "You're just showing him he has a place in your home. That you're willing to make changes for him. He's a smart kid—it won't take long before he realizes that also means he has a place in your heart."

He stared at her. "How did you get so wise?"

"Comes with age," she said. "You'll catch up."

"You make it sound like you're ancient." He wasn't sure why this bothered him, but it did.

"When I graduated high school, you were ten."

He winced. When she put it that way… "That's different. The maturity difference is bigger then."

She moved then, because Sam had rounded a corner and they couldn't see him. It seemed instinctive to her, and he wondered if it was something in the female DNA. Which brought back to mind what he'd learned from the trace she'd asked him to run on her own DNA. It had explained a lot about her, from her light brown skin to her determination.

"Ah. Here we go." She gestured toward some shelves of bedding. "I'll bet if you dug around in there a bit, you could find some stuff from that video game he loves."

"That might work," he said. He glanced past a couple standing behind Daria, who were discussing when and where to meet up later, and saw a display that looked like it had potential. He had to dig a bit, but he found a bedcover that had the characters he recognized. "We've gone from sleeping with the fishes to sleeping with zombies," he said with a shake of his head.

"Same effect," Daria retorted. "Come on, Sam's over here, and I think he may have found the perfect bed for this."

He glanced that direction and saw his son sitting on a twin bed. It wasn't, Stefan saw to his relief, one of the elaborate things he'd likely have to spend days putting together. It was a bit high, but not so high it made him nervous the boy would fall out and get hurt. There were two steps attached to one end, and the entire thing was painted to look like it was built of stone.

"It's the castle!" Sam was so excited Stefan couldn't help smiling. "From my game!"

"So it is," Stefan said. Then he tossed what he'd found to his son. "Which means this should go with it."

Sam's eyes widened as he recognized his zombies. "Wow!"

"And look who's in the middle," Daria urged. "In the picture on the other side."

The boy turned the plastic-wrapped cover over. "It's the dragon!" He could hardly contain himself now.

"So is this it? What you want?" Stefan asked. "No changing your mind later," he added.

"Well, maybe when he's twenty," Daria said teasingly. The boy laughed, as if the idea of being that old was ludicrous.

Twenty. For a moment Stefan just stared at his son,

tried to picture him at that age. *You're still surprised by him at five. Twenty's beyond your imagination.*

Sam shifted his gaze. Gave his father a look that seemed equal parts hope and doubt. "Did you mean it? I can have this in that room?"

That room. Not *my* room. Daria had been right.

"It's your room now, Sam," he said quietly. "So yes, you can have this in your room."

After a moment, when Sam didn't speak, Daria said, "I'm sure your room would have been ready if your dad had known sooner you were coming." She gave Sam a wide-eyed look. "But who knows what he would have picked out? Maybe something really babyish, because he remembers when you were a baby."

Sam looked horrified. "No! I want this."

They ended up buying the bed, a shelf that could be hung off the end to make a night table, a small dresser and a couple of pictures for the walls. And, when Daria pointed out—tactfully—that as tall as Sam was for his age, he couldn't reach clothes hanging in the closet, they added a clever setup that hung a lower pole from the upper one, right at Sam's height.

Stefan managed not to wince when the clerk rang up the total. But Sam was quite disappointed when he realized they couldn't take it all with them, and that the furniture and some of the other items would have to be delivered in a few days.

"It won't all fit in the car, plus we have to get the other stuff out of there," Stefan explained, "so there's room for your stuff."

"Oh," the boy said. Then, warily again, "Are you mad?"

Stefan blinked. "About what, son?"

"Your stuff."

For a moment Stefan couldn't think of what to say. So he tried to imagine what Daria would say. And running on that impulse, he reached out and ran a hand over the boy's soft, short curls. "You're worth a lot more to me than any amount of stuff."

Sam stared at him as if he wasn't sure whether to believe him or not. They were on their way back to the car when Daria's phone rang. She answered as Stefan got Sam in and situated in the booster seat. The boy didn't like it, and Stefan understood; he was tall enough it seemed extraneous. But it was the law, and so into the booster seat he went.

"That was Fiona," Daria said as she got in and fastened her own belt. "She suggested this Saturday for the playdate. They've got a covered patio with heaters, so the boys can have lunch outside and if the weather holds play on the fort, as they call it."

Stefan turned to look at her. "Just like that?"

"Fiona," Daria said, "is the mother every kid wishes they could have. He'll have fun and be safe. Can't ask for much more than that."

"No," Stefan said gruffly. "I…thank you."

"Thank her. All I did was facilitate."

"Still…if not for you…" He drew in a breath. "If not for you, a lot of things."

And suddenly it was there, in the car with them, the memory of last night and that hug of thanks that had become an entirely different kind of embrace. And he knew, by the way she averted her eyes and became suddenly busy adjusting her purse, that she felt it, too.

Where that left them, he had no idea.

Chapter 7

"We should probably explain to Sam what's going on, don't you think?" she said as they drove.

"Yeah. Sure."

Something in the way he said it told her his mind had gone exactly where hers had gone—to last night. But that way lay nothing but trouble, and so she quickly turned to Sam and explained about her friend and the invitation.

Sam took the prospect of this new venture Saturday well, even with a little excitement, although he seemed more enthused about his new bed.

It was a few minutes later when Daria said, with no particular intonation, "We're not too far from Max Hollick's place." Stefan gave her a sideways look, and she shrugged. "Just saying. It's early yet."

"You're determined to get me into this, aren't you?"

The corners of his mouth were twitching, and she knew he wasn't upset.

"Not like you'll go home with one," she pointed out. "As I said, they're all spoken for already."

"Safe enough, I guess. Unless somebody starts nagging."

"Make it incentive. For good behavior, I mean."

Stefan surrendered with good grace and made the turn she pointed out.

"Where are we going?" Sam asked.

Daria turned in her seat to look back at the boy. "Do you remember how you felt when you first got here? Like your world had been turned upside down?"

Sam frowned, clearly wondering what this had to do with his question. "Yeah," he said hesitantly, and Daria hoped the hesitation wasn't because he still felt that way.

"Well, sometimes when—" she chose the easier word for the five-year-old to understand "—soldiers come home from where there's been fighting, they feel the same way. Like they don't know how to fit in back home anymore. Does that make sense to you?"

"Yeah," the boy repeated, more certainly this time.

"Well, I met someone a while ago who helps them with that, in the coolest way."

"How?" Sam was clearly intrigued now.

"He finds dogs who have no one to love them, and he matches them up with the soldiers who need them."

"Dogs?" Sam's eyes had gone wide.

"Yep," she said cheerfully. "So the dogs get a home and somebody to love them, and the soldiers get a best friend who will always understand when they're not feeling quite right. Isn't that cool?"

"Yeah." With enthusiasm now, until the boy added sadly, "My mom hates dogs."

"No surprise there," Stefan muttered.

She wondered if Stefan realized his son was testing these particular waters. She went on rather briskly, "Anyway, that's where we're going. To where Mr. Hollick keeps the dogs for the soldiers. He's not there right now, but someone will be."

Sam's eyes went saucer big this time. "Really?"

"They all belong to someone else already," she said carefully, "but it would still be fun to meet them, wouldn't it?"

That Sam could hardly sit still after this gave them the answer to that question. And when they arrived at their destination, and were greeted by an excited cacophony of happy barking, she thought Sam just might lift off, he was so excited.

The fact that within minutes of their arrival Sam was giggling, surrounded by a pack of clearly delighted, gamboling dogs of varying sizes and breed combinations, proved her right better than anything else could have.

The woman who'd greeted them, a grandmotherly sort who said she had become a volunteer at K-9 Cadets after one of Max's dogs had saved her son's life, had been quite happy to oblige when Daria explained.

"It's great for the dogs to encounter all sorts of people, like they will once they're paired with their veteran. It's a wonderful thing Max is doing here."

"Absolutely," Stefan said, but his eyes were on his son, whose joyous laughter as he played with the animals was something Daria was guessing he hadn't heard much of.

When he finally turned to look at her, he caught her watching him. "Convinced?" she asked hastily.

His mouth quirked. "Maybe. Still doesn't give my house any more room for a dog."

"Details," she said rather airily, then added with a

grin, "Of course, details never matter to the person who doesn't have to handle them."

When they got home and Stefan told Sam to look at his room and decide where he wanted his new bed, the boy scampered off happily, looking for the first time like a normal five-year-old.

"Thank you," Stefan said to Daria again as she prepared to leave. He wanted—oh, how he wanted—to hug her again, but he didn't dare. "I really haven't been thinking in his terms, and I should have been."

"Oh, yes," she answered lightly. "Here, on two days' notice, for the first time in your life, instantly start thinking like a five-year-old."

"You're cutting me a lot of slack," he said, but he couldn't help smiling.

"Somebody has to, since you're certainly not," she returned, smiling back in a way that made him want to hug her even more.

But she left, and he felt a little adrift without her quick, easy and wise support. And when she texted him a couple of hours later, asking if he could take a call, he immediately dialed her cell.

"How's it going with Sam?" was the first thing she asked.

"Better. You really nailed it."

"I'm glad. But listen, I had a thought. About the case."

He was surprised at himself, and the fact that he felt almost disappointed that she hadn't just reached out because she wanted to talk to him.

Business. Colleagues. Serial killer. Hello, Roberts, get with the program.

"Shoot," he said.

"Remember that couple in the furniture store, behind us when Sam was sitting on the bed?"

His brow furrowed. What that had to do with anything escaped him. But he said, "I remember."

"Were you close enough to hear what they were saying?"

"Yeah. They were talking about where to meet up later, after they—" It hit him. "You think Bianca met Blue Eyes before she went upstairs?"

"It's a thought. If she did, then kept her…assigned date, but after he passed out went back downstairs…"

"To wherever they planned to meet up," he finished.

"It's a thought."

"Indeed it is." He let out a breath. "And a better one than we've had yet."

"It also means we need more lobby and bar video, from earlier in the evening."

Which meant more hours spent searching that video. Hours spent alone with Daria.

And somehow he didn't mind.

"Another day of this and I'm throwing away my cell phone, my tablet and my laptop," Daria muttered, hitting the pause button on the video. "If I never have to stare at another screen again, it would be fine with me."

"I was thinking more along the lines of taking mine back to Illinois and throwing it in Lake Michigan," Stefan said, sounding as weary of this as she felt. "Along with every other screen within reach."

She leaned back in her chair. They had been working backward a half hour at a time from the moment they already knew Bianca had come downstairs for the last time. The security video ran at fifteen frames per second, but they were watching at one-third speed, so an hour took them three times that. Add in that they had to do it twice, once for the lobby video and once for the bar video, and they had only managed to get through two hours of frame-by-frame scrutiny.

Daria's eyes were burning. Stefan was rubbing at his as well, so she guessed they must feel the same. He got up, stretched. Daria tried not to watch, but it was hard to take her eyes off the sheer muscled beauty of him. He moved like…she tried to think of an analogy and couldn't. He was simply, purely male, on such an elemental level it was impossible to ignore. Although when he started to pace to the office door, images of a restless, prowling big cat came to mind.

Then he stopped, apparently to look out the single window that gave them a view out into the rest of the building. But he didn't speak, and so she broke the silence.

"There must be something we can do that doesn't involve—" she waved vaguely toward the flat screen "—that."

Stefan went very still. Then he turned his head to look at her, and for just an instant she saw something in his eyes that reminded her once again of that embrace. Not that she needed reminding; it was never far from her mind. Which was ridiculous, really. It wasn't like they'd shared some long, passionate kiss or something.

And that had been a very poor choice of comparison, she told herself as she had to fight down a jolt of heat at just the thought. She'd simply been closed up in this room alone with him for too long. It was making her mind go crazy places. That was all it was.

"I'm going up to The Lodge," she said abruptly. "I

want to see where the places not covered by the cameras are again."

She wasn't sure what she expected to find—they already knew where the few places were—but maybe something would occur to her if she looked again. And if not, at least they would have a break in the eye-straining monotony of going over and over slo-mo video for hours.

"All right," Stefan agreed easily enough, so easily she wondered if he wanted to get out of these close quarters, too. "But," he added, "you might want to be aware that it's snowing."

"What?" she said, startled. He gestured at the door, and she jumped up and went over to look through the window. Sure enough, the white stuff was coming down outside. Rather steadily.

The cold white stuff. Her spoiled California bones shivered.

"They didn't predict this," she said, a bit crankily.

"What a shock. A wrong weather prediction."

Her gaze snapped to his face. He was grinning at her, the smart aleck. She wanted to be mad, but she simply couldn't be in the face of that heart-melting grin. She threw up her hands and laughed instead.

"All right, you found me out, I'm a true cold-weather wuss."

"You've been here how long now?"

"Four years," she said with a grimace. "And my blood shows no signs of thickening up, if that's what you're hinting at."

"I wasn't going to hint, I was going to come right out and say it."

She turned and gave him a mock glare. "Didn't you say your parents moved to Florida?"

"Only three years ago, and after spending their whole lives in Illinois," he pointed out. "And," he added, "Mom says sometimes she misses it. The seasons, I mean."

She gestured toward the falling snow. "Then she should come here to visit you and Sam."

Stefan's teasing demeanor faded. "I've been thinking about that, ever since you mentioned it. And you're right. They would want to be part of Sam's life, now that the major…roadblock is out of the way."

"Then ask them," she said simply. "Surely Sam's happiness and him adjusting to this huge change is the most important thing right now?"

"Yes. Yes, it is."

"You've got the troops, Roberts. Call them in."

A different kind of smile curved his mouth. *That mouth.* But this wasn't that killer grin—this was a softer, maybe hopeful, kind of expression. Then, to her surprise, he reached out and ran the back of his fingers over her cheek.

"I thought I already had," he said quietly.

The shiver she felt this time had nothing to do with the thought of snow.

Chapter 8

It would help, Stefan thought as he stared out at the falling snow, if she wasn't so damned cute. And funny. And wise. And helpful.

And sexy. *Oh, yeah, Roberts, let's not forget that one.*

If he were going to be honest, and he usually tried to be, he'd admit he'd known he was in trouble the first moment he'd been introduced to the sheriff's deputy who would be the liaison to the FBI on this case. But thanks to her tough-as-nails demeanor and take-no-prisoners attitude, he'd managed to keep it under control and strictly business. Even when he'd done that trace for her on her mother, and found out Ava Bloom's sad, tragic fate, he'd kept it professional. And admired her for how well she'd taken it.

But he was learning that the brusqueness covered a softer side, a gentler side, as she'd shown to Sam. And that his son had clearly fallen for her at first contact had...complicated things. The change in the boy was priceless to him, but at the same time it was harder and harder to be around Daria outside the job. He kept wanting to—

He abruptly cut off his own thoughts. The long list of what he kept wanting when it came to Daria was not something it was wise to dwell on right now. Besides, given how much help she'd been with Sam, the last thing he wanted to do was drive her away. She'd been pretty clear she wasn't interested. And he couldn't blame her. Who'd want to take on the chaos his life was in right now? Then again, that chaos had calmed considerably since the first moment Sam had met her.

And, of course, that had been before that hug that had become more than a hug.

Maybe it hadn't been more, for her. Maybe he'd misinterpreted her response, and the occasional look in her eyes he saw when he caught her looking at him. Maybe it was just him. He hadn't had time for any kind of relationship, even a hookup, for longer than he cared to remember. Even before Sam, and this case, his job had been all consuming. It had eaten up his marriage, although he was now distanced enough from that to realize that would likely have happened, anyway. Because his wife had not been the woman he'd thought she was.

But regardless of that, it had been so long it was only to be expected he'd...overreact to the first attractive woman he'd spent any real amount of time with. He'd been so wary—and distrustful of his own judgment—since Leah that he'd gone beyond careful and all the way into doing without. For a long time. And Sam had only intensified that; no longer could he be bringing someone back to his...bachelor pad, as Daria had described it.

Well, unless it was her. Because Sam had already made it quite clear he adored her.

Understandably.

"You okay?"

Her quiet question snapped him out of his pointless reverie. "Just thinking about Sam." Which was, to a certain extent, true.

"It will be fine," she assured him. "It will just take time." She put a hand on his arm, clearly intending only to comfort. But all he could think about was all the ways he wanted her hands on him, and he had to suppress a shudder, so strong was the need that swept over him.

"If we're staying here, we might as well get back to it," he said brusquely, as if the merest touch from her hadn't nearly sent him into a tailspin.

"I suppose."

She walked back over to the chairs they'd set up before the flat-screen display and picked up the remote. She pressed a key that turned off the screensaver that had come on and then hit the play button. And they began again.

He wasn't sure how much longer they'd been at it when Daria suddenly hit the Pause button. Only this time she wasn't leaning back, closing tired eyes. This time she was leaning in, staring at the screen. It was stopped at almost exactly an hour before the lobby camera had caught Bianca walking toward the bar.

He looked, but he couldn't see anyone in the frozen image from the hotel bar that even vaguely resembled Bianca. Still, he stayed quiet as she moved the video frame by frame until she reached a spot where she stopped it again. As far as he could tell, she was focusing on a table in the back corner of the bar, mostly hidden in shadow, where Stefan could just tell that a man sat by himself. Then, with a quickly typed command on the laptop keyboard, she zoomed the video in. Definitely a man, and definitely alone.

"Well, well," she murmured.

"Feel like sharing?"

She glanced at him. Her eyes were alight with interest, but the interest of a hunter who had just spotted her prey. "Back at the beginning, I interviewed The Lodge staff. And then when we turned up the body of a Colton cousin, I talked to all of them, including the brass. Including Russ Colton."

Her voice changed a little when she said the Colton name, but that seemed endemic to just about everyone in Roaring Springs. Some spoke it with awe and respect, others with envy, some with downright dislike. Although he'd never had much interaction with them, he'd always been aware of the wealthy, important family. He'd found it fascinating how they were scattered all over the country, each branch holding a unique place wherever they were. One branch had even spawned a president.

And he knew that the discovery of the body of a Colton cousin had kicked the investigation into high gear.

"Russ Colton, the emperor of The Colton Empire?" he said, purposely keeping his tone light.

She grimaced. "That's what he calls it, yes."

"You sound like you don't care for the man much."

"I don't care for anyone who tries to pressure us into rushing through a case to keep the family name clean."

"I'd say that seems typical of a Colton, if I hadn't met Trey."

She gave him an odd look he couldn't put a name to. But then she went back to her original point.

"One of the things he mentioned in passing was that staff and employees were not allowed to frequent the guest areas on their time off."

He caught her meaning and looked back at the screen. "And him?"

"That," she said, gesturing at the enlarged and rather blurry image, "is Curtis Shruggs."

"Rings a bell," he said, but his brow furrowed as he tried to place the name.

"He's the director of personnel at The Lodge."

"Oh?" His brows rose, and he leaned in for a closer look. "And who would know personnel policy better than the personnel director," he said slowly.

"Exactly."

She started the video again. But now she ran it slowly forward, and he quickly guessed she wanted to see exactly how long The Lodge's director of personnel had lingered in the off-limits hotel bar. They watched as the man gradually emptied the glass before him.

Stefan looked at the time stamp at the bottom of the image. They were at ten minutes before Bianca would exit that elevator. In the next moment Shruggs's head moved, as if to look at something on the table. At this magnification the image was very blurry, but there was a small, different-colored shape there.

And then he got up. Picked up the object and slid it into a pocket. Upon closer examination, Stefan would swear it was a cell phone. The entire action was clear, familiar, even if the image wasn't. And then the man headed farther back into the bar and vanished into the shadows where the camera didn't—couldn't—reach. The man he supposed women would think handsome, if they went for the salt-and-pepper-hair look.

Daria paused the video once more. The time glowed at the bottom of the screen. She looked at Stefan.

"That could have been a text coming in. He could have been going to meet her."

"And he went out the back, through the employee door. Where the camera wouldn't catch him if he met someone."

"And he would likely know that. He could have told her to meet him there."

Stefan let out a breath. "That's a lot of hypotheticals."

"I know. We still need to go back and see if there's anything on the lobby video earlier of them connecting."

"That should only take the rest of the night," Stefan muttered. Then the reality of his new life snapped at him, and he was reminded yet again that was no longer an option for him. He had to get home to his son.

"There's more," Daria said, turning her gaze from the video to him. He saw in those lovely, golden-brown eyes a spark of something beyond excitement; she was into this hunt just as much as he was.

"I interviewed him, back when this started. He never said anything about even being in the hotel, let alone the bar, the night Bianca disappeared."

He frowned. "But he had to know we'd be going over the video surveillance. Although, if you hadn't recognized him, I never would have noticed him, back in the shadows like that."

"Maybe that's what he was counting on."

Slowly, Stefan nodded. "There's at least a chance he saw Bianca that night."

"And he didn't even mention that he'd been there. Maybe he's not the killer, but that alone is worth pursuing."

"Indeed it is. Even if he's just one of those people who thinks the rules don't apply to him. Since he's the director of personnel, he could think he's above such things. Or maybe he was checking up on some other employee who might be the exception to the rule."

"Yes. But there's one more thing."

"What?" he asked, knowing from the undertone in her voice that it had to be something important.

"Curtis Shruggs," she said, "has very, very blue eyes."

Chapter 9

"That was a great catch," Stefan said after they'd gone over it again. "I don't think I would have noticed that anytime soon."

"Thanks. I'm just sorry I didn't see it until now."

They screen grabbed an image from the video, because she wanted proof in case Shruggs tried to deny he'd been there. Of course he could still negate that this was him—it wasn't the clearest image ever—but Stefan had also sent a copy to the Bureau's tech guys, who would clean it up and sharpen the image.

"Back in the corner, in the shadows like that, it's amazing you recognized him at all," Stefan said, still sounding admiring, which warmed her in ways she couldn't afford to think about right now.

"Makes me wonder if he knows perfectly well that table's half-hidden from the cameras."

"It does, doesn't it?" Stefan glanced at his watch and grimaced. "I'm sorry, I have to get home."

Daria glanced at her own watch; she'd gotten so immersed in the time ticking by slowly on the screen's images that she'd lost track of the time in the real world. And when she saw it was nearly ten, she was surprised.

"Of course you do. Sam's probably worried."

Stefan gave her a sideways look. "I don't think we've come quite that far yet, that he'd be worried about me."

She arched a brow at him. "I meant worried you might have changed your mind about his new furniture," she said, making her tone purposely light and teasing.

"Now that," Stefan said with a wry smile, "I could believe."

She studied him for a moment, wondering if it was prudent to say what had just occurred to her. It truly wasn't any of her business. But she decided it was important enough that she should.

"Have you thought any more about legal arrangements for him?"

"You mean getting full custody?" He looked puzzled, no doubt since they'd already talked about that. "I will, now that I have…some hope this will work. Thanks to you."

She smiled at that, but shook her head. And her tone was very serious when she said, "I meant what would happen with him right now, if something happened to you."

It was grim, yes, but in their line of work, a reality they both lived with every day. "It's handled," he said, rather gruffly. "A trust, and guardians."

She merely nodded, ignoring his tone. "I figured it would be. You would see to his welfare, no matter how things are between you."

"Was that a character assessment, or what?"

It had been, she realized. And her certainty of it, that this was a man who saw to his own no matter what, only added to her surprise. "Did you need one?" she countered.

"Sometimes. Lately, anyway."

The gruffness had vanished, and what she heard was a man weary of trying to deal with two of the biggest things the world could have handed him—this case and the full, lone responsibility for his son.

"You'll make it," she assured him. "Both of you. Just remember how long it took you to adjust when he was first born."

"I'm not sure I did," he muttered.

"You're not sure of anything regarding Sam right now. And that can't be easy for a guy who's usually so decisive."

Again the sideways look. "More character assessment?"

"That," she said pointedly, "was from firsthand observation." She grinned at him then, trying to lighten the mood. "Besides, your reputation did precede you, you know."

He went very still, and for a moment he just stared at her. She wondered what she could have said that had apparently hit so hard.

"I'd better get home," he finally muttered. Then, after a sharp shake of his head, as if he were trying to rid himself of something, he added, "The Lodge in the morning?"

She nodded. "I'll go over what we have on Shruggs again tonight. He probably won't even be there on a Saturday, but I want to talk to the staff about his habits. They'd likely know if he violates the order they have to live by, and maybe be miffed enough to say so. But you don't need to come along." At his puzzled look, she added, "Sam has a playdate tomorrow, remember?"

"Oh. Yeah. But that's afternoon. And I have the sitter already set anyway."

"All right, then."

Then he asked, "How far do you have to drive?"

"Home?" She realized it had never yet come up. "I'm just outside town, so not too far."

"So you'll be okay getting there? With the snow?"

"I've learned to deal. Just because I don't like it doesn't mean I don't respect it," she said, surprised anew. And wary of the fact that what had popped into her head at his question was her own earlier thought—that this man would see to his own. No matter what.

"Drive carefully."

"You, too. Get home to your son." His expression changed, tightened slightly, and she added hastily, "Sam would love my place. The backyard, at least. It's huge. He and that dog he wants could play for hours out there."

"Better than my little concrete patio, huh?"

He didn't sound offended, so she answered truthfully. "From a five-year-old boy's point of view? Yes. There's even a little tree house—well, more of a platform, really—in an old mountain mahogany."

He drew back slightly, but was smiling. "You have a tree house?"

"I've even been known to use it on a nice day. Which," she added rather sourly, "would exclude today."

"Better not tell Sam—he'll be showing up."

"He'd be welcome to visit," she said.

"He'd like that."

And you?

Daria groaned inwardly at her instant thought. This man was off-limits for so many reasons, but she seemed to keep forgetting them. Especially when they were working together. It was just proximity, that's all. And when this case was finally over, that would end and so would these crazy feelings.

Her voice a little brisk, she said, "I'll secure everything here. You get going."

"All right."

"Tell Sam hi for me."

"Will do. It'll please him."

She managed a smile but didn't trust herself to say anything more.

When he'd gone, she shut down, considered taking the laptop home and decided she'd had quite enough of watching video for the moment, and locked it up. She stowed away all the paper files, then gathered up her personal things. Flipping out the lights, she turned the lock on the door and stepped out into the hall. As she pulled the door closed, she heard footsteps approaching, looked and saw Keith Parker coming toward her. He was working the night watch this month, so he had to be coming, not going.

"Hey," he said when he spotted her. "How goes it on the case of the century?"

"Too slow, of course," she answered.

"You're keeping some late hours."

"And early," she said wryly.

"I'm glad Trey picked you, not me," he joked.

She laughed. "You're better off, trust me."

He smiled as they parted. That smile that was as warm as ever. She smiled back, even as it struck her that if she'd felt a fraction of the spark she felt around Stefan Roberts with Keith, they'd still be dating. Or more.

She thought about that as she made her way to the door that led out to the employee parking area. She usually tried to avoid thinking about this particular subject, but the only thing that was powerful enough to replace it was this case, and she knew she needed to give that a rest. She had come very close to frying every circuit tonight, with all that video.

But it had paid off, in the end. The Shruggs lead might come to nothing, but at least it was a shot, something they hadn't had in far too long. She had been living and breathing this evil for ten months now. She could barely remember her life before this, before Trey had entrusted her with this case that could likely affect him in a personal and permanent way. Trey, who had been through his own share of crap and yet had still teased her about having to fight even harder than he did; she wasn't just biracial, she was also a woman. But if they didn't break this case soon, Trey might lose the election. She didn't think she could bear that.

And now she was at the third thing occupying so much of her mind, and there was nothing she could do about it except what she was already doing—working as hard as she could on the case.

When you're not having inappropriate feelings about a certain FBI agent...

"Full circle," she muttered to herself as she reached the back door and pushed it open.

For an instant she was startled. She'd almost forgotten about the snow. But it was still coming down, although not as fast as before. There were a couple of inches on the ground, and she could see trails of dark footprints where people had walked to and from their parked vehicles.

She was *not* ready for this. Couldn't it have waited until next month, when it would have at least fit her idea of Christmas weather? She hadn't even worn her sheepskin-lined boots, so her feet were going to be freezing by the time she got to her car. And it would take a while for anything but cold air to come out the heater vents.

Spoiled California girl. Just get it done.

Taking a deep breath, she stepped outside.

Chapter 10

The snow had stopped overnight at a lovely three or so inches. Just enough to make everything look white and pristine, Stefan thought, without causing a ton of problems. Much better than the nearly foot and a half most of Illinois had gotten in November a couple of years or so before he'd transferred here.

"Thanks for driving," Daria said as they headed for The Lodge.

"This is nothing," he replied, gesturing at the small, neatly plowed piles by the roadside. They had this snow thing down to a science in Roaring Springs. They probably had to, being that all the great skiing conditions in the world were of no use if people couldn't get there. And the kind of clientele they catered to would likely have little patience with unnecessary delays. "Piece of cake," he added.

"That's why you're driving, because you can say that,"

Daria said with an arched brow. Which drew his attention to her eyes, of course. They really were an amazing color, the highlights almost like a piece of amber he'd seen in a wealthy man's collection once. And he wondered yet again why some lucky guy hadn't scooped her up yet. What was wrong with these Coloradans, that they let a woman like Daria stay footloose? Or was it her choice? That made more sense to him, because he couldn't imagine guys were not lining up at her door.

He forced his attention back to the road ahead; slight or not, it was still snowy, they were climbing Pine Peak and he should be paying more attention. No matter how hard it was with her next to him in the car.

Professional, Roberts. Just keep it professional.

"Was Sam excited about this afternoon?"

"Very excited." *Eventually.*

The boy wasn't, at first. He was back to sulking, glaring at Stefan and telling him he didn't want to go. The magic turnaround was when he found out they were friends of Daria's and that she had arranged it.

They're friends of hers?

Yes.

Oh. I guess I'll go, then.

Stefan had added something about not getting into trouble because it would reflect on Daria, but he kind of doubted the five-year-old got it.

And then of course there was the rest…

"I'm glad," Daria said.

"You may not be," he said dryly. "He assumed you were going with us, to introduce us."

"Oh."

She frowned, and for a moment he figured he was going to have to explain to Sam why she wasn't going with them.

Then, slowly, she nodded, and when she spoke he realized she'd only been trying to work through Sam's thought process.

"Okay, I get it—strange place, strange family, kids he doesn't know… I can see that he'd want a familiar face there. At least at first."

As they reached a stoplight and he halted the car, he took the chance to look at her. "Does that mean…you will?"

"What do you think?"

He blinked. *Me? I think you should go with us. I think you should always go with us.*

The shock of that thought rendered him speechless. He stared at her. Afraid to open his mouth for fear he'd look like a landed fish.

"I mean," Daria explained as if he hadn't understood, "I can see it would be easier for him, but would it be better in the long run to have him do it on his own? Or do you think it's too soon for that?"

Sam. She was thinking of what would be best for Sam. That touched him somehow, yet at the same time he was wrestling with the remnants of that unexpected thought. It took him a moment to regroup, but then the light changed and it gave him an excuse to look away.

And he felt like two kinds of coward when he said, "Right now I think easier would be better if you came along."

While that was true, it was so far from the complete truth that he winced inwardly. *Easier for who?*

He'd always thought of himself as a pretty up-front kind of guy personally, with the only subterfuge he did related to his work. But right now he was suddenly holding more back than he was saying, and it was an uncomfortable feeling.

"All right."

Was that all right she understood, all right she agreed or all right she would come? And why the hell did it matter so much?

Stefan focused more than he needed to as they approached the massive, covered entrance to The Lodge, with its stone pillars and colorful slate surface, free of any snow. He pulled to a halt just under the rough-timbered, beamed roof, out of the way of traffic, then turned to look at Daria again. "Does that mean you'll come?" he asked bluntly.

She looked surprised. "Of course, if you think it's best."

He wasn't sure that shouldn't be the other way around, since she was clearly much better at this than he was. But it didn't really matter—what mattered was that she would be there.

For Sam's sake, of course.

Stefan seemed a bit scattered this morning, but Daria supposed every morning was like that for him now. Working nearly every day, weekend or no, he hadn't had anywhere near the time off he needed to settle in with his son. If he hadn't already been knee-deep in this case by the time Sam had arrived, it would have been reason enough for them to assign someone else. But Stefan had actually been involved indirectly ever since he'd fielded a random call from Detective Kastor at RSPD, asking for the name of a surveillance expert, and had heard the rumblings that they were possibly dealing with multiple murders.

Of course, the avalanche that had uncovered the bodies and given their serial killer his moniker hadn't happened until months later, but Stefan had immediately connected things and so was elected to be the agent to get involved when Trey had made the request. And then his own life had been upended by the unexpected arrival of his son. When it came down to it, Daria was amazed he was as focused as he had managed to be so far.

Stefan cleared the vehicle with the head valet, who either let nothing ruffle him or had grown used to having law enforcement show up over the last ten-plus months. Daria watched as a low-slung Italian sports car pulled up, the driver apparently giving a long string of instructions before he let the valet take the vehicle. One day she'd like to ask the guy what the craziest request he'd ever gotten was, but this was hardly the time.

She noticed Stefan looking up at the rather intricate structure of huge timber beams that held up the portico roof. When he caught her watching him with curiosity, he shrugged.

"My dad's a builder," he explained. "He'd love to see this."

"Then you'll have to bring him here when they visit."

He looked at her then, and smiled. "Yes," he said. "I called them this morning. They never hesitated."

She couldn't help it—she grinned at him. "I knew it. Just from the way you described them."

He looked a tad sheepish. "Dad's finishing up a project, but they'll be here by the end of next week. And stay for Thanksgiving, even."

"Well, if this keeps up, that'll be a shock," she said, gesturing at the snow.

"Illinois," he reminded her, but then he grimaced. "God help me, my dad wants to learn to ski."

Daria's grin widened. "And your mom?"

His mouth twitched. "Knowing her, she'll want to snowboard." She laughed in delight at that. He stopped just inside the big wood-and-glass doors and turned to face her. "Mom even said if Dad couldn't get clear, she'd come. And they never go anywhere without each other."

"Obviously their son and grandson are worth an exception," she said, both amused and touched by the wonder in his voice.

"Yeah," he murmured, still sounding a bit amazed. "I…um…thanks."

"Sometimes it's hard to see the path when you're in the middle of chaos," she told him with a smile as they went in and crossed the lobby, so familiar from the hours of video, and yet so different in person from the ground level.

And different now than it had been even last year; the place was practically empty. Not many clamoring to visit or vacation here when there was a serial killer on the loose. If they didn't wrap this up soon, not only could more women be killed, but the economic base of Roaring Springs might never recover. She had already wondered if the name of the town was going to be forever linked to that Avalanche Killer moniker.

But now she found herself, perhaps because of the fewer people milling about, noticing the building itself more than she usually did. Then, curiously, she asked Stefan, "What does your dad build?"

"Houses, mostly, and the occasional small commercial project. Nothing like this," he said, gesturing around at The Lodge. "He'll love to see it, though."

"It is pretty impressive."

"Yes. And he'll see that. But he'll also think of how many people were employed for how long, how many other businesses got paid along the way." At her quirked brow, he shrugged. "He's a big-picture kind of guy. He likes seeing how a big project like this plays out."

"I like how you sound when you speak of him," she said, meaning it.

"He's my hero," Stefan admitted. "I mean, I went through the usual rebellion stuff when I was in college, figuring I'd learned to be smarter than this guy who had made a solid living and supported a family of six for twenty-five years. Took me until Sam was born to get that completely out of my system and see the real worth of who he was and what he'd done."

By now he was reaching for the door to the hallway that led to the administrative offices of The Lodge. Impulsively Daria reached out and touched his arm. She was startled when he flinched as if burned, but after a moment he only turned to look at her.

"You really want to thank me?" she asked. For an instant something flared in his eyes. She felt a responding flush of warmth and tried not to acknowledge what it was. "Then bring your folks here one night after they arrive. Buy them dinner at the steak house, and tell your father word for word what you just said."

His eyes changed then, to radiating a different kind of heat. "That is a great idea. And I will do it. But how does that thank you?"

"Because I never had that chance," she said softly.

She'd never spoken about her adoptive family for fear she would let something slip about the secret she'd kept since she'd come to Roaring Springs. Being a former president's adopted daughter was complicated, but here amid a ton of other Coltons, it would be even more so. What was it about this family? They couldn't seem to quietly blend into the fabric of any place they landed.

But this somehow seemed too important for her to keep to herself. For Stefan, anyway. And he already knew she didn't know who her biological father was—she'd told him when he'd agreed to try and trace what had happened to her mother. The results hadn't been what she'd hoped for, but they had been what she'd expected. And although she'd thanked him profusely at the time, she had never quite felt as if she'd thanked him enough. But now, maybe she'd at least made a payment.

As she'd expected, Curtis Shruggs was not in his office on this Saturday morning. What she hadn't expected was when his assistant, a middle-aged woman who managed to look both efficient and harried at the same time, told them he usually was around on the weekends, but he'd been out for the last three days with the flu. In the process, Shelly Bates showed herself to be one of those who, with an upward inflection at the end of her sentences, seemed to make every statement a question. Daria knew it was just a vocal tic some people had, but usually it was in people young enough to be uncertain about most things. Before they became positive about everything, she thought, stifling a smile.

"He doesn't answer his phone or texts, which worried me, so I went by his place to check on him, but he wasn't there at all? It's so unlike him?" the woman said, sounding anxious.

"So he's a dedicated-to-his-job sort of guy?" Daria asked.

Shelly nodded. "He never even takes a real vacation, just some long weekends or a few days here and there, you know? Sometimes even just a few hours now and—"

"We'll need those dates," Stefan said.

The woman gave him a rather shy but appreciative look. But she still managed to look surprised. "For Mr. Shruggs?"

"Well, we need to include him, of course, to be thorough," Daria interjected quickly, sounding almost dismissive of the idea of including the man, "But what we really need are those records on The Lodge personnel, staff, management, everyone, dating back to January."

Stefan glanced at her, then gave the barest nod, agreeing that there was no point in doing anything that might give Shruggs a heads-up. Best to keep him thinking they were looking at everyone for as long as they could.

"I thought you had all that?" the woman asked.

"I believe the police department does, but that was before the FBI was called in," Stefan explained with a charming wink Daria had no doubt got him just about anywhere he wanted to go with any breathing woman. "Sorry to put you to work again, but as long as we're here anyway, it would really help."

"Oh, of course!" For the first time it wasn't a question. "Do you want the paper schedules, too?" She sounded apologetic. "We do post them on the bulletin board, so if any of the staff make switches among themselves, there's a record."

"Then yes, we'll need those, too," Daria said.

"It must be tough," Stefan mused sympathetically, smiling at the woman, "working for a guy who ignores his own rules."

Shelly blinked. "I…well, he is the boss? And he can be kind of…intimidating, sometimes, you know?"

"Still," Stefan said. "I had a boss once who demanded no one make personal phone calls, but he went ahead and did it all the time. Kind of like Mr. Shruggs hanging out in the hotel bar when you're not allowed to."

Daria saw a faint tinge of color rise in the woman's

cheeks. But Stefan kept giving her that sympathetic look and captivating smile, and after a moment she gave in.

"We do talk about it, sometimes, that he goes in there. But we figured he was just kind of lonely, and maybe didn't want to go home to an empty house, you know?"

"You think he's lonely?" Daria asked.

The woman shrugged. "It's just…a feeling, I guess? He's always nice here at work, very professional, but—"

"Professional except for this?" Stefan asked. She nodded. He gave her an even wider smile. "He's lucky he has you to count on to keep things going when he's gone. So if you could get us those schedules, we'll let you get back to it."

The woman truly blushed this time.

"Well, you flustered her right into hurrying that through," Daria said with a smirk as the woman instantly went to do as he'd asked.

"And you had the presence of mind to not make it look like we were zeroing in on Shruggs." He seemed to be looking at her rather intently when he said, "We make a good team."

They did, investigatively. Together, they were able to bounce ideas off each other without fear that the other would find them without merit or even stupid. He saw things she hadn't, and vice versa. And they were in tune; he was quick to pick up on where she was going, and she often got to what he was thinking before he had to tell her.

They were a good team.

And professionally was all he meant, she told herself sternly.

Chapter 11

Stefan saw it immediately, but he didn't say anything. He wanted to be sure, and so he silently let Daria go over the data provided by Ms. Bates as he drove them back to the office. She was interrupted only by a text, which she read and frowned over, before putting her phone away again.

"Still nothing on the newest missing girl," she said. "I asked them to keep us updated."

He nodded. "What's your feel on that? When does she become ours?"

"Hopefully never. But as for a time element, since she'd already been missing a week, I'd say not much longer."

"Agreed."

They were pulling into the secured parking lot behind the sheriff's office when she released a long sigh.

"Do those dates he was away match as closely as I think they do?" he asked quietly.

"Yes." She gave a shake of her head. "And those that don't match are the ones where we aren't sure exactly when those girls vanished."

"Under these circumstances," he said flatly, "that should be enough to buy us a warrant to search his place."

"I'll call Trey. Just for the judge on call's name. I need to update him anyway." She pulled out her phone again, and he saw her notice the time on the lock screen. "We need to go get Sam and head to Fiona's."

"I...yes."

"He'll do fine, Stefan. Her boys are great, and they'll welcome him. And some good rough-and-tumble time might be just what he needs to get some of that anger and uncertainty out of his system."

"If it accomplishes that, it'll be a miracle," he deadpanned.

"If it does, maybe that means you need to keep him too worn-out physically to have the energy to stay mad."

"Maybe I'll start him running marathons."

When Daria's gaze narrowed, he had to suppress a teasing smile. He didn't quite succeed. "Will you be running with him?" she asked, just a shade too innocently.

He went suddenly still, the bit of humor vanishing as the ugly memories connected. "I've run one," he said quietly.

"Oh?"

"Boston, 2014."

He saw the change in her, in her demeanor and in those golden eyes as she understood immediately the significance of the date: the year after the bombing.

"A good choice," she said softly.

He nodded, acknowledging her understanding. "Yes. It was."

For a moment they just looked at each other, not as agent and deputy, not even as man and woman, but as warriors in a battle that never seemed to end. They were part of that wall between the innocent and the ugliness, and he knew instinctively that Daria Bloom would stand, as would he. No matter the insanity from the outside, or even from within, they at least would stand.

She called Trey up on her contact list. And smiled as she said, "He told me he assigned me a unique ring on his phone, but he won't tell me what it is."

He smiled back at that, and her lightening of the mood. He thought of suggesting it was probably something sexy, but that seemed wrong after the moment they'd just shared.

"He said it's so he won't inadvertently dodge me when he's avoiding the media. They're hounding him more and more as the election gets closer. Even the governor's on his case about it, because it makes the whole state look bad."

"Sucks," Stefan said succinctly.

"Yes. I feel so bad for him—he's such a good man."

"Seems he's taking most of the heat for what's happening, even though Roaring Springs itself isn't his responsibility," he said.

"Exactly. But civilians don't care about jurisdiction—they just want this over. Not that I blame them, but still, it doesn't seem fair when the rest of the county that is his responsibility is calm, quiet and peaceful, with the lowest crime rate it's had in years."

"You should do an ad for him," Stefan said. "Except

I'm not sure anybody who saw it and didn't know you would believe you were a deputy."

"And why not?" she demanded.

"They'd think you were some actress they hired because of your looks." When she stared at him as if she wasn't sure what he'd meant by the compliment, he tried to save face. "Not their fault. They'd only see the surface—they wouldn't know how good a cop you are."

"Oh." He thought he saw a tinge of pink in her cheeks, but he wasn't sure. And then she was making the call, putting it on speakerphone.

Trey Colton answered almost immediately. And was obviously relieved to hear that they had a lead, at least. He didn't ask for anything more; when he'd turned this case over to Daria, he'd meant it. Because he was an honest man, Stefan thought. This was one vote—maybe the only one in recent memory—he would cast without qualm.

When Daria asked about the judge for a possible search warrant, Trey answered quickly. "Judge Cruz is on call this weekend. He's been following the case, so he won't slow you down. I can get you his number—"

"No, I'll find it," she told him. "We haven't started on the affidavits yet. Besides, I want to be able to swear all you gave me was a name."

"Copy that," Trey said, sourly enough that even Stefan noticed. "And now, lucky me, I have a meeting with Mayor Dylan."

Stefan raised a brow at her when she ended the call. "It's wearing on him. The case, the election…"

"It's amazing he's still upright. Says a lot about him." She sighed. "I'm so glad he has Aisha now. She helps him stay level."

By the time they reached The Lodge gates, she had the judge's number, but there was no point in making the call until they had the paperwork done, or at least their reasoning outlined.

"How fast do we need to move on this, do you think?" he asked.

"My instinct is to jump instantly, because it's the first small break in a long time, but in reality I don't know."

"I don't think we tipped Shruggs—you took care of that nicely. But…"

"But it might be easier to search his premises without him there," she countered.

"True."

"Let's get Sam over to Fiona's," she suggested. "And after we get him settled, we can drive by Shruggs's place for a building description, then we can go to the office and get going on the paperwork while we call the judge."

"Agreed. We can have a plain clothes meet us at Shruggs's place, watch for him and sit on it until we get back with the warrant."

Daria nodded. "Good idea. And have them stay either way, keep an eye on him. And if he is there, we'll want more backup. If he's our guy…"

"He's not going to come quietly," Stefan concurred. "Not with all this hanging over his head."

They made the necessary arrangements, then headed back to Stefan's car. On the way, he made a call to the sitter to tell her they were coming and to make sure Sam was ready.

He grimaced as he ended the call.

"Problem?" Daria asked.

"No. She just said Sam didn't want to get ready."

"I thought he was excited about going," she said.

"He was. Is. She said he didn't want to get ready because he thought we weren't coming. That he holed up in his room after he told her I hated him." He sighed. "I swear, sometimes I think he's actually scared of me."

"Of course he is. You're so much bigger than he is, and he doesn't really know you. Maybe try getting down on his level a bit more."

Something clicked almost audibly in his brain, a memory of days back in training when they'd covered how to deal with children. He hadn't had to use that often in his career, and so it had never occurred to him to use the techniques—such as what Daria had suggested, crouching down to their level—on his own son. That alone told him how thrown he'd been by this whole thing.

He shook his head, as much at himself as at his son. "Where'd he get the idea we weren't coming?"

"That sounds like a kid who's been let down too often."

"Yeah."

"Well, you'll just have to make sure you don't let him down," she said softly. "And if you ever have to, then you'd better make it up to him."

"And just how do I do that?"

She gave him a sideways look and a teasing smile that did weird things to his pulse. Which was crazy—it was just a smile. "I know someone who has a cabin, out of the reach of cell and internet."

"I'm afraid he'd consider that cruel and unusual punishment."

"To actually have to talk to and get to know his father? Perhaps. But it might be worth it."

She might have a point. Although he had to admit when he thought of retreating to a remote, private cabin with no interruptions, it was Daria who immediately came to mind as a companion. Which in turn made him feel guilty, because he needed to get to know his son as much as the other way around.

Damn, things had gotten deep and murky in a hurry. One day he was cruising along thinking life was pretty good, and the next he was in the middle of dealing with a serial killer and a five-year-old, and he wasn't sure the kid wasn't the worst of it. He knew how to go after a killer, but his son too often had him at an utter loss.

As for Daria, he wasn't at a loss there. He knew exactly what he wanted.

He also knew he couldn't have it.

Chapter 12

"Daria!"

Sam's happy cry did things to her insides. And as he ran across Stefan's sleek, rather cold living room, clunking a bit in snow boots, she could see his father in the shape of his face, his nose, even the way he tilted his head to look at her. She was willing to bet that in about ten years, the resemblance would be even more obvious, as Sam proceeded on the journey from boy to man.

"Hey, kiddo, you ready for this?" she asked as he skidded to a stop before her. "It's cold out there."

"Aw, there's not that much snow here."

"Not enough to build a snowman?"

"Maybe a snow head."

She laughed, and he grinned, looking delighted. "Well, you might find a bit more at the Alvarezes'," she said. "They've got a yard almost as big as mine, so you've got a lot more room to gather it from."

Sam gave her another of those head-tilted looks. "You have a big yard?"

"Huge. Too huge sometimes." She leaned down and whispered conspiratorially, "You could get lost out there and have to climb up to my tree house to see your way back."

Sam's eyes widened to huge, dark saucers. "You have a tree house?"

"Sort of. It doesn't have walls or a roof, so it's not the best when it's snowing, but when it's nice you can sit up there."

"You should put walls and a roof on!"

"I'm not sure the tree's big enough for that. But I can guarantee you'll have a full-on fort to play in today. Oh, and I understand there'll be sledding."

Sam lit up. "Really?"

"They've got a little hill in back, just steep enough to really get going. Their dad cleared a nice path for them, too, so no crashes." Sam looked almost disappointed and Daria barely managed not to laugh. "Cool boots, by the way," she added. The boy grinned and stuck a foot out. "Do you have a change of clothes, for when you get all wet in the snow? Especially warm socks?"

Sam's brow furrowed. "I didn't think of that."

"Got something to stuff stuff in?" she asked, and he grinned yet again at her words.

"I've got my backpack," he said and whirled to run and get it.

Stefan had been quiet throughout their exchange, just watching. "What?" she asked, when he just looked at her.

"I didn't think of extra clothes, either," he said. Then, with a shake of his head, "You're amazing with him."

"I just talk to him."

His mouth quirked. "Then maybe it's just that I'm so bad with him."

"You're probably just feeling awkward, still. It hasn't been that long, and you haven't had time with him, with this case."

"Still making excuses for me?" he asked.

"Maybe. You certainly don't seem inclined to."

"My family wasn't big on excuses for not doing what you needed to do."

"And you had to do it right the first time, every time? And fast?"

His brow furrowed. "No. You just had to keep honestly trying."

She said nothing, just looked at him with raised brows. And after a moment he let out a wry chuckle. "All right, all right. Point taken."

"Have you always been good at everything you've ever tried?"

He laughed. "Hardly. You don't ever want to hear me try and play music."

"Sports?"

"Lousy at football, good at baseball, liked tennis."

She leaned back a little, registering again his considerable height. "I'll bet you have a smashing serve."

"Pretty rusty now," he admitted, and she liked that he didn't deny it.

"The Chateau has some good tennis courts. Maybe you should sharpen that up when the weather's better."

He gave her an assessing look. "Know anyone who could help me get that rust off?"

"I might," she said rather airily as Sam ran back, carrying his school backpack by one strap. She could see the sleeve of a shirt hanging out where it wasn't zipped all the way closed.

"Where's your school stuff?" Stefan asked.

"I'll put it back later," Sam said, sounding a bit defensive.

"I wasn't criticizing, son," Stefan said mildly, "just wondering if that big bed was actually helpful for once."

Sam looked surprised. "Yeah, maybe. That's where I dumped it."

"Get your jacket on, then, and let's get this adventure started."

Sam stared at his father. "Adventure?"

"Sure," Stefan said. "What's an adventure except something exciting you've never done before?"

Pleasure dawned on Sam's young face. "Yeah!" The boy ran to grab up the heavy jacket that lay across the back of the tailored gray couch.

"You're getting the hang of it," Daria said softly.

He looked at her. "I've been watching an expert."

They heard a slight thump and looked to see Sam wrestling with trying to get his jacket on without putting down the backpack. Stefan started to take a step toward him, but Daria stopped him.

"Let him figure it out," she whispered. "Aren't you curious to see how he does it?"

He didn't speak but stayed put as they watched Sam stop, appear to be thinking for a moment. Then the boy set down the backpack, untangled his jacket from it, put it on and then picked up the pack again.

"Thanks," Stefan whispered back to her as his son turned around.

"Acknowledgment might be in order," she suggested.

Stefan nodded and shot her an appreciative grin that

gave her an entirely new feeling inside. "Nice job," he called out to Sam.

Again the boy look surprised, but he did smile.

"Ready?" Daria asked.

Sam nodded enthusiastically, and they were off. And as the child scrambled into the back seat of the car, Stefan startled her by reaching out to take her hand and squeeze it.

"Thank you," he said again, rather fervently.

"My pleasure," she returned without thinking. Then had to look away to hide the evidence of what had slammed into her mind at the words.

Stefan would give anything to know what had just gone through Daria's mind, but he didn't dwell on it. He didn't dare; his own mind was already skittering far too often into that dangerous territory.

Besides, for the first time he felt…hopeful that he and Sam would reach some kind of accord. It seemed so simple when Daria did it, so obvious, yet he couldn't deny it worked. He'd even gotten a smile out of the boy with the simple praise she'd suggested.

"So, living here might not be so bad after all, huh?" she said to the boy in back.

"Maybe."

"Not the best way to come here, though."

"You mean 'cause my mom sent me away."

It wasn't a question, and the flat, carefully emotionless tone his son said it in dug at his gut. He was going to have words with Leah one of these days, but not until he thought he had at least a chance of doing it calmly.

"My mother gave me up, too," Daria said softly.

"She did?" Sam sounded astonished. "Why?"

"She was sick and couldn't take care of me."

"Oh. My mom's not sick."

"That," she said rather sourly, "is still up for debate."

Stefan managed not to let out a sharp laugh, but she was right; Leah had to be a certain kind of sick to just kick her son out of her life like this.

"She just doesn't want me." The boy's voice dropped to a pained whisper, but he still heard the words. "He doesn't, either."

In the first moment after Sam said it, Stefan assumed his son had meant Leah's fiancé. But then Daria flicked a glance at him, and he realized with a bit more of that roiling guilt that Sam had meant him.

Daria didn't, as he'd half expected, deny the boy's words. Instead she said quietly, "You know how I felt, after a while, after my mom gave me up?"

"How?"

Sam's voice was so tiny, so scared that Stefan's stomach knotted.

"I felt like nobody would ever want me. And that was the scariest time of my life."

"Yeah." Stefan nearly pulled the car over, so strong was the urge to grab his son and hold him. But Daria, as usual, had gotten the boy talking better than he ever had, so he stifled the urge.

"But Sam," she said, "there's a big difference between having to get used to a big change in your life, especially when it happens without warning, and not wanting that change."

"Huh?"

"I'm saying when things change so much, so fast, it takes time to get used to it. That doesn't mean you don't want the change."

There was a moment of silence before Daria laughed lightly. "Too complex, huh? Okay, it would be like…if you got a dog without knowing you were getting one ahead of time. You'd need dog stuff, a bed, toys, a collar and leash, right?" At his nod, she went on to say, "And then all of a sudden you'd have someone else to worry about, to keep safe and protect, and you'd have to learn what he likes and doesn't like, and he'd have to learn about you the same way."

"Oh. That's a lot."

"Yes. And it would be confusing, but it wouldn't mean you don't want each other."

"Oh," Sam repeated, and now he sounded thoughtful. And a lot less scared.

And once more, Stefan found himself appreciating the amazing woman fate had partnered him with on this case. And denying the other thoughts that word *partner* kicked off in his head. *It's the proximity, that's all. We have to work closely together—can't avoid it. It's natural, but controllable.*

He just wished he was more convinced of that last part.

He wasn't sure what he'd been expecting, but the house they pulled up to wasn't it. Of course, he'd grown up amid tall city buildings and nearby houses built on tiny lots. He should have realized that when Daria said they had lots of room, it meant…well, lots of room.

Stefan also was a bit startled when Fiona Alvarez came to the door. He somehow hadn't envisioned a petite, almost tiny woman with strawberry blonde hair and bright green eyes.

He was also surprised when the first thing she did

was cry out in exaggerated happiness, "Sam! My boys are so excited to meet you! Come on in."

Sam looked startled, too, but then shyly pleased. They stepped inside. Daria exchanged a hug with her friend, then introduced him to her.

"We met online years ago," Fiona explained. "And when Daria was thinking about moving, I pestered her unmercifully to come here."

"For which I will be forever thankful," Daria said with a wide smile.

"And which reminds me, Stefan, we should exchange phone numbers, just in case. That should guarantee we won't need them."

He nodded and resisted even the thought of saying that she could just call or text Daria. Because it wasn't like they were together 24/7. And that made him feel… he didn't even have a word for how that made him feel.

"Might as well keep the jacket on," Fiona said to Sam. "Everybody's already outside." She stepped back and looked at the boy assessingly. "My, but you're tall. It makes you look much older."

The boy looked pleased at that, too.

"Slipper is just going to love you," Fiona told him.

"Slipper?"

"Our dog. He's named that because as a puppy he was always chewing on everyone's slippers."

Sam's eyes widened even more. "You have a dog?"

"Oh, did I forget to mention that?" Daria said with a thoughtfulness exaggerated enough to tell Stefan she'd known exactly what she was doing.

Sam was smiling so widely now Stefan barely recognized him as the same sullen, withdrawn child who had gotten off that airplane, tagged like a piece of luggage.

He felt a jab of renewed anger that Leah had done that, hadn't even cared enough to bring him here herself, but he quashed it. It was easier now, he realized, now that he'd seen the boy stirring out of that brittle shell since Daria had stepped in. He knew he hadn't done nearly enough to stay in his son's life, but he would make up for that now.

While Fiona went to put on a jacket and snow boots, Stefan looked around the house. It was nicely furnished, but there were toys scattered about, and the big, cushy-looking sofa simply invited a kid to jump onto it. There was an air of comfort, warmth and…solidity, he thought.

"I see what you mean," he murmured to Daria.

"It's a very welcoming house," she said. "To match the owners."

He nodded. He could see that. It wasn't his taste, exactly, but then when it came down to it, neither was his place. That had been a decorator's taste, or at least their idea of what a newly divorced guy should have. He had this vague memory now of the guy asking him about his son, and he'd brushed it off, saying he'd be going back to Illinois to visit, not the other way around, so not to worry about it.

Talk about tempting fate...

"Come on," Fiona said. "Come see the fort and meet Miguel and the boys. And of course the dog."

Stefan was surprised anew when he stepped outside onto a covered patio with a large table, chairs and a couple of lounges still sitting outside. The explanation came with the heaters built in around the outer perimeter.

"Miguel is always afraid I'm going to get cold, but I like sitting out here when it's raining, even better when it's snowing. My Irish blood is a lot thicker than his," Fiona said.

"Kind of like California and Illinois blood," Daria teased.

He only smiled, because he'd just spotted the rather impressive structure they were headed for in the large backyard. It was like a two-level tower, open on the bottom and closed in with a roof on top. It had a ladder, knotted ropes for climbing up and down, a slide out of one opening up top, swings and climbing bars on one side, and a large pit that he guessed was filled with sand when not covered with snow on the other side.

Stefan looked down at his son, who was staring wide-eyed at the contraption. The man who was with the boys saw them, spoke to the kids, then headed their way. He was just under six feet, Stefan noted automatically, with black hair and dark eyes.

"Miguel Alvarez," he said, introducing himself as he pulled off a glove to shake hands. "Welcome to the zoo."

"That," Stefan said, gesturing toward the fort, "is amazing."

"They like it, and it keeps them busy and tired," the other man replied with a grin.

"I'll go get Sam started," Fiona said, "while you get acquainted."

The boy went with her unhesitatingly, clearly as excited as Stefan had hoped about this.

"He'll have fun, I promise," Alvarez assured him.

"I'm pretty sure he will indeed," Stefan said. "I sure would have as a kid."

"This is the whole family Saturday, so you picked a good time to call, Daria."

"Whole family?" Stefan asked, confused.

"They have a system," Daria explained. "The twins—who are inseparable, by the way—have Dad to themselves one Saturday a month, Casey gets him the next, and the next the whole family spends together."

"And the last?" Stefan asked.

Alvarez's grin widened. "Oh, that's for the hot redhead and me," he said with an exaggerated leer.

Stefan smiled—there was no way not to—but inside he felt a sudden tug. They had it down, these people. And he realized what he had felt since stepping into their home was the same sort of total connectedness his parents had. They would make it, this couple. No one who stepped into their home could doubt the strength of their bond.

And he wondered what that said about Daria, that these were the friends she valued most.

You know what it says. That she'd want the same thing. And you already failed at it miserably.

And once again he had to shake himself out of his thoughts, wondering why he couldn't stop thinking about the woman who was his partner in this investigation only as an entirely different kind of partner.

Chapter 13

"Are you all right with leaving Sam here?" Daria asked as they got back in the car.

"Fine. They seem like really good people."

"They are. The best. They had to fight to get to wherc they are now. His family didn't approve."

He blinked. "Of her? What about her family?"

"Welcomed him with open arms. And he used that to shame his own family into coming around, although I think she would have managed that herself, once they saw how much she adored their son."

"People," Stefan said, "are strange."

"And wonderful," she added. "Sometimes both at once."

He smiled at her. "That, too," he agreed.

"As long as there are those at least working toward wonderful, we should make sure they're safe."

For a moment he just looked at her. Then, softly, he

said, "Best definition I've ever heard. Wish DC thought that way. It should be in the job description."

It was a quiet moment of accord, something she could only think of as kinship. And an odd sort of quiet reigned in the car as he drove. Not the awkward sort of silence she'd experienced sometimes with him, but a companionable sort, and it was puzzling. She'd felt kinship with people she worked with before, and on difficult cases, but this was different somehow. This was…more.

Because you're attracted to him?

Even as the words ran through her mind, she set her jaw. *Fine, admit it. Who wouldn't be? He is one fine-looking man, smart and with integrity, and that's a powerful combination.* What he also was was a man coping as best he could with a life turned upside down at the moment, a five-year-old son who didn't want to be here, and just to add spice, he was eight years younger than her.

And he has no idea who you really are. There's always that. That would nip whatever this was in the bud.

She'd always thought that if she ever really got involved with someone, she would have to tell them. Being secretive wasn't really in her nature, but she'd learned early in her…other life that sometimes it was a requirement.

As they drove, the silence in the car seemed to change. She knew it was only in her mind, that she was putting this pressure on herself, but suddenly she felt she had to say something, anything.

"I sure hope this is enough for the judge," she said abruptly. "All we have is that Curtis is older than Bianca was, has blue eyes like millions of other people and that he was there that night, in an area he normally shouldn't have been. And regarding the other victims, that he was not at work or his time isn't accounted for at the times of their disappearances."

"Maybe in a normal case it wouldn't be, but this one passed normal a while back. Sure, I'd rather have had a run at Shruggs, see how he reacted, but unless we can find him quickly, I don't think we should wait."

"There is that. And Trey said Judge Cruz is pretty current on the progress—or lack thereof—on this one. But he may really narrow it down," she warned. "Like only things related to his whereabouts on the dates in question."

"Then we'll just have to do our best, won't we?" Stefan said, almost airily. "Who knows what we'll come across in plain sight."

"Spoken like a true fed," she remarked wryly.

His gaze shot to her face. "Problem?"

"Envy," she said.

"That's all right, then," he said with a grin.

She started to roll her eyes but found herself laughing instead. She reached into her bag and pulled out the laptop, figuring she would start working on the forms for the judge. Stefan glanced at her.

"Motion sickness not an issue, I gather?"

She looked up. "Not usually, no. And you're a smooth driver."

He smiled. "Thanks." He hesitated, then said, "People tend to think I push to drive because I'm a control freak. But really it's because passengering makes me queasy."

"And here I thought it was because you're the guy."

He blinked. "Seriously? That's what you thought?" Her straight face failed, and she laughed. And Daria was glad when he joined her. "Are you kidding?" he said.

"I've heard about your range scores. You could probably outshoot me with a peashooter."

"I know that's not true—you have to qualify just like we do."

"But there's qualifying and then there's excelling," he said. "Now, you give me a long gun and we'll talk."

"Good to know," she retorted.

They drove toward the address they had for Shruggs. Daria made a call to find out the nature of the neighborhood and any recent activities, suspicious or otherwise. The report she got indicated it was a very quiet subdivision, with only the occasional loud music or kid-generated mischief. Worst incident had been a house fire, but that had been determined to be from a faulty space heater.

The area lived up to the billing. There was little activity, although there were signs of earlier playing in the snow, including a tiny snowman—there hadn't been much accumulation here at this lower elevation—that made her smile, thinking of Sam's snow head. All the houses seemed to be variations on a theme—tract homes trying to look like log cabins.

When they reached Shruggs's street, Stefan drove slowly. "Green roof," he said as they neared the address.

Daria spotted it quickly. "Got it."

They went by slowly, without stopping. As they did, she inputted the detailed description of the building any search warrant request required. She was a little surprised at the cozy-looking, log-style home with the green metal roof, set amid tall cottonwood trees. It was very... picturesque.

"Looks like a freaking postcard," Stefan muttered.

"Exactly what I was thinking," she concurred as she made a note about the mailbox sitting on a stone pillar out at the street, then the large spruce tree in the front yard and the bright red front door that looked a bit Christmassy with the green roof.

"Wonder whose idea the door was?" Stefan mused aloud as he turned the car around and slid it in behind a large truck parked on the street that would hide it from view of the Shruggs house.

"And again," Daria said as he hit upon her thought. "Someone with a Christmas thing?"

"Maybe. It could—"

He stopped suddenly. Daria's head came up. "What? See something? Or someone?"

"I—no. Sorry. Nothing about this. It just hit me that next month I've got a five-year-old's Christmas to deal with."

"Oh, my, lucky you!"

His head turned and he stared at her. "Lucky?"

"Of course. A child's joy in Christmas is a precious thing. I'll bet yours as a kid were special."

"Very. The best," he said, thoughtfully, as if memories were flooding him. "My mom saw to that."

"Ask her then. Tell her you want Sam to feel like she made you feel."

He stared at her for a moment. "Are you sure you've never met my mother? Because you sure know how to get to her."

Daria laughed. "Thank my adoptive mom for that." The moment the words were out she froze. She never, *ever* brought up her adoptive family, and she couldn't believe she'd done it now, with him.

His gaze changed, as if he'd realized she'd never even mentioned them before, except when he'd done her that incredible favor and found out about her biological mother. "You're still close?"

"Yes. She's impossibly busy, but we keep in close touch."

She said it rather briskly and went back to her notes. While she did so, Stefan pulled out his phone and put in a call to Detective Kastor about arranging someone to stake out the house while they pursued the warrant.

"Well, that was easy," he said when he hung up. "Liam was so hyped that we had an actual lead, I think he'll come out and sit here himself if he has to."

"I don't doubt that. He's sharp, too. He put together the resemblance between Bianca and April Thomas before anyone else."

Stefan nodded. "I thought that, too. I think we're safe turning it over to him or whoever he sends." He looked back at the house. "Place sure is quiet."

She nodded. "Wonder if Curtis really is home sick?"

Stefan sat looking at the house they were focused on. "I think a little recon is in order," he murmured.

"I could—"

She stopped when he shook his head. "He knows who you are. I've never met him or been face-to-face with him."

"Good point."

"You have a cell number for him there, don't you?" he asked.

"Yes."

"Good. If all looks quiet, you can call it when I get close enough, see if I can hear it."

"All right," she replied. "Got a story if he's there and catches you?"

"Me?" He gave her a look that was so innocent she

almost laughed. "I'm just an accountant, checking out the neighborhood, looking for a house for me and my son where we can have an old-fashioned Christmas."

She blinked. "An accountant?"

He reached into an inner jacket pocket to pull out a small case, extracted a business card and held it out to her. "Sure hope there's good internet here so I can work from home," he said, still in that tone of utter innocence.

"'Steven Barker, CPA, Barker and Associates,'" she read out loud. Obviously he had this—and quite possibly others for other occupations—on hand for occasions just such as this. She supposed many agents did.

"I do so love numbers," he said with an exaggerated sigh.

She was still laughing when he got out of the car and started toward the house, looking around at the other houses as much as the target house, as if he were truly just checking out the neighborhood. She watched him go and tried to imagine him tied endlessly to spreadsheets and account books. She couldn't.

So instead she just settled in and allowed herself the pleasure of simply watching the way he moved.

And for the moment hushed the inner voice warning that she was edging closer and closer to very big trouble.

Chapter 14

After confirming Shruggs was not at the house, and that the officer Detective Kastor had sent had arrived to keep watch, they headed back to the station to start the process of getting a search warrant.

Stefan looked over the affidavits Daria had prepared while they were on the way. She'd asked him to, to see if she'd missed anything. And as he'd expected, she had not. Deputy Bloom was very thorough, and she had worded things in a way that made it seem a bit more impressive than it was, yet stopped short of blowing smoke, which would likely tick the judge off.

She paced the office while he read. He understood—he was antsy to get going on this, too.

"I'd add a cursory description of the houses on either side, especially the one with the carved bear in front, just to avoid any problems with the houses all resembling each other. Other than that, perfect."

She smiled as she nodded and made the addition. And then she'd picked up the phone and called the judge, going through everything with Cruz after she'd emailed the now-encrypted documents to him.

And as they waited for the call with the judge's decision, they were both pacing.

"Is your gut screaming at you?" she finally asked him.

"Yeah. It is."

"I keep telling myself it's only because this is the first thing that looks like a real break in a long time on this case."

"It has been a long time. But it takes more than that to get my gut going like this."

She looked at him curiously. "I suppose you're more used to cases that take a long time."

"We've had a few," he said. Then, wryly, he added, "Of course, we've had a few that shouldn't have taken as long as they did, too."

She studied him for a moment. "Do you miss the city? That life?"

He smiled, chuckled and shook his head at the same time. "Not one bit."

She smiled back. "Me, either."

The phone rang. Caller ID verified their hopes. "That was fast," Stefan said appreciatively.

With a nod Daria answered, listened, checked for the email that had arrived and said, "Yes, Your Honor," a couple of times, then, "Thank you very much."

Before she'd even hung up, the printer in the corner of the room hummed to life and began to spit out the paper copies they would need to actually serve the warrant, to be handed to Shruggs if he was there, or left openly visible if he was not. Stefan walked over to get the pages.

It wasn't bad, as warrants went. Judge Cruz had narrowed it down more than he'd have liked, limiting them to the Bianca Rouge case. But he'd given them full range on the search itself, for anything connected to that or to Shruggs's whereabouts at the time of her murder. So who knows what they might turn up, or what they might find in plain sight? And he suspected the judge knew that.

Daria was already back on the phone arranging backup. He took out his own phone and, as they'd discussed on the way here, called the FBI office in Denver to arrange for forensics to respond if necessary. It was a three-hour drive on a good day, so a heads-up was definitely in order.

And Daria hadn't protested at all, as some locals did, not liking the feds getting involved in their cases. *Turn down the FBI lab capabilities on a serial killer case that's been dragging on for over ten months? Gee, let me think about that...*

He smiled at the memory. He did like her sense of humor and her way of putting things. And the way she treated everyone, even the doorman at The Lodge, with the utmost respect. And how she chose good, solid people for her closest friends. And the way she—

He cut off his thoughts, which had somehow turned into a catalog of everything he liked about Daria Bloom.

And you didn't even get to the X-rated section yet.

But he could. Oh boy, could he. But if he started listing all the things about her that fired him up, all the things that woke him up at night in the grips of a dream worthy of some hormone-crazed teenager, not only would it take all day, but he'd end up saying or doing something unforgivably stupid.

"Ready?" Daria asked.

He blinked. He knew she meant the search warrant, but his body still shouted. *Oh yeah. Seriously ready.*

"Let's roll," he said, rather gruffly, hoping she'd take it as impatience to get a move on and not guess he'd just been daydreaming about kissing that luscious mouth and running his hands over her trimly curved body.

It was just as well that she again let him drive. It gave his hands something to do when everything in him wanted them to be doing something else.

It was only, Daria told herself, that they were at last doing something besides going around in circles, combing over the same old information in the futile hope that something new, some fresh approach or angle or thought, would pop out. That was why she was so revved up. Why she was tapping a finger on the armrest of the car, why her pulse was elevated, why she had to work so hard to keep her gaze anywhere except on the man behind the wheel.

She played back all the sound, logical reasons those things were impossible in her head. There were more than three strikes, so it should be enough to outweigh six-plus feet of tall, broad-shouldered, muscled male with those stunning light brown eyes and that gorgeous mahogany skin.

As long as he doesn't smile at me.

Yes, she had to admit, that heart-stopping smile, from the no-nonsense, very by-the-book Agent Roberts, was enough to throw any calculation into chaos.

"If it's there to be found, we'll find it."

His words snapped her out of her reverie. She spared a moment to be grateful he'd assumed it was the case that had been consuming her.

"Yes," she said. "And I think it will be."

"Agreed. It feels…right."

It did. But Daria wished her mind would apply that feeling strictly to the case at hand and not her temporary partner. There were so many concrete reasons why getting involved with him would be wrong, and only one on the other side.

Of course, the fact that that one reason was that she hadn't felt this attracted to someone in a very long time carried a lot of weight.

And then they were there, and she pushed all of it out of her mind. It was her efficient, all-business partner she was with now, and he would expect the same of her. They were on the verge of a huge break, she could just feel it, and no amount of telling herself she'd had her hopes up before on this case could tamp them down this time.

The house, the officer who'd been staked out told them, was still empty. No one had even driven down the street except a minivan full of kids in sports uniforms of some kind. She hoped for their sake it was an indoor sport; the snow was melting and making the ground a soggy mess.

She spared a brief moment to hope Sam was having the time of his life at the Alvarezes', then narrowed her focus strictly to the matter at hand.

They let the tactical team breach; just because there'd been no sign of anyone around didn't mean Shruggs wasn't holed up inside. They didn't think they'd tipped him off, unless his assistant felt inclined to warn him they'd been there, although even then they'd covered all their bases by asking for all the records, not just his, and Stefan had managed to make it sound boringly routine.

Once the house had been declared clear, they gloved

up and went in. Daria left a copy of the warrant in plain sight on a bare dining table, then looked around.

"A bit tidy for a guy supposedly living alone," she said.

"Hey," Stefan protested.

"Even your place looked more lived-in than this. I mean, look," she said with a gesture toward a coffee table in the living room where two stacks of magazines were lined up perfectly square, "not even a magazine out of place, no jackets hung by the door, no dishes in the sink." She walked into the kitchen to check, then continued. "Not even in the dishwasher."

"Maybe he's just a neat freak."

"Mmm," Daria said, wondering what percentage of serial killers turned out to be manically tidy in their personal spaces.

"Fridge is pretty sparse," Stefan said, following her and opening the appliance door. "Beer, half a bottle of wine and…leftover something."

"That looks like it should have been tossed days ago."

"Charming. And technically outside the purview of our warrant."

"Not if we need to know if he's actually living here," Daria remarked.

"Point taken," Stefan said with a nod.

She walked around the rest of the kitchen, opening each drawer as she passed. Found utensils, a tray of flatware, some towels and…nothing. She stopped, frowning.

"What?" Stefan asked.

"Just looking for the junk drawer." She glanced at him. "Everyone has a junk drawer, don't they? Where all the appliance manuals, notepads and the like get stuffed?"

"Um..."

She widened her eyes at him. "If you tell me you don't have a junk drawer, I may have to give up hope."

He went still. "And what, exactly, are you hoping for?"

She'd meant him relaxing enough to make Sam feel at home, but something in the way he said it, and in the hot gleam that suddenly came into those eyes, made her want to answer something entirely different. And of all times and places, this was probably the worst.

She had to struggle to get her original answer out. "For Sam to feel he can leave out a glass and not get in trouble."

The gleam faded. "Yeah, right," he muttered.

She turned away, trying to deny to herself that that look in his eyes told her he wanted the same thing.

Chapter 15

They continued the search in silence. Stefan noted that each room matched the living room and kitchen—not just tidy but immaculate. The master bedroom and even the bathrooms were spotless and without a thing out of place.

"Not even a shoe on the floor," Daria murmured as she looked into the master closet.

Even his place looked well lived-in compared to this. "Manic?" he wondered aloud.

"Or overcompensating," Daria murmured as they continued down the hallway.

He saw what she meant. "For the other, messy part of his life?"

She nodded, then looked his way. "Am I letting my suspicions override the evidence?"

"You're just thinking. And as long as you're asking that question, no, you're not."

She smiled at him, although under the circumstances it was fleeting. It still warmed him in ways he doubted he would ever get used to.

They were getting close to breaking this case wide-open. He knew it. He could almost *smell* it. And so, in hindsight, he appreciated her caution. He'd seen other agents act too soon on those gut feelings and end up completely blowing a case. Not that they were wrong, although that happened occasionally, but because they rushed ahead before they had the evidence to justify each step, and the case then fell apart in court, hacked to pieces by viciously clever attorneys who cared about nothing but the win.

So they would proceed methodically, only as fast as the evidence would allow. And they would build this case brick by brick, until the walls were so high and thick this madman would never escape.

He had a sudden vision of the end of this case, of the day when they caught this twisted psychopath. It would be a day of triumph at stopping him, yet sadness that he had killed so many. It would be a day—probably days—of media circus come to town. It would be a day of satisfaction for a tough job finished, but another layer of pained belief in the ugliness possible from humankind.

It would also be the end of their partnership.

No longer would he drive to work every morning looking forward to seeing Daria, to being in the room with her, to looking into those beautiful golden-brown eyes, to watching her move, seeing that smile.

He was surprised—no, make that stunned—at what that realization did to him.

And he didn't want to think about what it would do to Sam. Maybe she would still want to see him. She seemed to genuinely like the boy, so maybe she'd keep in touch, for his sake.

And you can be the side beneficiary?

The realization that he was hoping his five-year-old son could be the reason he would still see Daria after this was over rattled him nearly as much as the realization this would be over soon had in the first place.

He gave himself a fierce mental shake and followed Daria as she walked down the hallway of Curtis Shruggs's house toward the only room they hadn't yet looked at, at the end of that hallway. They stepped inside.

In one corner there was a rather ornate desk, oversized for the space. On the opposite wall was a floor-to-ceiling bookcase about four feet wide. There wasn't room for much else.

"Picked the smallest room for an office," Stefan said.

Daria nodded again, then looked back toward the desk. "And so it continues," she murmured.

"Indeed," Stefan concurred, also looking at the spotless surface of the large desk. The only items on it were an old-fashioned inkwell that looked as if it should have a feather quill sticking out of it and a pristine blotter. Some stationery was tucked into one side, blank except for the name in fancy script across the top. *Curtis Allen Shruggs III.*

Daria blinked. "He's a third? I don't remember...in fact I'm certain that's not in the info we have."

Stefan pulled out his phone and did a quick search. "No. He's not even a second or junior."

"Unless they skipped a generation. His father's name was Charles Ellis Shruggs."

"It's a stuffy-sounding kind of name. Delusions of grandeur, then?" Stefan asked.

"Or perfection. Goes with everything in here," Daria said, gesturing toward the bookcase. "Look at that. Every book a hardcover, no dust jackets, leather- or fake-leather bound, and every last one of them the same height."

"And not a one looking as if it's ever been cracked."

"Then again," she mused as she walked over for a closer look, "given some of these titles, perhaps that's not surprising." She tilted her head to read out loud. "'*Dewey Decimal Classification and Relative Index.*'"

"Seriously?"

"And there's four of them," she said.

"Maybe he wanted to be a librarian."

"Classifying books instead of people? Maybe." She ran her fingers over the row of books. Stefan tried not to think about her running those graceful fingers over every part of him. "Although you'd think if that was true at least one book would have been opened—" She broke off suddenly.

"What?"

"It won't move."

"They are jammed in there pretty tightly. All in that perfect row."

"No, I mean it truly won't move." She tried the next book. Same thing. "It's like he's got them glued down or something."

Stefan stepped over and tried a book farther down, then one on a different shelf. Neither gave even a fraction of an inch. "Boy, they really are just for show, aren't they?"

Daria stepped back, staring at the rows of perfectly matched and lined-up volumes. They weren't only the exact same height, they were each the exact distance, about an inch, back from the edge of the shelf.

“Is that what it is? They simply must always be perfectly in line?”

“I guess it would keep them that way if you bumped the shelf or something,” Stefan mused.

Daria’s breath caught. “Or…if you moved it.”

“Moved—” Stefan started to ask her, then stopped short. He pivoted back to look at the bookcase. Then at her. “How tall is Shruggs?” he asked quietly.

“Shorter than you. Five-ten, five-eleven, maybe.”

He raised one arm, easily reaching the top shelf. Then he felt along the row of books, tugging on each, but they all appeared to be as solid as those she’d looked at. Dropping his hand down one shelf, he repeated the action. And when his hand stopped suddenly, Daria’s breath jammed up in her throat.

“Well, well,” Stefan murmured and shifted his strong fingers over the book he’d stopped at.

It moved.

He pulled the book forward. As it slid off the shelf, the books on either side of it stayed exactly where they were, upright and securely fastened just as all the others had been.

“There’s a switch,” he said in a very low voice. “Get the breach team back in here.”

And she knew he’d reached the same conclusion she had.

It wasn’t a bookcase.

It was a door.

Chapter 16

Stefan stood outside in the chill, staring at the back of the house. In his mind's eye, he tried to gauge where the interior walls were, to get an idea of how big the hidden room would be. Not very. If the office had originally been the size of the other bedrooms in the house, then it was missing maybe four feet in width. Which meant that if the secret room ran the length of that room, that would make the space about four feet by ten.

Forty square feet. Not much. But enough for a serial killer to hide...*whatever* he was hiding in there? The possibilities for that were pretty grim. He'd seen some ugly things in his career, and he hoped this wasn't going to be another gruesome scene to add to the memory banks.

He heard the crunch of footsteps on what little snow there was remaining here and looked up to see Daria approaching. She had her heavy coat buttoned up to her throat, the collar pulled up and held by the thick, knitted scarf she had wound around her neck multiple times. It was a deep gold that, wrapped so close to her face, made her eyes look the same impossible shade. Had she made it herself? If so, she was good—the intricate cables looked beyond difficult to his untrained eye. And he smiled inwardly as he remembered her warning about very pointy tools.

Other people count to ten to hold on to their temper. I count stitches.

Point taken. Er, no pun intended.

Too bad. It would have been a good one.

He almost smiled outwardly at that memory. He did like her sense of humor. Besides, with the big scarf and her heavy, fur-lined boots, she looked ready for the Antarctic, which also made him want to smile. He stopped himself, because he didn't really want to explain what he was amused about.

"They're ready," she said as she came to a halt.

And just as she said it, he heard the call of, "Ready team!"

He looked over toward the team leader, who had ordered his crew to suit back up in vests and full tactical gear. Stefan didn't really think Shruggs was in there, but more than one agent had died going on a wrong assumption. He didn't want anyone to be a statistic, so they had left the house and turned it back over to the pros at CQB—close quarters battling without the proper gear was a chance he didn't want to take.

It was a chance he could *no longer* take.

He had a sudden vision of Sam, already lost and scared, having to go through that. He'd arranged for him to go to his parents, but what if Leah had other ideas? She hadn't wanted him now, but she'd never really gotten along well with his parents—they were far too unsophisticated and traditional for her taste. Would she demand to have Sam back to keep him away from them? Unlikely, but he didn't like even thinking about his son having to go back to a mother who hadn't wanted him and a stepfather who actively disliked him.

And for the first time in his career, it had really, truly struck home that he had a responsibility to take care of himself. For Sam's sake. He'd always known his death would devastate his parents, but as long as they had each other, they'd get through it. Sam had no one else. No one who would feel about him as he did. Because he loved his son, even when he wasn't liking him very much.

But he really liked the boy Sam had turned into around Daria. That was the happy child he remembered, the child he wanted back. And he had to stay alive to get there.

Stefan wasn't surprised it only took moments for the team to reappear and declare the small hidden room clear. And to tell them they had, in a macabre sort of way, hit pay dirt.

"We didn't mess it up—it only took a visual sweep from the doorway to be sure it was unoccupied," the team leader said grimly. "You're going to want forensics in there, in a big way."

And so again they waited, he and Daria, as the crime scene unit arrived, and in their own gear to prevent contamination, went into the little room.

Daria started pacing, rubbing at her arms. Gloves, too, he noted. Thick, warm ones. Not knitted like the scarf, though. Could you even do that? With fingers? Clearly his pointy-stick education was lacking.

"You want to go back inside?" he asked as she kept pacing. "It's warmer in there."

"Only temperature-wise," she said with a grimace. "I'll stay out here, thanks."

He nodded in understanding. "Don't blame you." He didn't want to spend any more time in that house than he had to, either. The evilness of it was much, much chillier than the weather outside. "Sometimes I wonder," he said, staring at the house, "if when you see sickness like this…it seeps into you somehow."

"To paraphrase what a wise man once told me, that you ask that means that it's not."

Startled at hearing his own words quoted back to him, his gaze snapped back to her face. Slowly he smiled. "Wise?"

"Definitely," she said.

He had been complimented on a few things in his life—his looks, his brain, his smile, even his height…but nothing had ever pleased him quite like that did. And he was afraid whatever he would answer would come out all wrong, make her think the wrong thing.

Except she wouldn't be wrong.

"I think my son might argue that," he finally managed to say.

"For now, maybe. But he's young."

Finally the forensics team emerged. "I'll get the blood type to you ASAP," the blonde woman said to his rather urgent request, her expression showing she understood quite well what they were dealing with and what was at stake.

The first thing Stefan thought when he stepped inside the small room behind the fake bookcase was that it reminded him of the room he'd told Daria about before.

Photographs tacked on the walls, notes beside each one that he sensed were going to be grim and ugly. And… the trophy shelf. This was typical, this kind of collection, something from each victim, so that the man with the twisted mind could joyously relive the thrill of each of his kills.

But what riveted his attention now was the opposite side of the room.

The side with the cage.

It looked like the kind of metal crate used for large dogs. Except those didn't usually have shiny new padlocks on them. Well, it had been shiny, until forensics had blackened it with fingerprint powder, finding nothing but a faint smear that might have once been a print.

But most riveting of all, most *haunting*, was the fact that there was relatively fresh blood on the side of the cage opening.

"I can't believe I sat across an interview table from him and didn't pick up on this." Daria sounded devastated. "If I had, this new victim might not have been taken. If I had—"

"Funny," Stefan said grimly, still staring at the cage, "I don't remember seeing mind reading on your stellar résumé."

He heard her take a deep breath, and when she spoke again, she sounded steadier. He hoped he'd helped with that. He was more…not *inured* to cases like this, because if the day ever came where this kind of thing didn't disturb him, then it would be time to hang it up. But he had seen more of them than she had, probably a lot more, and so was less prone to be shocked at the existence of such human depravity.

Daria moved over to look at the wall of photos. In a

sick twist, there appeared to be two of each girl—one alive, one dead. He'd already noted that any image of the new girl, alive or dead, was missing.

"I know her picture's not here, but I still think it has to be the new missing girl," she said.

"My gut agrees," he answered. "Maybe he takes the photos right before he kills them."

"He probably likes to capture the utter terror in their eyes," Daria said, with a loathing in her voice that told him Curtis Shruggs had better be very careful when they finally caught up with him.

"It would fit," he agreed. "I told them to advise us on a match to the blood type ASAP. Not that they wouldn't anyway, but a reminder never hurts." She'd been standing a few feet away at the time, and he wasn't sure she'd been listening.

She was still staring at the wall. "He didn't even want to have to take the time to call the photos up on a computer or phone," she murmured. "He wanted them right here in front of him all the time."

"And in front of them," Stefan added. "That's probably half the reason he brings them in here."

Daria shuddered. "Mental torture. They would know the minute they saw this wall what was going to happen to them."

He felt the strongest urge to put a comforting arm around her. Had they been alone in here, had not a dozen other people been on scene, he might have done it. He remembered his first serial killer scene, remembered the nausea it had caused, being forced to truly confront how evil some people could be.

"But he doesn't kill them here," he said, looking around again. "Maybe he doesn't want the mess."

"A fastidious serial killer?"

"One behavior often comes in conjunction with others."

"Or he thinks he's making up for being evil by being tidy?" she asked, sounding steadier now.

"I've seen stranger thought patterns," he answered. "But the most important thing right now is…we've got him."

He looked at her then and saw the belated realization dawn in those golden-brown eyes of her. She'd been so busy processing all of this, the enormity of it, that she hadn't hit the bottom line yet.

They now knew for sure who the Avalanche Killer was.

Chapter 17

Energized, they spent a few more fruitless hours trying to track down where Curtis Shruggs might be. There was still the sense of urgency, but it had a different cause now. There was a chance, although Daria thought it a very slim one, that the most recent victim might still be alive. That put the entire situation into overdrive, and every police officer and sheriff in the county and beyond now had the bulletin they'd sent out.

A thorough crime-scene processing was not something you could hide from the neighbors. The locals had done a house to house and had reported back that the man seemed to mostly keep to himself—one rather dramatic young man speculated that he was mourning a lost love—but that was no guarantee one of them wasn't friendly enough with Shruggs to warn him about what had been going on.

She and Stefan batted around the possibilities, and she sensed that he was as antsy as she was. Would Shruggs run? Or would he stay on his home turf? More importantly, where was he now? With his victim? Or did he have her stashed away in some secret place, where he could indulge his twisted fantasies? Was part of the torture leaving her there alone, giving her hope she could escape? Or would he be one of those sickos who liked to taunt his victims with what he was going to do to them for hours, even days before he actually took their lives? And when he did it, when he killed them, he did it with his bare hands, up close and personal. That spoke of a particular kind of drive and made it all the uglier.

"I think we need to talk to whoever hired him," Stefan said. "I can't believe the Coltons would employ someone for such a high-level position without vetting him pretty thoroughly first."

"They would," Daria agreed, "but I asked, and the person who actually hired Shruggs over ten years ago was the prior personnel manager."

"The background check must be somewhere."

She nodded. "All of that is in Decker Colton's office, and he's the only one who has access to it."

He gave her a smile then that warmed her. "You don't miss a trick, do you? So where do we find Mr. Decker Colton on a Saturday night?"

"I checked—he's gone until Monday, off the grid with his wife."

"Be nice if serial killers took weekends off," Stefan muttered.

"I know. But it's what we have to work with."

"Hard to feel stalled when there's maybe a still-alive victim out there."

"Tell me about it," Daria muttered.

Stefan gave her a sideways look. "You're still convinced Sabrina Gilford wasn't one of his victims?"

"Yes. And that her murderer knew who the Avalanche Killer was."

"He knew a lot," Stefan agreed, "to make it look like one of his kills."

After the hours spent hashing over it all, dozens of phone calls and several reports from the further door to doors Liam Kastor had set in motion for them, they had a slightly clearer picture. Shruggs had many coworkers and several direct employees, but few friends, which seemed significant to Daria.

Stefan had one of the Bureau's IT people start scouring for signs of his life—open or secret—online. Daria knew that people who had few personal contacts often had many online, and with the illusion of protection that step removed gave some people, they sometimes told those contacts things they would never say to anyone in person.

"If that doesn't net anything," Stefan said as they finally headed out to pick up Sam, "since we didn't find a computer at his house, we'll have to go for his work computer."

She nodded but felt doubtful. "I just can't imagine anyone as careful as he seems to be not keeping his two…lives completely separate."

"Agreed. But people make mistakes. If they didn't, we'd never get anywhere."

"Point taken," she said.

He gave her a sideways look. "Point reminds me to ask, did you make your scarf?"

Surprised but pleased, she smiled at him. "I did."

"You weren't kidding, then. You seriously knit."

"I knit seriously," she corrected with a grin. "Why, you want one?"

He reached out and ran a finger along the line of one of the cables. "Might look a little silly on me."

"I think you could carry it off." *You could carry just about anything off.* "Maybe in a more masculine color."

In the process of pulling back his hand, his fingers brushed her jawline. She gave a start at the little electric shock it gave her. Had he done it intentionally? Of course not, she answered herself. It was just an accidental touch. She almost had herself convinced when something caught her peripheral vision and she realized his hand—the hand that had touched her—was tightened around the steering wheel far more than was necessary.

She didn't dare look at him again and was relieved when they got to Fiona's place. Sam was happily worn-out. But that didn't stop him from chattering away excitedly about his day from the moment they got into the car. And the longer he went on, the wider Stefan's smile at his son became.

"And they said I could come back," Sam crowed. "Mrs. Alvarez said she could get me from school. Then I could come and play."

Stefan glanced at her. "How do you thank people for that?" he asked softly.

"We'll think of something."

This got her the smile. And damn, it was a killer smile.

"C'n Daria fix dinner?" Sam asked innocently.

Stefan gave her another glance, this time wincing, as if he thought the boy was saying she belonged in the kitchen. She nearly laughed.

"Why would you want me to do that?" she asked the boy.

"'Cause you fix stuff that tastes good."

She looked back at his father. "Sometimes," she said with a grin, "it really is that simple."

"How about we hit the burger place?" Stefan suggested. "You can order it however you want."

"Okay," Sam said agreeably.

Apparently a happy day with the Alvarez boys took the angry right out of him, which was what she'd hoped for.

"I mentioned to Fiona that we could be heading into a very demanding phase of the investigation," she said.

Stefan gave her a sideways look as he drove, then lifted one shoulder in a half shrug. "It's not as if she doesn't know what we're working on. The whole town knows."

"Yes. And both she and Miguel instantly said Sam could stay with them whenever necessary."

"Told ya," Sam piped up from the back seat.

"Guess you made a good impression, buddy," Stefan said.

"What's that mean?"

"It means they liked you," Daria said, beaming at the boy, who grinned right back at her.

Dear heaven, he was going to have that same killer charm when he grew up, she thought. She tried to picture it, an adult Sam with an older Stefan. For some reason her mind kept wanting to put herself into that picture, so she veered away quickly.

"They're nice. Really nice," Sam said. He was looking at Daria rather pointedly. "Casey said they come play at your house sometimes."

"They do," she confirmed.

"They said your tree thing was cool."

"They like it because it has other trees all around, and if you're quiet when you're up there, you can see all sorts of birds and animals."

"Really? Like squirrels and stuff?"

She laughed. "More like deer, raccoons, hawks, now and then even an eagle."

Sam's eyes widened. "An eagle?"

"If you're lucky. No wapiti, though."

"What's a—" Sam enunciated carefully "—wapiti?"

"An elk. Like a deer, only way bigger, with *biiiiig* antlers," she answered, drawling out the *big* and spreading her hands as far apart as she could in the car.

"Wow! I've never seen anything that big."

"I saw some down on the golf course just the other day," she told him. "They come down during the winter to eat the grass, because it's hard to find food up in the mountains."

"I wish I could see one."

"I bet you will, kiddo, now that you're here."

"Cool."

They spent a cheerful half an hour eating burgers and fries at the local supplier of Sam's choice. And sitting at the table across from the two of them, listening to Sam tell yet another tale of his exciting day—this one involving a snowball fight that had lasted until they'd run out of snow—she felt something she'd rarely felt in her life. A sense of…something. Wholeness? Completeness? Something she hadn't felt since she'd made the decision to make her way without the weight of her adoptive family name—and the power and prestige of President Joe Colton—behind her.

When she realized it was that sense of family she was feeling, she suddenly found the last of her fries very interesting and stared downward as if she were counting them.

"I can't get over the change in him," Stefan said after he'd gotten the boy back into the car.

"He's already feeling more secure."

"And you did it in a little over three days."

"I didn't do it all," she protested. "So did you. He's starting to believe that you want him here." She hesitated, then went ahead. "You've changed, too, with him. You're not quite as tense, and he senses that."

"Thank you for that, too," he said, and there was so much sincerity in his voice, she couldn't stop the warmth that bubbled up inside her.

When they reached the sheriff's office so she could pick up her car, Sam looked around with interest.

"Is this where you work?" he asked Daria.

"It is. And where your dad works for now."

"On the 'lanche killer," Sam answered knowingly.

She felt rather than saw Stefan tense. Slowly he turned to look at the boy.

"Where'd you hear that?"

"Casey said Daria was going to catch him," Sam said, sounding rather blasé. "Can I go inside and see?"

It took her a moment to get past little Casey Alvarez's complete faith to say, "It would be pretty boring after your exciting day."

"But I wanna see where you work."

She glanced at Stefan then, questioningly. He tilted his head and let out a breath in that "I hate to ask, but..." kind of way.

"I could give him the quick tour," she said.

"Please, Dad?"

Something changed in Stefan's expression then, and she wondered if he had ever heard such a normal, wheedling request from his son.

"All right," Stefan said, "but only because you asked nicely."

Surprise then thoughtfulness flickered across the boy's face, and when they got out of the car, before he opened the back door for his son, Daria looked at Stefan across the roof of the car. "Speaking of nicely, nicely done," she said. "That registered."

"Even as a brand-new shooter, I hit the target now and then," he said with a wry smile, clearly referring to her earlier reassurances.

"In six months it will be like he's been here forever, and you'll have a happy, well-adjusted kid on your hands."

"Can I get that in writing?"

She grinned back at him, but as he opened the door to lean in and unstrap Sam from the booster seat, it faded away. Because now that they knew who they were after, she had every confidence they would wrap up this case in short order.

And once they did that, Stefan—and Sam—would be gone.

Chapter 18

Not for the first time in his career, Stefan felt a jab of impatience on Sunday. He felt as if they were treading water, when he wanted to be powering full speed ahead. Especially now that there was another potential victim, who might—however tiny the chance was—still be alive.

They knew who the Avalanche Killer was now, and it was just a matter of finding him. They knew Curtis Shruggs had been at work at The Lodge as recently as Wednesday—the three days since were mostly a mystery. The blood at the house, in that obscene little room with the cage, was fresh enough for them to say it was likely he'd been there with the girl sometime in those three days. Yet none of the neighbors had seen or heard him. Or her.

But then, they universally said, they rarely did see Shruggs. They'd all tended to think of him as a hard worker, because he left for The Lodge early and came home late. He was more likely to be seen by the garbagemen, one woman had joked, clearly unaware of what all the fuss was about. But Stefan had made a mental note to check with the waste-management company and whoever handled this route. Who knows what they might have glimpsed in the man's trash? At least they wouldn't need a warrant for that.

It all came back to not knowing enough about their quarry to even begin to predict what he might do. And so far, no one they talked to had been much help.

Feeling restless, he began pacing his living room. He stopped a couple of times to look at the room, mentally comparing it to the warm, welcoming feeling of the Alvarez place. Realized that not only did it not feel kid-friendly, it didn't feel particularly friendly to him. And suddenly he wanted to clear it all out and start over.

He heard the clump-clump of Sam running down the hallway. He turned, and the boy skidded to a halt and looked at him warily. He tried to think, to imagine of what Daria would say.

Talk to him, Stefan, not at him. And more important, listen to what he says.

"Hey, you're just in time. I need your help," he said.

Sam looked startled. "Me?"

"Yeah." He gestured around the room. "I'm thinking all this stuff—well, most of it, not the TV—needs to go away."

Sam looked around rather cautiously. "Go where?"

"Anywhere but here. I'm thinking we need some stuff like the Alvarezes have, where a guy can put his feet up and watch TV or play a video game without worrying about it."

He wasn't sure if it was the video game mention or the *we* that did it, but the wariness vanished. And in its place came a small smile that bolstered Stefan's hope for a future with his son.

"Or maybe even a different place," he said. "Someplace with a bigger yard to play in."

Sam's eyes widened. Then he looked thoughtful. "Daria said her house has a big yard. We could move there."

If the boy had kicked him in the gut, he couldn't have driven the breath out of him any more completely. The easily spoken *we*—had it really only taken him saying it?—was enough, but the innocent suggestion that they simply move in with Daria not only stole his breath but made it hard to remember how to get it back.

He struggled for something, *anything* to say. The best he could do, after a gasping moment, was, "You haven't even seen her place."

"But it sounds cool. And Daria wouldn't lie," Sam added with a childlike certainty Stefan envied.

"No," he agreed quietly. "No, she wouldn't."

He was still pondering his son's more-than-accurate assessment of his temporary partner when his phone chimed, alerting him to a text coming in. He walked over to the kitchen counter where it was, swiped the screen and for a moment just stood staring at the name. Because, as if conjured up by Sam's cogent assessment, it was Daria.

But then he read it and found himself smiling.

"Hey, Sam?"

"What?"

"Daria says the wapiti are on the golf course right now."

The boy ran over, instantly excited. "They are?"

He held the phone out to his son, who stared at the photo Daria had sent. "Wow!"

Driven by a few impulses at once, he said, "You want to go see them?"

Sam's eyes got even wider. "For real?"

"If you can get your shoes and your heavy jacket on in the next three minutes. I don't know how long they'll stick around."

The boy didn't even answer but ran for his room. Stefan was smiling as he texted Daria back and she answered. Because even if the elk headed back to the hills, Daria would wait for them there.

As it turned out, the majestic animals stayed, seemingly unconcerned—or unimpressed—by the humans who were gawking at them mere yards away. By the time they arrived, there were ten or so people in various spots along the golf course, pointing and taking pictures.

"Do you suppose they know there won't be golfers out because of the snow?" Daria asked Sam as he excitedly exclaimed at the size of the animals.

The boy took her question very seriously. And after a moment of thought, he nodded. "Prob'ly. 'Cause they live here."

"I'll bet you're right," Daria said, and Sam gave her that beaming smile. Then he looked back at the small herd, brow furrowed as he made some gestures with his fingers.

"Thanks for thinking to text us," Stefan told her. "I've been here for a while, and I've never seen them like this."

She smiled at him, nearly as widely as Sam had grinned at her, and Stefan had that same breathless feeling he'd had before. Damn, this woman got to him, in ways he didn't fully understand. They'd been working side by side for months now, and he'd been fighting it from the first moment he'd laid eyes on her. And sometimes, despite all his best efforts, he wanted nothing more than to grab her, whisk her off somewhere private and find out if the chemistry between them was truly as explosive as he thought it would be.

"There's 'leven of them!" Sam exclaimed, and Stefan suddenly understood what the boy's hand motions had been.

"Good counting," Daria said. "Now, can you find the leader of the herd?"

"The leader?"

"The boss. He looks different than the others."

"Oh!" Sam exalted. "The one with the…the…" Failing to find the word he wanted, the boy put his hands to his head in a descriptive gesture.

"Antlers," Stefan told him. "And he is a big one, isn't he?"

"Yeah," the boy said.

"Where were you off to this morning, that you ended up here?" he asked Daria as Sam went back to watching the herd.

"Nowhere in particular," she said. "I just wanted to get out of the house. Quit pacing, actually."

"I know the feeling," he muttered.

"It's so hard to be so close and yet be able to only tread water because we don't know enough."

"Maybe the new door to door will turn something up," he stated. "Somebody who wasn't home before might know something."

"Maybe."

He noticed Sam had moved a little closer to the elk.

Which put him on the edge of the rather steep slope that led from the pavement down to the course itself.

"Hey, buddy," he called out. "Watch the edge."

Sam looked down, as if he hadn't noticed how close he was or how far the drop was. He swayed, and Stefan moved so quickly Sam looked startled. He wobbled just before Stefan got there and grabbed his hand.

"Don't want to scare them off," Daria said to Sam as she got to them. "They're calm now, but if we get too close, that boss elk will show you why he's the boss."

Sam laughed at the way she said it, and the startled look vanished.

And when they walked back toward the pavement, the boy reached up and took Daria's hand with his.

It was such a simple, natural thing, walking along with his son between them, hanging on to both their hands. But Stefan had that same sense of breathlessness for the third time this morning. And when he finally worked up the courage to look over at Daria, the soft expression on her face and the warm glow in her golden eyes made him feel something he didn't even have a name for.

Sam was chattering away about the elk, but Stefan barely registered what he was saying. At least, until the boy interrupted himself.

"And—hey! Look!"

Stefan turned to see the Alvarez family piling out of a large SUV that had pulled up a few yards away from where he and Daria were parked.

"I texted them, too," she explained. "They like having the boys see the local wildlife."

"Hey, you three," Fiona called out cheerfully, waving toward the herd of elk. "Beautiful, aren't they?"

They chatted while the boys greeted each other and

excitedly watched the big animals. Since he and Daria couldn't talk about their work, they chatted about other things, and he learned that she and Fiona had both once tried skiing and had quickly decided it wasn't for them, but that Daria had somewhat of a knack for ice-skating. Now that he would like to see someday. He could just imagine her, graceful and beautiful, sliding across the ice.

"We're off to go sledding at the big hill," Fiona said when the boys finally started to get restless with just standing and watching the grazing animals.

Sam's head came around. "Sledding?"

"Yeah," Casey, the oldest boy, said excitedly. "There's this really cool place we go, at the bottom of the mountain. It's a lot bigger than our little hill at home, so you can go really fast. Dad found it."

As he started to tell Sam all about it, Miguel stepped up to say to Stefan, "Sam's welcome to join us, if that would be all right. This will probably be the last chance with this snow, it's melting so fast."

"That's very kind of you."

"The boys would love it. They really liked him."

Stefan smiled at that. "I'm glad. More than you know."

"We would have called and suggested it, but we know you're so busy with this awful case," Fiona said.

He didn't want to admit they were not at a dead end but helplessly immobilized temporarily, so instead he looked at his son.

"Sam? The Alvarezes have very nicely asked if you'd like to go sledding with them."

The boy's dark eyes widened. "Really? Can I?"

Stefan couldn't stop himself from smiling at the boy's hopeful expression. "I think it would be all right."

"And he can stay and have dinner with us, too,"

Miguel said. "We're having spaghetti, and Fiona always makes a ton."

"Because my boys eat a ton," Fiona said with a teasing grin at her husband. "You can have him back about seven, since it's a school night."

There were a few more minutes of scrambling and making arrangements, and then they were gone, Sam so enthused he was practically dancing.

"It's good to see him so happy, isn't it?" Daria asked.

It was way better than good. It was something he'd been afraid he would never see. And in less than a week, Daria had accomplished this.

Miracle worker was the only description that came to mind.

Chapter 19

"They're amazing people," Stefan said, watching the Alvarezes drive off.

"They are. They live for those boys."

"That's like my folks were. I never really appreciated it until Sam was born, how their lives revolved around us kids."

Daria was silent, and when he looked at her, she was gazing out over the golf course again, but not toward the elk. In fact, she looked as if she were a million miles away. "Good parents," she murmured.

It hit him then. Her mother. He instinctively reached out, took her arm and turned her to face him. "You know she did what she thought would be best for you," he said quietly. "She knew she couldn't take care of you the way she wanted you to be taken care of."

Surprise flickered in her eyes for an instant. But then

she smiled, a soft, gentle curve of those lips that sent heat rocketing through him.

"You're a perceptive man, Stefan Roberts."

"I…thank you." He didn't know what else to say.

"No, thank *you.* If not for your help, I would have never known. I wouldn't even have known what she looked like."

He knew Daria meant the old driver's license for Ava Bloom he'd gotten for her, which showed a young woman with lovely features, whose daughter was nearly a carbon copy of her—only Daria's skin tone was lighter.

He heard her let out an audible breath before she said what he'd guessed had to have been the most crucial question to her. "I would have always wondered why she gave me up."

"I'm sorry she had to," he said. "I wish…"

She looked at him as he trailed off awkwardly. "You wish what?"

"That everybody could have had my parents."

She smiled at him again, brighter this time. "I don't even have to meet them to bet the world would be a better place if everybody could have."

He had a sudden vision of that meeting happening, of introducing Daria to his parents. Speaking of bets, he'd make a sizable one that they'd like her. There was no snobbery about her, even though she had as much reason as some of the snootier sorts they'd encountered on this case.

Perhaps that's why she never mentioned the connection she had to the Coltons; it wouldn't surprise him at all that she purposely avoided it. Daria was a woman who had made it on her own. That's why his parents would both like and appreciate her. He'd kind of skipped that step with Leah—they hadn't met her until after their whirlwind courtship and elopement, and when they had, they'd been welcoming but reserved.

Because they knew what you'd gotten yourself into. That's what you get for not letting them vet her first.

But Daria… Daria was what his mother called good to the bone. He was certain of it, in a way he'd never even thought about with Leah. And he knew his parents would see that. He truly could picture it—

He gave himself a sharp mental shake. What the hell was with him? Imagining taking her home to Mom and Dad? When they hadn't done…anything more than that single impulsive hug?

They hadn't even really discussed this powerful pull between them.

Or maybe it's only you that feels it, Roberts. Ever think of that?

He didn't want to believe that. Which sounded childish to him even as he thought it.

"Stefan?"

He snapped back to the present. And was immediately irritated with himself. He wasn't usually given to mental meandering. "Sorry," he muttered. "I was thinking about…my parents."

"They'll be here soon," she said.

"Yeah."

"Is Sam excited? Does he even remember them?"

"I…don't know." He'd almost forgotten about that. In fact, in the midst of the case and everything else that had been changing so rapidly, he'd overlooked a few things. Including telling his son they were going to have company. "I've been a bit consumed."

"I know the feeling," Daria said. "I feel guilty every minute I'm not working on the case."

"So do I."

"But I was going crazy, spinning my wheels. I was hoping getting outside for a bit would help."

"Did it?" he asked.

"I don't know."

"I suppose," Stefan said slowly, "the only way to find out is to try, but the thought of going back to the office makes me cringe."

"Me, too," she agreed. Then, rather hesitantly, she said, "I have most of the stuff on my laptop at home. That's where I was working before the walls closed in on me. We could…go there instead, if you think it would be better."

He was smiling at her correct assumption they would both rather be working than pretending there was such a thing as time off during a case like this one. And then it registered what she'd suggested. She was inviting him to her home?

To work, idiot.

But he couldn't deny he was curious.

Daria said her house has a big yard. We could move there.

Sam's words echoed in his head. He could only wish life was as simple as a five-year-old could make it sound.

And he caught himself again. His mind was careening out of control. How could he be wishing it were that simple, with a woman who was not only a work colleague, but one he'd never even kissed, and who had made it pretty clear she considered him off-limits?

"Okay, obviously that was a bad idea."

Daria's words snapped him out of his reverie yet

again. "I…no. No, it wasn't. I was just…thinking about something Sam said this morning. About…your yard."

God, he sounded like a complete idiot. He was usually reasonably articulate, but when it came to anything outside of work with this woman, he seemed to trip all over himself.

He tried to recover. "He'll be jealous I got to see it."

"Well, he'll have to come another time, then."

And so he ended up following her, since he'd need his car to go pick up Sam later. She'd mentioned she lived just outside the city limits, so he wasn't surprised when they left the density of town behind and headed into the foothills. But he was when she turned into a long, curving driveway that led up to a ranch-style house with a touch of The Lodge's log finish, a prow sort of front with huge windows, sitting on a slight rise. The way it was situated, he figured it would have a great view down over the hills, and that if you didn't know, you'd never guess there were other, similar houses on the way up to here.

And she hadn't exaggerated if that entire clearing behind the house was the yard she'd talked about.

A garage door rolled up as they neared, and she pulled into the shelter of it. He pulled up behind her in the driveway, stopped and got out.

"Wow," he said, looking back the way they had come. He couldn't see any sign of the neighbors he knew were there, except for a glimpse of a roofline off to the left. "Nice."

"It's bigger than I need, but it was a great deal, and my dream location." She walked over to him. "I like it. It's so…peaceful."

"You don't feel… I don't know, isolated up here?"

"There are neighbors closer than you might think.

Besides, I've had enough of living with a lot of people around all the time." Her expression shifted, as if she were remembering something specific. "I find it a nice change."

"I've always thought of myself as a city guy, but this could change my mind."

"At night, if it's clear, I get a bit of the sparkle of lights in town," she said. "And if I look the other way, I get the mountains. Seems perfect to me."

"Best of both," he agreed.

"And don't forget the backyard," she said, grinning now. Damn, it lit up her face, and those golden-brown eyes. "Come on, I'll show you, and you can decide if you think Sam would like it."

He was almost sure he already knew the answer to that, but he went along anyway. And the moment they rounded the corner of the house, the "almost" vanished. What kid wouldn't love this, a vast expanse of open meadow with occasional trees, intriguing paths and a small stream that wound its way down past the house? He saw a small, arched bridge that crossed it farther out, along a path that disappeared on the other side into thick trees. The whole area was groomed enough to be in control, but with enough wildness left to look natural.

"The stream is just a trickle in summer, but the rest of the year it flows pretty steadily," she said. "And the path that leads over the bridge continues on to the tree platform."

"Definitely five-year-old heaven," he murmured. "Or any other age, for that matter."

"I like it."

"How long have you been here?" Stefan asked.

"Three years now. I lived in town when I first started

with the sheriff, but I always wanted a place with more room."

He studied the yard, then her. "Who does your gardening?"

She laughed. "And that quickly he spots the problem."

"It just looks…intensive."

"It is. Usually I do most of the day to day, and I have a crew come in every month to handle the bigger stuff. But since this case… I hired a service some of the neighbors use. And I confess, it's been a relief."

"Might be worth it to keep them, then. Be more fun to enjoy than to worry about."

"I'll have to look at the budget," she said.

His gaze snapped from the bridge he'd been admiring to her face. Surely money wasn't an issue for her? With her connections?

And you think she'd use those connections?

He realized with a sudden shock that he not only liked this woman, he admired her. Not just for her smarts and work ethic, which was a match for his own, but for the fact that she'd carved out a spot for herself in a job that wasn't always welcoming to women.

Add that to the fact that he was, plain and simple, hot for her, and he suddenly felt like he was in way over his head, in a very different way than he'd felt since Sam had arrived.

Maybe this hadn't been the best idea, coming here where they would be alone. Secluded. Unnoticed. And following her into the house seemed like an even worse idea. But follow her he did, when she walked back around the corner of the house and into the double garage. Which was tidy, although somewhat full, with boxes stacked along one wall and metal shelving filled with various things on the other.

She stopped. "I'm sorry, I didn't think. If we're going to be working for a while, do you want to pull your car inside?"

He could think of a lot of other things he'd like to share with her besides garage space. Before he could descend into crudity—but not before a few images had flashed through his mind that made him very aware just how close to being out of control he was—he thanked her and went to move the car.

At least it would be warmer when he went to get Sam, he thought as he got out and she closed the garage door behind them. And as if she'd sensed where his thoughts had gone, which he wouldn't put past her at this point, she said, "When it's time to get Sam, there's a shortcut over the hill to the Alvarezes' place. You can be there in less than ten minutes."

"Thanks," he rasped, his voice sounding oddly tight, even to him.

The garage entrance put them in the kitchen. Where his was sleek, modern and rather cold, hers was…homey, he guessed was the word. The appliances were modern, yes, but the butcher-block countertops gave it a warmer feel, as did the artful arrangement of branches with dried fall leaves that graced the large island.

Beyond that island was the great room, a wide-open space boasting a big river-rock fireplace, which, judging by the stack of logs beside it, was not just for show. There was a large, cushy chair at an angle to the hearth, and beside it a large basket of yarn, with something half-knitted lying on top. He could see the needles with their indeed pointy ends. He found himself smiling again at the memory.

The rest of the room looked just as homey. There were two comfortable-looking couches, one arranged to take advantage of the view out the front, which was as spectacular as he'd envisioned, the other facing the fireplace, where he guessed it would be warm and cozy on a cold winter night. Maybe with snow falling outside, reducing the world to a soft quiet.

He yanked his thoughts off that path when he realized he was picturing them together on a night like that, on that couch before a roaring fire, wrapped in each other as the snow fell.

As if reading his mind, she went to that fireplace and quickly, efficiently built a fire. She had obviously learned what worked, for the paper and kindling she'd laid out neatly were almost immediately aflame, and when she added a couple of bigger logs, they caught quickly.

The fire completed the image. And he faced the simple fact. Her home was everything his wasn't. Warm. Welcoming. Just as Daria herself was.

He wondered just how much trouble he'd gotten himself into by coming here.

Chapter 20

Daria had a moment to be grateful she'd instigated what she called her full-schedule protocol: when things were normal, she tended to get a bit lax about keeping things picked up, but when things got crazy she was a lot more strict, knowing she had no time to deal with looking for things she might have left here or there.

And things hadn't been normal for months now.

"Coffee?" she suggested. "Hot chocolate, maybe?" She gave him a sideways glance. "Or, if you're insane enough to want it, something cold?"

"Let's keep it warm," he said, and there was a rough note in his voice, slight yet enough to have her thinking of other contexts in which that comment could be meant. "Coffee's fine," he added quickly.

She only nodded, because she didn't quite trust herself to speak, and went to the kitchen to set up the coffee maker. While it was running, she got out two coffee mugs from the cupboard. Her glance fell on the mug that Keith Parker had given her as a joke, before they'd ever gone out, with a scene of a California beach and the caption "If I was here, I wouldn't need hot coffee." He'd known she was from California, but nothing else. No one here knew the full truth of her California roots except Trey.

Stefan took the mug of coffee she offered him, and then she led the way to her home office. She booted up the computer, sent the display to her larger, separate monitor, and a few minutes later they were looking at the data they had on Curtis Shruggs. Not that it did any good, because after going through it all yet again, and then again, after nearly three hours spent retreading worn, unproductive territory, they had nothing more than they'd started with.

They went for refills on the coffee then walked into the living room. It was warm, that special kind of warmth that only came from a wood fire. She added another log, aware as she did so that Stefan was pacing the room. She stayed in front of the fire, both for the warmth and the distance from this man who so unsettled her.

Finally he said, "I know we didn't turn up any registered weapons, but I was thinking we should check for a fishing or hunting license in his name tomorrow. It might give us a clue if he frequents wilderness areas or lakes."

"Good idea. Parks and Wildlife would have the records." She grimaced. "Although a fishing license is for the entire state, all fresh water, so it wouldn't narrow it down. I'm almost hoping there's nothing, because the range that would open up would be huge."

"Too bad they're not like a passport, with entry stamps."

She nodded, thinking. "But if he has a hunting license, the stamps might tell us something. There are places that are prime for waterfowl, others for elk, whatever stamps he might have. It's more than we have now, anyway."

"Of course," Stefan said rather wryly, "we're assuming a serial killer gives a damn about permits to hunt or fish or anything else."

"Our lives would be easier if it worked that way, wouldn't it?" she agreed, feeling a bit morose about it at the moment.

"They call 'em outlaws for a reason," Stefan quipped.

She had to laugh at that one, even though it was a rather grim laugh. "We sure don't have much else."

"I know," Stefan said, starting to pace the room again as he ran through what they'd gleaned so far. "To his assistant's knowledge, he doesn't play golf, or tennis, or ski. The most she had on his leisure time was that he's used The Chateau spa for a massage now and then."

Daria suppressed a shudder. "Can you imagine being one of the staff who did that? Especially if you were a woman?"

"Frightening," he agreed. He shook his head, slowly. "I've been thinking his assistant is lucky she doesn't fit the victim profile."

Another shudder, and Daria began pacing, as well. "Is it making you as crazy as it is me that we know who he is, but have no idea where?"

"Well, at least it's a fairly narrow search area, since he's likely still in Colorado," Stefan said. "I mean, he hasn't bought a plane, train or bus ticket, and we've got a watch on his credit cards and there's been no activity, no gas purchases, or food."

Daria stopped pacing to look at him. And then she chuckled.

"I said something funny?" he asked, clearly puzzled.

"No. It's just sometimes I forget. That to you, the entire state of Colorado is a small search area."

"Well…yes." He smiled back at her. "But we've got a lot more resources, don't forget."

"Lucky for us," she said. Then she looked at him curiously. "Did you always want to be an FBI agent?"

He laughed. "No. I wanted to be a baseball star."

"Understandable." She tried picturing him in a baseball uniform. The image came quite easily. "So how'd you end up where you are?"

He hesitated, then shrugged. "They sort of recruited me."

"The FBI?"

He nodded. "Something…brought me to their attention, and they came calling and told me to come see them as soon as I finished college."

"'Something'?"

"An incident when I was nineteen. A shooter, at a restaurant."

Her eyes widened. "What happened?"

He gave her a rather sheepish look. "In reality? I got mad. I figured if he was going to kill me, he was going to have to work for it."

"And?" she prodded. "What did you do?"

"It was a pizza place. I had just gotten mine, so I offered him a slice. It kind of took him off his stride, and he instinctively reached out to take it." Another shrug. "I grabbed his weapon and threw it across the room and shoved him back out the front door."

"That was you!" she exclaimed. "I remember that incident. You were a hero across the country."

And, she realized with a little jolt, he'd visited the White House. If the timing had been different…

He grimaced rather ruefully. "I kept telling them I was just saving my own ass, but people needed a hero, I guess."

And that, she thought, was what made a true hero. One who didn't see what they did as heroic, but just as what had to be done. "I can't believe I didn't remember your name."

"Not the rarest name around," he said with equanimity.

"You really were unimpressed with yourself." She flashed him a smile. "Which impressed me."

"My folks saw to that. My dad said he was proud of what I'd done, but if I let it go to my head he'd take me down a peg." He grinned suddenly. "I've got about four inches and thirty pounds on him, but I have no doubt he could take me out even now."

"Because you'd let him," she said softly.

The grin faded, changed to a slow, loving smile. "Yeah. Yeah, I would."

And Daria was seized with a strong, very real desire to someday meet the father who had raised this man to become who he was, from pizza-parlor hero to honest, tough, smart FBI agent.

And an even stronger desire to have that kind of loving smile from this man turned on her.

She turned away before he read the longing in her eyes. Then headed back for the warmth of the hearth and the fire, since she was denying herself a different kind of warmth.

But an instant later she knew she'd been too late, because he came up behind her and said huskily, "Are we going to just keep ignoring this?"

She opened her mouth to say, in her best innocent tone, "Ignoring what?" Knew she couldn't manage it. She thought about simply saying, "Yes, we are." Couldn't manage that, either.

In the end, what she said came out a little desperately. "We have to."

"Why?"

"So many reasons."

"Such as?"

"You need to settle in with Sam. I'm older than you." She swallowed tightly. "And there are things you don't know."

"You're secretly a video-game addict?"

She blinked. "What? No, I—"

"As for Sam? Yes, it's been a struggle, but we've made great strides, thanks to you. He adores you, and I think you like him. So there's that argument shot down. Older?" He made a dismissive sound. "Big deal. If it was the other way around, it wouldn't even occur to anyone to think about it. So strike a blow for equality. As for not knowing everything about each other, well, that's half the fun, isn't it? Discovering all that?"

She turned and stared up at him. He was so close. So big. Couldn't he be less gorgeous? She could feel his heat. She could feel an answering heat building in her, no matter how she tried to fight it. It made the warmth from the fire seem a mere flicker. She couldn't even imagine what it would be like if he actually touched her.

And she couldn't think of a thing else to say.

"You told me Aisha made Trey make the first move, and you approved."

"That's different."

"Is it?" Something in his expression changed then, and when he spoke, his voice was softer. "So, when this case is over, we just go back to our regular jobs, our regular lives? Forget about…this?"

He leaned in then. Slowly, giving her a chance to pull away, to dodge.

She did neither.

And when his mouth—that mouth that could create that smile that melted her—came down on hers, the heat that had been building in her exploded, sending fire along every nerve.

She felt a moment of stunned shock. She'd lived forty-two years, some of them hard, some of them wonderful, but she had never in her life felt anything like this. Faint echoes of it, yes, and she'd thought that's all there was to it. But this…this was as if those prior feelings had been tiny candles leading to this impossibly deep, impossibly rich explosion of sensation.

And it was just a kiss.

Even as she thought it she dismissed the idea jubilantly. This was no mere kiss—this was fire as surely as the one going in her fireplace. No, not just fire, because it was hotter, more insistent than mere warming fire. This was…inferno. Conflagration.

And she, who had ever and always been cautious, flung herself into it without hesitation.

An awareness of how solid and strong he was came to her. She'd known it before just by looking, but now she knew, because she was touching. Sliding her hands over him so eagerly it would have embarrassed her had she been capable of such an emotion just now. But she wasn't. There was no room for anything except this blazing heat and the sensations the feel of him erupted in her.

He deepened the kiss, stole her breath. It didn't matter, because he was touching her in turn now, and having those big, strong hands stroking her so gently was more fuel to the blaze. He cupped her breasts, and she instinctively arched toward him, a tiny moan escaping her. His thumbs rubbed over nipples already achingly taut, and this time his name broke from her on a gasping breath.

He broke the kiss, and she felt a shudder go through him.

"If you're going to say stop, say it now," he said, his voice sounding hoarse and strained.

"No." It was all she could manage. Another shudder, and he started to pull away. She realized what he thought she'd meant. She grabbed at him, tried to hold him close. "I meant…no, not saying stop."

She looked up at him, and what she saw in those gorgeous eyes had her breathing even more quickly. "Daria by firelight," he whispered. "I can't think of anything more beautiful."

And she knew it was going to happen, right here, right now. And it felt so right, so good that her heart began to hammer in her chest, her body rising to the promise in those eyes.

She didn't know or care who undressed who—all she knew for sure was that she wanted to see him, *all* of him, wanted to run her hands over every inch of him, wanted to claim him in whatever way she could. And when they'd untangled themselves from their clothes, something seemed to snap inside her. Triggered by the simple fact that he was power and strength made visible, that he was even more magnificent than she'd imagined, need rocketed through her.

Once unleashed, her hunger overwhelmed her and she was stroking, kissing, even nipping at him, everywhere she could reach. She'd become some wild thing that astonished her. She was glad he'd thought of a condom, because she certainly hadn't.

She heard him swear, low and deep and heartfelt, that gruff, rumbling male voice kicking her pulse up a notch higher. And then he'd scooped her up and taken them both to the soft rug on the floor in a smooth flow that spoke of the power in that big body. The beautifully sculpted body that, for now at least, was hers to touch, to caress, to ravish.

The body that moments later was surging into her, the ease of his passage telling her the truth of how much she wanted this man. And then he was in her, stretching her until she would have sworn she couldn't take any more. But he kept on, until the exquisite sensation made her cry out at the joy of having that empty place inside her filled.

He said her name, low and harsh, and she knew she would carry the sound of it in some sacred part of her mind forever. She felt a shudder go through him, felt his entire body go rigid.

"Can't go slow," he ground out. "This has been building too long."

"I know," she whispered and lifted her hips to him.

And then he was moving, stroking, caressing as he withdrew and plunged deeper, until she was crying out with every thrust. He drove her higher and higher, his hands seemingly everywhere, his mouth on her lips, her cheek, her neck, all while the rhythm he set nearly drove her mad.

And then he reached between them, to where they were joined. He stroked with a single finger once, twice, and she reached that peak of madness. Every nerve in her body seemed suddenly to lead to that place, and they all fired at once. Her body clenched, then exploded, so fiercely all she could do was wrap herself around him and hang on.

Chapter 21

Well, having your first wild, crazy sex in the middle of the day was one way to avoid the dreaded morning after, Stefan thought.

He kept his eyes closed. He was full of so many sensations he was having trouble sorting them out. Uppermost was the feel of Daria draped over him, her skin as silken as he'd known it would be. She felt good. More than good. He thought he might just lie here forever with her delicious weight on him. Well, maybe eventually move to a bed. Her bed. His bed. He didn't care, he just wanted more. Much, much more.

He'd gone a little crazy with her. Or maybe she'd made him a little crazy. He wasn't sure which, wasn't sure it mattered. All he knew for certain was that he'd never felt anything in his life like sex with this woman. And he had the feeling it was just as much because of who she was—smart, determined, quick, kind—as it was because she was so damned intoxicating. But whichever it was, she'd fried every nerve in his body.

And in that moment when he'd exploded inside her, he hadn't been a hundred percent sure he'd survive it. Nor did he care, because that would be a hell of a way to go.

He realized abruptly he was almost falling asleep. A warning bell went off in the back of his mind, that this was not a good thing to do the first time with a woman. Especially one you genuinely cared about. But he hadn't been sleeping much lately, and she felt so damned good, naked against him. So good that even now, even just moments later, other parts of him were declaring rather fervently that sleep was not on the agenda.

He wasn't surprised at that. What he was surprised at was himself. Because he was lying here thinking a guy could face almost anything if he had this waiting for him every night. Or afternoon, he amended with an inward smile. But the image conjured by those two words, *every night*, lingered in his mind. And the thought of a never-ending stretch of moments like this filled a place inside him that he'd never even known existed, let alone that it was empty.

Maybe it hadn't existed, until he'd met her.

"Why did we wait so long?"

He hadn't really realized he'd spoken it aloud until her head came up. "Because it complicates things," she said, and the husky note in her voice completed what the feel of her skin had begun—his body started clamoring for a replay.

"Regrets?" he asked, carefully keeping his tone neutral as he thought maybe he hadn't avoided the morning-after minefield after all.

But a slow, pleased-looking smile curved that mouth that had driven him to that crazy state. "No. It does complicate things, but no."

Belatedly it struck him that it wouldn't complicate things unless she expected it to continue, would it? So she wasn't going to pull away, change her mind? Relief at that flooded him, because he couldn't understand how anybody could not want more and more of this.

It did complicate things, but only logistically. Between this case and Sam, free time was at a premium. But relegating what they'd just discovered together to only that minimum of free time seemed…impossible.

"I want more," he declared.

"I noticed," she said with a grin that made him feel oddly light even as she left a fiery trail along his body when she slipped her hand downward to curl around flesh already eager for a repeat. "Hard not to."

"Hard's the word all right," he growled, and he had to fight not to roll her under him right now. "But I meant more than just today. And more than just until the end of this case."

"Stefan—"

"Don't even try, unless you've got better excuses than before."

"But—"

He stopped her with a feverish kiss, giving in to the demands of a body that had nearly begun to shout, "What are you waiting for?" She was the one with the excuses, so if he had to show her again why they didn't matter, he would. Happily.

He forced himself to take it slower this time, vowing to himself he'd make her crazy for it before he slid into her welcoming heat. He wanted to hear her cry out his name again, wanted her legs wrapped around him, wanted her fingers digging into his back, wanted to feel the incredible clasping of her body as she climaxed around him.

He blazed paths with his hands, traced every luscious curve, then followed with his mouth until she was moaning, twisting under his touch, his kisses, his tongue. She was the most delicious thing he'd ever tasted, and on some gut-deep level he knew he would never, ever get enough of her. That should have rattled him, but it didn't; it only filled him with a joy he'd never known and a soaring feeling that he finally, finally understood.

And in the end, she didn't cry out his name—she screamed it as her body bucked beneath him, and the feel of her sent him hurtling over the edge right after her. And he thought he must have shouted her name as he went.

It was much later, in the dancing light of the fire, that she gave him a shyly wondering look. "I've…never been like that. I'm not sure what got into me."

"I'll refrain from making the obvious joke," he said, grinning at her.

She blushed slightly, just enough for him to see beneath the color of her skin. He found the fact that she was blushing beautiful. In fact, he couldn't think of a damn thing about her he didn't find beautiful.

And he didn't feel the slightest urge to back off, the way he always had with any other woman since his hideously faulty judgment about Leah. He'd worked beside this woman for three months; he'd seen her smarts, her dedication and her integrity. If he was wrong about Daria, then he should just give up altogether. And he wasn't going to give up. Wasn't going to give *her* up. He wanted it all, no matter what they had to do, how they had to arrange things.

"I was serious," she said after a moment when she'd regained her composure. Which, considering they were sprawled naked on her great room floor, was saying something. "I have never, ever been like this."

"I'm glad. Because you blew circuits I didn't even know I had." When she gave him a fleeting look that was almost bashful, he shook his head. "No inhibitions. Not with us. We blew right past that."

"Apparently," she said, with just a touch of wryness that told him she was regaining her humor, too.

When his cell phone chimed an alarm, he was startled. Because he only had one for today—the one he'd set when he'd sent Sam off with the Alvarezes. He scrambled over to the spot on the floor where their clothes lay as entangled as they had been, and tugged it out of a pocket. He'd been half convinced he'd set the time wrong, because it couldn't possibly be—

It was.

"Time to go get Sam?" she asked, getting to her feet and, sadly, reaching for her own clothes.

"Unbelievably, yes. Although I've got a little margin, because when I set this I assumed I'd be coming from…my place."

"Lucky you're here, then."

He covered the short distance between them in one stride, grabbed her shoulders. When she was looking up at him, he said solemnly, "I have never, ever been luckier."

Again she blushed slightly, and he wondered what the

hell was wrong with whatever men had been in her life that such a simple compliment got to her so.

"And here I was thinking I was the lucky one."

"Remember that," he said, rather fiercely, "the next time those excuses float through your mind."

Chapter 22

Daria watched as Trey Colton drummed his fingers on his desk. That was the only outward sign of tension, despite the fact that tomorrow was the day that would determine the course of the rest of his life. Election day.

"I read your reports," he said, looking across at her and Stefan. "Great work, both of you."

"It's finally going to be over," Daria murmured.

"We have to find him first, but yes, it is," Stefan agreed. His gaze shifted from her to Trey. "And maybe just in time. You could put word out that we know who the Avalanche Killer is now. Before tomorrow."

Trey's brows rose. "The election, you mean."

Stefan nodded. "It would be big, favorable news."

Trey looked affronted. "And could well spook Shruggs into running, lose us the chance to nail this guy, put him away for good. That's more important than any damn election."

Stefan smiled as if this was the answer he'd expected. "And that, Sheriff, is why I'll be voting for you tomorrow."

Daria saw a slight smile play across her boss's lips. "Just go find this miserable excuse for a human being, all right?"

"Yes, sir," they both said.

"Thank you for that," Daria whispered as they left Trey's office.

"Just confirming I was voting for who I thought I was voting for," Stefan said easily.

"What if he'd gone the other way? He never would, but what if?"

"Then I'd be voting for the lesser of two evils, which I hate, so I'm very glad he didn't."

And that little scene, Daria thought, told her a great deal about both of these men.

As they walked to the back of the station, toward the parking area, she said, "I meant to ask, how's Sam?"

"Remarkably compliant," Stefan answered as they got into his car for the ride to The Lodge. "Obviously the answer is keep him exhausted."

She laughed. "I talked to Fiona last night—she said he did marvelously. Even Casey likes him, which from his vastly superior position of two years older is saying something."

That wasn't all Fiona had said, of course. A great deal of the conversation had been taken up with the fact that apparently Sam had chattered even more about her than his father. And, Fiona being Fiona, with teasingly probing questions about how on earth Daria managed to resist the tall, dark and gorgeous Stefan.

And now that she'd stopped resisting, she wasn't sure

how to answer that. Except that she couldn't be unhappy about it. How could she possibly be unhappy about anything that made her feel so darn good?

She warned herself against making incredible sex into something more, something it wasn't. Warned herself against hoping this was the start of something bigger, longer lasting. Because once this case was over—and thank God it appeared it might actually be, finally—there would be no reason for them to spend so much time together, unless that itself was the purpose. And she was afraid to even hope for that.

I meant more than just today. And more than just until the end of this case.

His words played back in her head, and she felt a tiny shiver inside. He couldn't have been much clearer, so why did she doubt him? Why did she assume he didn't mean it?

You know why. Because you haven't told him the truth, haven't told him who you really are, and it could change everything.

She thought back to their conversation about the pressure of the Coltons being involved in this case, and his rather pragmatic assumption that Colton pressure was why Trey had asked the FBI to step in.

Contrary to what some think, we don't always go around butting into local affairs if we're not asked.

When he'd said it, she'd merely observed that a lot of people made a lot of assumptions, and there was a good chance half of them were wrong. He'd laughed, commented her estimate might be a little low, and they'd moved on. At least, *he* had; the truth of what he'd said, and the secret she was keeping, had been nagging at her ever since.

But it had to wait. Because right now they were close, *so close* to ending this nightmare that she barely wanted to stop to breathe, let alone have what would likely be a long and possibly devastating conversation. At least, as far as her relationship with this man went. A relationship she very much wanted but had doubts would survive.

The trip to The Lodge was silent, although Stefan kept giving her sideways glances as he drove.

"Problem?" she finally asked.

"Not unless you have one," he said. "It's just, you're… quiet."

"Antsy," she clarified. "We're so close, and yet…"

"I'm glad it's the case you're thinking about."

And not…us? Did they qualify as an *us* now? He was certainly acting like it. And on some level, she knew it was her own guilty conscience that had her thinking anything other than that he'd meant what he'd said. He wanted more, and he wanted it beyond the end of this case.

But he doesn't know…and given who he works for, it could matter.

"When this is over," she began, but she had no idea where to go from there and so the words hung in the air unfinished.

"Then we'll work out the details," he said, as if the big decision was already made. She felt a tiny spark of… something. Speaking of assumptions, he seemed to be making a big one, since all she'd agreed to was that she didn't regret what they'd done. And she wasn't quite sure how she felt about that. All the reasons against it still existed—they just didn't seem to matter anymore.

When they arrived at The Lodge, they parked the car themselves in the lot rather than leave it under the portico, because this time they were going to be here as long as it took to get something, anything, that would tell them where Curtis Shruggs might be. And if that entailed talking to every one of the hundreds on staff, so be it.

"Great tennis weather," Stefan remarked as they got a glimpse of the courts and saw two people out playing. There was still a bit of snow lingering around the edges and in shady spots, so it did look a bit odd.

"Helps when the courts are heated," she said.

He turned his head to look at her. "Seriously?"

"Of course. This is the crown jewel of The Colton Empire. Unless you're talking to Mara Colton, of course, then The Chateau is the crown jewel and The Lodge merely the adjunct."

"No wonder she and her husband are having problems," Stefan muttered.

"Not to mention that little affair of the nephew who's really his son," Daria said dryly.

Stefan had facilitated the DNA testing that had revealed that bit of news that shocked the Coltons. And he'd done the same for her, although instead of finding out that she had a living parent, as Fox Colton had, she'd found out what she'd suspected was true—her mother had died years ago, after giving her up when she became so seriously ill. But she owed this man for the closure.

And a few other things.

"And speak of the devil," Daria said, suddenly realizing who was coming out of The Lodge's front doors.

Stefan looked. She heard him make a sound and knew he'd spotted Russ Colton approaching. A tall, broad-shouldered man, with once dark brown hair now mostly gray, the head of The Colton Empire had clearly passed his good looks on to his sons. He thankfully hadn't passed on his rather overbearing manner to any of them she'd spoken to.

"Wonder what he's doing here?" Stefan asked.

"Down from the Manor?" she said rather dryly, using the grand name for the building in the mountains that looked like what it was—some very wealthy family's home base. She knew it had been built ten years ago, and that before they had lived down by The Chateau. She had always had a suspicion the Manor existed so the Coltons didn't have to mingle quite so much with the regular folks. "He's pretty hands-on. He must work about twenty hours a day."

"I have no problem with people who work hard to get to where they are," Stefan replied. "But speaking of the Colton home, he's got a bit of that lord-of-the-manor thing going on, and that I find annoying."

"The business is his baby. More than his children ever were, I think. It's amazing most of them came out pretty decent people."

Stefan murmured as Russ spotted them and headed their way, "I wonder how he's going to feel about someone so high up in his company being a serial killer?"

"I vote we don't find out just yet," she whispered back.

"You win."

"Deputy Bloom!"

"Mr. Colton," she said. "You remember Agent Roberts?"

"Yes, yes, of course. What are you doing back here? Shouldn't you be out hunting down this maniac?"

"We have bloodhounds for that," Stefan said smoothly.

Daria shot him a look, both appreciative of the joke and startled that he'd risk it with the powerful tycoon.

Russ looked a bit taken aback. But he recovered quickly. "This just has everyone so on edge. It's very difficult to do business, which is in a horrible state with all this going on."

"Nothing like a serial killer to shake things up," Stefan said. Again Daria blinked. She supposed being an FBI agent gave Stefan the freedom to say things she only thought, since she was a lot more likely to encounter the Coltons on a regular basis.

"Yes, yes, it's awful, but I'm very tired of my family being blamed for any part of this when we're victims. Accusing us of getting special treatment when we've only tried to help. You have no idea what it's like, having people judge you for something as simple as your name!"

Daria and Stefan exchanged a pointed glance.

"Oh, really?" Stefan drawled.

They had no idea? She, even with her skin tone being lighter than Stefan's rich, deep brown, had had her share of being judged by something even simpler than a name.

"You know what I mean," Russ said, a little defensively.

"Yes," Daria said; this was not the time or place. "Now if you'll excuse us, we have work to do."

"Chasing after that maniac," Stefan added with a too-charming smile.

After Russ had hurried away, they continued inside. "He really does rub you wrong, doesn't he?" she asked.

Stefan shrugged dismissively. And then, with a slow smile, he said in a voice rich with the husky undertone she'd heard when she'd been in his arms and he'd been murmuring her name, "You, on the other hand, rub me very, very right."

She felt a frisson of sensation shoot down her spine, as if he'd touched her. And she wondered yet again what would happen between them when this case that had seemed endless just two days ago finally did wrap up.

Chapter 23

They started at the top.

The office of the director of operations of The Lodge quite suited the rest of the place, elegant yet fitting the majestic mountain setting. Since Daria had dealt with this side of things practically from the beginning, Stefan let her explain what they wanted.

Perhaps because they'd just encountered the senior Colton, Stefan thought he could tolerate Decker Colton a lot better. He'd not interacted with him much on this case, but when he had, he'd noted the guy had the air of someone who had learned there was more to life than business, a lesson it appeared his father had never learned—and likely would never learn.

He'd mentioned that once to Daria.

And he learned it by falling in love. With a whip-smart woman.

She'd said it with a wide smile. Obviously she approved of the idea, he thought now. So why was she so wary with him?

He suddenly went still as he realized the path of his own thoughts. Falling in love? Was that what he'd done? What he wanted her to do? Was that why it bothered him that she seemed so…cautious?

A tangle of emotions jammed up in him. Didn't he have enough on his plate with Sam and a serial killer? Shouldn't he resolve at least one of those before he added something new and all consuming? Did he even want to add the complication a serious relationship would bring?

But it was only because of Daria that he was where he was with Sam. If not for her, they'd likely still be at each other, with him searching for patience and constantly reminding himself his son was only five, and Sam giving him those angry looks and throwing out those hateful words. She had changed that, had set them on a path that he hoped would lead to a genuine bond with his son.

Not to mention he was not about to give up what they'd discovered together yesterday. That had been no casual encounter, no simple onetime hookup. He'd had enough of that to know the difference.

He wondered if he and Daria gave off the same sizzle Decker Colton and his wife, Kendall, did. The pretty blonde had been leaving just as they arrived and had stopped to greet Daria enthusiastically—Daria's boss had been instrumental in finding the kidnapper who had grabbed her, and in discovering it had been orchestrated by someone her family owed money—and Stefan more decorously. But her face glowed with happiness, along with that sizzle.

Of course, she and Decker were newly married. That put them in a different category. Didn't it?

The smile Kendall had left on Decker's face faded when he realized why they were here. Since Shruggs again hadn't shown up at work today, they'd decided there was little to gain by trying to hide that he was a suspect, although they refrained from confirming he was the only suspect. Decker looked shocked but thoughtful. Shruggs had been here since before Decker had taken over, and since they had relatively few personnel problems, he'd never had reason to question his effectiveness or look into his methods.

It was Daria who quietly made the suggestion that Shruggs might have used his office to hunt for victims among the job applicants. Decker went pale, but Stefan could sense the change as he went from shock to anger that a Colton executive would use his position in such a hideous way. He offered them his full assistance before they had to ask and quickly set them up in his spacious meeting room and began to personally send employees in to them.

From there it became an extensive string of interviews, some short, some longer. They began with all the people who worked in Shruggs's department. Including his assistant, whom they had now concluded Shruggs had chosen because she was the most uncurious being he could find. The only thing this interview with her accomplished was to have Daria say sourly, after Shelly Bates had left, "If I ever start uptalking like that, shut me up, fast."

"Well, now you've got me hoping you do," Stefan said, thinking of the ways he'd like to quiet her in that very unlikely event, most of which involved keeping her mouth otherwise occupied.

And for a moment it was there in the room, alive between them, what they'd discovered together. The power of it took his breath away, and that rattled him. He'd never felt this way, and he wasn't quite sure what to do with the roiling emotions she caused in him. All he knew for sure was that if she asked him for a replay, he'd do it, right here, right now on this expensive Colton table.

Sex is the easy part, son.

His father's words from long ago echoed in his head even as he had the arousing thought. And they were followed by the rest of what his father had said, which surprised him a little, because he would have sworn back then he hadn't been paying much attention.

When you find yourself wanting to make her life easier, even if you have to go out of your way to do it, when you put what you want on hold for something she wants, not begrudgingly but happily—and when she does the same for you—well, then you've got something.

He'd ignored that wise, fatherly advice with Leah, who had never put anything she wanted on hold. And look where it had gotten him.

But it did get him Sam. And for the first time, he had hope that it would work out, that he could do for his son what his father had done for him. And that truly was thanks to Daria. And somehow no amount of mental orders not to get ahead of himself seemed to stop his mind from racing wildly in the direction of forever with this woman.

Forever.

He had a sudden image flash through his mind, of them years—hell, decades—from now, still together, as solid and unbreakable as his parents. He'd spent so long thinking he wasn't capable of that kind of bond that it was beyond startling to realize that he was thinking about it now, easily, with Daria. And he felt both thrilled and scared about it.

He wasn't sure if he wanted to know how Daria felt. Because if she hadn't had the same kind of thoughts…

He made an effort to yank his wandering mind back, which in itself was a warning. He never had trouble focusing on a case. That alone told him how much deeper Daria had dug into him, and without even trying.

If she ever did try…

This time he slammed the door on his thoughts and issued a stern order to his unruly mind to focus. He didn't want to be the reason they missed some hint or clue, not now that the end was nearly in sight.

They moved on to the managers at Shruggs's level, people he would have felt were worth his time, if they were judging his character correctly. Most of them recalled the man attending various social functions, but always alone. A couple of the women even admitted to offering to set Shruggs up with a friend, but he had always declined. They'd finally written him off as a confirmed bachelor who didn't want any change to that status.

And when they realized what this interview meant, that Shruggs was suspected of being the Avalanche Killer, even the most composed of them were completely shaken.

But once they got over that, every one of them made an obvious effort to remember anything about the man that could offer a clue to where he might be now. And as they'd expected, once they realized what was up, everybody seemed to have a memory of some creepy thing Shruggs had done or said. Stefan and Daria were both familiar with this Monday-morning-quarterbacking aspect of an investigation, so they dismissed the more general observations, but made note of everything anyway and highlighted the ones that seemed more solid.

But one stuck out to them, from the head of housekeeping, who had mentioned how, whenever she encountered the personnel director on a Monday, she would politely asked him how his weekend had been.

"He always said something like 'Beautiful,' or 'Wondrous,' but he said it with the creepiest expression I've ever seen. A hundred times worse than my ex-husband when he thought I didn't know he was cheating again." She'd paused then before adding, "He did say something once about there being lots of fish in the pond. I remember that because my mother used to say that, but it was fish in the sea, not pond."

Her words had made Stefan think of their discovery this morning, just before their meeting with Trey, that Shruggs had once had a fishing license but it had not been renewed in the last decade.

"Which proves nothing, really," Daria had said, sounding frustrated.

"Except that he might know some remote places to hide."

She'd brightened slightly. "True. And it's not likely a killer's going to worry about something as mundane as keeping his fishing license up to date."

"You might be surprised, some of the things serial killers obsess about. They can go either way."

"But still twisted."

He nodded in agreement.

They plowed on now. Swearing they'd talk to every employee if they had to had sounded good enough back at the office, but they hadn't really factored in the time the interviewees' shock would eat up, and they weren't moving as fast as they wanted, not when the chances of Shruggs's latest victim still being alive were shrinking rapidly.

They were down to the last couple of managers on the list when the door to Decker's conference room flew open. A woman burst in without knocking, making them both tense. Stefan rose out of his chair, but took no action as he recognized her as the director of guest services here at The Lodge.

"Is it true?" the woman demanded. "You know who the monster who killed my sister is?"

"I think," Daria said quietly, also getting to her feet, "you'd better sit down, Molly."

Chapter 24

"It's…really Curtis? The Avalanche Killer is Curtis Shruggs?"

Molly Gilford trembled slightly as she sat across the table from them. Daria saw the tremor in her fingers as she brushed a strand of blond hair back from blue eyes that were suspiciously bright. She could only imagine how she must be feeling right now.

And Daria quickly decided that this woman had been through enough—the murder of her sister, that terrifying incident on the gondola and then being kidnapped herself by her half-crazed sister-in-law who wanted her then unborn baby. True, she was now married to the baby's father—Max Hollick of K-9 Cadets—apparently happily, but nothing could change the fact that she had been terrorized and her sister had been viciously murdered. And she deserved every bit of the truth Daria was able to give to her.

"I'm afraid it's true," Daria said gently. "We found definitive evidence in his house." She left it at that—no need for the woman to know about the hidden, soundproofed room, the cage where he apparently tormented his victims before he killed them.

"But… I've worked with him for years. And he's always been…very vocally pro-women. Supportive. In his hiring, too. I never…he never…"

She stopped, took a deep breath.

"I know it's hard, feels impossible to believe," Daria murmured.

Molly took another breath, then looked Daria in the eye. "My sister and I weren't as close as some, because of the seven years' difference between us. I used to wish she would—" Her voice broke, but after a moment she went on. "I used to wish she would hurry and grow up, get through the partying stage. And now…"

She never will.

The words echoed in the room as clearly as if she'd spoken them. And Daria had no idea what to say, because deep down she knew nothing she said could adequately ease what the woman was feeling.

Even as Daria thought it, Molly drew herself up and said with remarkable steadiness, "But she was my sister and I loved her. I named my baby after her." She looked at both of them. "I want the truth."

Daria knew the woman meant it, but since she had little but a gut feeling to go on that Sabrina Gilford hadn't been one of the Avalanche Killer victims, she kept her own theories to herself. Right now she needed to focus on the facts at hand, the evidence they had and the man they knew had a woman in his clutches right now. And if Molly could help them with that, they had to push to find out anything she might know. If it turned out that she'd been right about Sabrina, they'd deal with it then.

"How closely did you deal with him?" Stefan interjected, his tone very gentle, and Daria knew he, too, realized what this woman had been through in the past few months.

"Sometimes very, sometimes not," she answered, her voice hanging on to that new steadiness. "I always check with guests during their stay to make sure everything's to their satisfaction. If I came across an employee who handled a guest's problem or a request well enough that the guest mentioned it to me, I made sure he knew."

"And complaints?" Daria asked, genuinely curious.

Molly gave her a fleeting smile. "If it was a first complaint on an employee, I let it go. We have some…very particular guests."

Daria presumed that was her tactful way of saying some of their guests were a pain. She could imagine, having lived both sides of that divide. "The type no one can please?"

"Exactly. So unless it became a pattern, I let it go. If there was a second time, I'd talk to the employee, but if it came to a third—unless it was all from the same guest who clearly just didn't like the employee—then I'd let Curtis know." She gave a shake of her head. "And he always handled it well enough, I thought. Fairly, anyway. I just can't believe this. Curtis, a…a serial killer?"

"I understand the shock you must be feeling," Daria said. "But we need you to just set that aside for the moment, because right now we have to focus on finding him."

Molly nodded, although her expression made her feelings clear. Daria didn't blame her in the least; finding out someone you'd known and worked alongside for years was truly that monster she'd mentioned was enough to rattle anyone to the core.

Daria thought about speaking some platitude that it might turn out Curtis was innocent, but they had to find him to prove that, so she didn't. This woman had asked for the truth, and if she was this solid after all she had been through, she had earned it.

"Think back, Molly," Stefan urged. "Did you ever hear Curtis say anything that might be a clue to where he would go to be…alone? Anyplace that was a favorite haunt, maybe someplace he went on vacation or something?"

"I don't think he ever really took vacations. Not like other people, you know, for a week or two. Just extra days here and there."

Stefan nodded; that tallied with what his assistant had told them. But Molly went on and instantly had Daria's complete attention.

"But he did mention once that a friend of his had a place near here that he'd gone to."

"A place?" Stefan was just as on alert as she was.

"A fishing cabin. I remember it because Curtis never seemed like a fisherman type to me."

Not for fish, anyway. Daria tried to rein in the inner kick of excitement that hit her. "Do you have any idea where, exactly?"

Molly shook her head. "I don't think he ever told me exactly, just that it was up above the biggest of the springs, at the west end. Except…"

"What?" Stefan encouraged her, and Daria heard the change in his voice, sensed the same wiredrawn tension in him that she was feeling. This was something, she was *certain* of it.

"He mentioned how…isolated it was. He said you could scream at the top of your lungs and no one would hear you." Daria felt a shiver go down her spine at the description of the perfect serial killer hideaway. Molly swallowed visibly. "I thought it was an odd thing to say, but that was all. I never… I should have…"

She stopped, gulping now. Daria reached out and put a hand on her arm. "You had absolutely no way to know, Molly. He's obviously very, very good or he wouldn't have gotten away with it for this long."

"Did he ever mention this buddy's name?" Stefan asked.

Molly shook her head. "He only said something about him being pretty nice for a…well, he used some nasty slang for someone who's Japanese."

Stefan was already on the phone, probably to his office, as Daria tried to soothe the understandably upset woman.

"You promise you'll find him?"

"I promise I will not give up until I do, one way or another," Daria said fiercely.

And she meant it. If it took years—which, God help her, it had better not—she would take down the man who had slaughtered those innocent women for no better reason than they matched his "type." She didn't care what justification for murder his twisted brain might come up with. All she cared about was stopping him at all costs.

"I believe you," Molly said. "It's why I'll vote for your boss tomorrow. And I don't care what the Colton haters say about having a Colton for sheriff."

Tomorrow. One more thing to deal with, Daria thought as the grief-stricken woman left. And Molly had no idea that what she'd said had a double meaning for Daria. That Trey wasn't the only Colton connection in the department.

Stefan was ending the call as she turned back. "They're on it, cross-referencing property owners around the springs with any Japanese names. It shouldn't take too long."

"Assuming he could even be identified by last name," Daria said, thinking he could have divided parentage like her own.

"All we have to go on," Stefan reminded her. "And," he added with a gentle rub at her shoulder, "a heck of a lot more than we had when we started."

"Yes." She turned to look at him then. "Let's start that way."

Stefan blinked. "I called for a team, but it'll be a while before they can get rolling, especially since we don't have a location yet."

"But we can be in the area, check it out first."

"Get the lay of the land, you mean?"

She nodded, so antsy to do something, *anything*, that she thought she might go on her own if he refused.

"I'm not sure that's a good idea," he said.

"I've got to do something," she insisted, feeling as if she were about to jump out of her skin. "I can't just stand around and wait, not when we finally have him!"

"I've had that feeling," he said cautiously, "but a lot of times that's when mistakes get made."

"Look, all I want to do is look around, see what we'll be dealing with. If he's even there. And if he's not, we can search the place for any evidence."

"All right," he finally agreed. "But that's all we're doing. We're not going after a guy with this many kills to his name without backup."

Daria knew better than to think it was his own safety Stefan was concerned about. He was just worried about Shruggs getting away. And he had a point, she admitted. It just wasn't enough to tamp down her impatience.

"And," Stefan added, "I take the lead." She pursed her lips. Waited for an explanation of what had sounded rather peremptory. Because she knew this man now, and knew he usually had a good reason for such decisions. When it came, it made perfect sense. "Just like at his house. He's seen you, but I've never been face-to-face with him."

"All right."

It wasn't until they were gathering up gear—Kevlar vests, tear gas, the Remington 700 rifle Daria hoped never to have to fire in a real-life sniper situation, and for good measure a couple of flash-bang grenades—that it occurred to her to wonder if maybe, just maybe, it wasn't just Shruggs escaping that Stefan was thinking about.

Maybe it was her.

Chapter 25

As he drove the department SUV, Stefan's instincts, honed by intensive training, warned him this was not what he wanted to do. Not what the Bureau would do. Barring interference from above, thankfully rare this far from the halls of power, they would wait until they had all the pieces in place, all possibilities they could think of covered. But Daria was so determined he knew there was no stopping her. And if he let her go alone, it could all too quickly devolve into disaster. Because he knew she'd risk herself, if it came down to it, to take this beast out. She was too damned fearless for her own good.

And for his peace of mind.

And that simple realization—that he was worried as much about her as this case—was a screaming warning that he was in way over his head with this woman. Never before had his emotions interfered with an investigation, and most especially a case like this, particularly when they were this close.

He tried to focus on the fact that she did have a point, about scouting the area. They needed to know the surrounding terrain, scope out possible escape routes, and if they could get that done before the backup team arrived, they'd be that much further ahead. And if they came across the target alone, he would just have to keep Deputy Bloom reined in until help arrived. No way in hell was he letting her go in after Shruggs without a full team, including a sniper—maybe two—in place and ready.

The old nightmare rose in his mind, and full daylight made no difference. That horrendous night, back in the killing fields of Chicago, when bodies had been strewn in the street, among them two agents who had moved too fast, without backup. True, they had done it because they had to—the suspect and his gang were shooting random citizens—but the aftermath had looked like a battlefield.

And two of their own had been among the dead.

This isn't the city. And we're going after one man, not a mob.

Not, of course, that one well-armed psychopath couldn't do a great deal of damage. And just because Shruggs had no concealed carry permit meant nothing. Less than nothing. Expecting a serial killer to abide by the law was a fool's game.

But he didn't do his kills with a weapon—he killed with his hands, up close and personal. Stefan had seen interviews, and done one himself, where the killer professed his delight in seeing life fading out of his victim's eyes.

He gave himself an inward shake; this was accomplishing nothing. Right now he needed to focus on keeping Daria out of trouble while they gathered the intel they could pass on to the backup team. At least she had realized he was right about him taking the lead, just in case the worst happened.

"Thank you," she said suddenly.

"For?"

There was a half second of silence, enough to make him glance at her. The slight smile that barely curved her lips warmed him inside in a way such a minute expression shouldn't have been able to. And the warning bells sounded again.

"Many things," she answered just as he had to turn back to driving, "but right now, for agreeing to this. I know you didn't want to."

"No, I didn't. I'm more of a get-your-ducks-in-a-row-first kind of guy."

"And what if while you're lining up those ducks, the vulture escapes?"

He glanced at her. "I wouldn't have thought of you as...impulsive."

Before he had to look back at the road ahead, he saw her expression change slightly as the word registered. "I'm not," she said. "I make very sure I know what I'm doing before taking a big step." He had time to wonder if that applied to what had happened between them yesterday as she hesitated for a moment. But then she said, very quietly, "I have a feeling my mother acted on impulse, and look where it got her."

He thought of what else the DNA testing he'd arranged had shown, but this was hardly the time for that discussion. He'd never pushed her about her parentage, and he wasn't about to now—not when they were heading into a situation that required them to be completely focused.

"She did what she had to. To give you both the best chance."

"I know." His next glance at her caught a very speculative look in her eye, but all she said was, "And it probably did work out for the best."

"You were adopted."

"Yes. And they were…wonderful to me." Again that speculative look, but it was the last time he was able to notice her expression, because they'd reached the area above the west end of the springs the town was named for, which also meant they'd reached the end of paved roads. Hence the SUV. Daria had known the roads up here were gravel at best, more often dirt and too often mud. He could already see she'd been right.

He paused the vehicle once, to get oriented in his mind. They'd called up the satellite imagery and he'd studied it until it was set in his mind, a knack he'd often put to good use. He was looking at a thick stand of trees off to the left when she spoke again.

"Isolated," she said, "could mean different things to different people. Did he mean out all alone with no neighbors close enough to hear, or just secluded among trees, so no one can see, either?"

"Could go either way," he replied. "But…"

"You're thinking trees?"

"Just a gut feeling." He knew she'd get this. Most cops of any persuasion did.

"Me, too. Something about his house, the log cabin look…"

"So…north-facing?"

"A good place to start," she murmured.

"Then that narrows down the escape routes, unless he's got a plan to get out on foot if he has to."

"He struck me as even less of a hiker than a fisherman," she said.

"All right. We'll go with that."

It took Daria a moment to realize what had caused the oddly emotional reaction she had to what should have been a strictly businesslike, even grim decision-making process—to hunt for a serial killer was hardly a heartwarming subject.

But what was heartwarming was Stefan's easy acceptance of her assessment of Shruggs. He'd always been respectful of her and her skills, but this, so close to what she hoped and prayed was the end, was bigger, and if he'd ever been going to take over it would be now. But instead he respected her instincts, her training, trusted her judgment as a cop, and she was a little taken aback at how much that meant to her. That he took her word as an equal, not just as a woman to a man, but a small-county sheriff's deputy to a federal agent.

But then she realized she must have already known it on some level. Because if she wasn't certain, even subconsciously, that she had that respect from him, yesterday afternoon never would have happened. And the very thought of having missed what she had found in his arms, the sheer joy his hands, his mouth, his body had given her, was chilling. She was old enough to know such perfect matches came along rarely in life. What she didn't know was where they went from here. He'd said—

A bounce that jarred her teeth interrupted her thoughts.

"Sorry," Stefan muttered. "That was more of a pot fissure than a pothole."

She found herself grinning at that, and given the circumstances, she took it as a sign of how far gone she truly was for this man.

The road got even rougher, and Daria saw some patches of lingering snow as they entered the shade of the evergreen trees standing amid the deciduous ones.

"At least the leaves are mostly gone from the cottonwoods, or we'd probably have some branches down," she said.

"And it means we can see farther," Stefan added, not looking at her as he negotiated another rut in the rural road.

"It's nice out here, and I'll bet the view of the mountains is spectacular, but…"

"I like your place better."

She turned her head to look at him. "You do?"

"I like your place a lot."

"I'll…keep that in mind." The emphasis he'd put on that last word sent her mind racing in a direction she couldn't deal with right now. She needed to focus. How would she feel if they lost Shruggs because she was mooning around planning a rosy future she wasn't even sure he wanted?

But Stefan had said he wanted more.

With great effort, she tamped down thoughts of forging the kind of future that she'd almost given up even hoping for. Because if this failed and Shruggs got away because she wasn't focused, Stefan would find that hard to forgive.

And if this failed and it was her fault, she would never, ever forgive herself.

Chapter 26

When the steering wheel jerked yet again as they went over a rough spot in the dirt road, Stefan realized he missed that aspect of the city. It startled him, because he hadn't missed anything about the city for quite a while.

Spoiled. You want the whole planet paved? Even beautiful places like this?

Of course, that beauty was tainted at the moment by the presence of the human scum that was Curtis Shruggs. This place—and the planet—would be a lot better off once he was put away.

He glanced over and saw Daria studying something on her phone. It gave him a chance to see her in profile, to appreciate the delicate line of her jaw, the way her hair caressed her neck, the place in her throat where her pulse beat, where he had nuzzled and licked and kissed her...

He snapped his eyes back to the rough road. He was going to drive them into a tree at this rate. But the combination of her strength of will and body, her quick mind, and her unassuming beauty was intoxicating. And unlike this place, nothing could ever taint that beauty.

He had a sudden vision of her a quarter century from now, her hair perhaps gray, or even his mother's almost glowing silver. She would still be stunning, probably regal, an elder who demanded and got respect. And him? He'd be pushing sixty then, maybe thinking about retiring. Or flying a desk, something that seemed anathema now, but if he had her to go home to…

Damn.

Rattled, he stared at the road ahead. But he still saw that picture, of his future life, so full and complete in his mind, as if it were a given. Complete with the woman at his side now still at his side then.

Then again, why not? He admired her. Respected her. He'd thought her beautiful from the first moment he'd turned to see her coming into Trey Colton's office. He'd already known she was sharp, smart, or the equally sharp and smart sheriff wouldn't have signed this case over to her. But he hadn't expected the lithe, graceful knockout that had walked in, hadn't been—could he have ever been?—prepared for those gorgeous gold-flecked brown eyes.

And now you know you're hotter than hell together.

Well, yeah, that, too. They'd damned near set her hillside on fire.

And he was about to drive off this one. He scrambled to regain control of his thoughts. This was not the time to be lost in envisioning a future like he'd never even dared hope for before.

He hit upon the one thing powerful enough to match his flooding thoughts of Daria. *Sam.* But even he was no longer the distraction he'd once been, and that, too, was thanks to Daria. They were tentatively finding their way to the kind of relationship he wanted with his son. And as for Daria, Sam adored her, and she clearly liked him.

Enough to want both of us?

And suddenly that future image in his mind shifted, altered. Sam would be…damn, he'd be thirty then. And what kind of thirty he'd be would depend on what kind of father Stefan was now. Just as the man he was now was because of his own father.

Tell your father word for word what you just said.

Daria's words echoed in his mind, as they so often did. And he added the thought he'd just had to the list of things he was saving up to do exactly as she'd suggested. Tell the man who deserved to hear it.

And suddenly he was looking forward even more than before to his parents' trip out here. Not only for the help they'd be, but…he wanted them to meet Daria. He was as certain as he could be of anything in this life that they would see her for the amazing woman she was. He could even picture his father taking him aside, as he never had with Leah, and telling him to hang on to this one. And—

"You want me to drive?"

His head snapped around, and he stared at her. "What?"

"You look a bit white-knuckled. I've driven on roads like these quite a bit, if you'd rather not."

"Oh. No. I'm fine."

"We're going to get him, Stefan."

Of course she thought that was what had him all wound up. Why wouldn't she? It was probably the only thing she was thinking about. She certainly wasn't sitting there fantasizing about them growing old together.

And he was coward enough to seize on the out she'd unknowingly given him. "I know we are."

"I wish we'd gotten to him sooner, but—"

"We've got him now. It's just a matter of reeling him in." His cell rang, and on this road he pulled over before he tugged it out.

"At least the call got through," Daria murmured. "Service is particularly spotty up here."

"It's my office," he said as he answered. "Lisa? What do you have?"

"Two names and locations," the woman replied. Stefan saw Daria was already prepared with her own phone to take notes. "Go."

He quoted back the names and addresses Lisa gave him, and Daria keyed them into her notes app.

"I'd tell them to text as backup," she suggested. "Sometimes texts get through up here when calls won't." He relayed that info, all the while watching her as she switched to a map and did two quick searches. "One's on the left fork we'll hit another half mile or so ahead. The other's that gray house we passed on the way up."

"Gray one seems too close to civilization," he said.

"Agreed."

He drove on as she did something else with the image on her screen. The track that branched off to the left from the one they were on looked little more than something a mountain goat would use. He wasn't even sure the SUV would make it. Yet if Shruggs was up there, he had to have gotten there somehow. So he kept going, at a pace that would lose to the proverbial snail.

The track veered slightly more left, and the surface was even rougher.

"Maybe we should stop here." Daria indicated a very small space to her right where they could pull over at least halfway. "And go in on foot."

"Maybe," Stefan said neutrally, "we should wait for the troops to go in at all."

"I don't mean go up and knock on the door," she retorted. "Just to get a closer look."

He smothered a sigh. He supposed there wasn't any harm in that, if they were careful to stay under cover. "Let me get some gear out of the back. We'll need binoculars and communications at least."

She nodded, back to looking at her phone. "I'll enlarge the satellite view, see if we can tell anything from that."

His brow furrowed. He pulled out his own phone, to see the "No Service" warning. She glanced at him, and he turned it toward her.

"I know," she said. "I figured that would happen, so I took a screenshot of it back there where we had a signal."

He stared at her. "You never miss a trick, do ya?"

She gave him a smile then that nearly sent his pulse into overdrive. And suddenly he wanted that future he'd imagined, growing old with her by his side, more than he'd wanted anything. Ever.

"Here," she murmured, holding her phone out to him. "It looks like there's a footpath here that goes up around the back."

He silently questioned what she considered a footpath. Decided he was definitely still too much of a city boy and said only, "The house looks smaller than the gray one, but it's bigger than what I'd call a fishing cabin."

"True. So maybe it's not the one. Maybe when we get closer, we'll see a family with the traditional two-point-three kids and a dog, and we'll know."

He'd never thought himself that bound by tradition, but somehow that sounded…wonderful. Even the dog. Sam would love a dog—she'd obviously been right about that. And maybe more, later. Adoption was fine with him, although he would have liked to have seen what kind of child he and Daria would have produced.

And the realization he was thinking in those terms barely rattled him anymore. But they had to get through this first.

They slipped their earpieces on and verified they were working and that they could hear each other clearly. Then he let her take the lead, staying close enough behind her to grab her if she slipped, which looked uncomfortably possible on this very narrow path. Branches brushed him as they passed, and once a bird chattered at him crankily as they disturbed him.

"So much for stealth," he muttered.

"I don't think it matters," Daria said. She'd come to a stop, the binoculars to her eyes. He came up behind her, and she handed them to him.

He looked. It wasn't the two-point-three kids—more like four, with three adults, all bundled against the chill, a Japanese couple and a single Caucasian female. The adults were watching the four kids, an equal mix of the same races, playing in what was left of the snow. All smiling happily. As they watched, another male exited the house, carrying a tray with cups of something steaming that made Stefan suddenly crave that hot chocolate Daria had once mentioned.

"If I have to believe that group knowingly has anything to do with the likes of Shruggs, I'm going to quit and become a hermit," she whispered.

"You won't be a hermit, because I'll be right there with you," he said.

"Promise?"

She said it teasingly, but he got the feeling there was

more behind it. He put a hand on her shoulder, and she looked back at him.

"Yes," he replied quietly.

Something flashed between them, something vivid and alive, and he knew she'd understood. And when she looked away, he didn't feel slighted, because he realized the intensity was too much right now, when they had no choice but to be focused on the matter at hand. The details—for in his mind that was all that was left—could wait.

Had to wait. Because they were close, he could feel it.

Although he agreed with her completely about the innocence of this group, he watched them for a moment longer. The biggest child had raced off toward a small outbuilding, a shed of some sort, likely to gather the snow that lingered on the side still in shade.

And Daria went suddenly still. She pulled out her phone and swiped it on. He could see from where he stood behind her that the satellite image was still there. She enlarged it, then moved it slightly.

"See it?" she asked softly.

He frowned, scanning the screen. It took him a moment to orient himself, to place the edge of the clearing they stood a few yards away from now, but then he had it. In a thick stand of trees, east of where they were, was another roof. He looked that direction and saw nothing but trees. So hidden. Then he glanced back at the screen, the nearly hidden roof in the image. Definitely smaller than this house.

Just about the right size to be called a cabin.

Chapter 27

"It's a bit far, but it could still be on the same property if they have acreage," Daria said as she studied the phone, glad she'd thought to screenshot the image. They'd moved away from the happy group at the big house; the last thing she wanted was such obviously innocent bystanders getting caught up in anything. When the backup teams got here, they'd either corral them safely in the house or evacuate them, depending on how the situation looked.

"And thus be under the same name in the records," Stefan agreed. "It looks pretty basic—just a rectangle with a simple roofline."

She nodded. "I don't see any path from here to there," she said, enlarging the area around that second roof.

"Trees are thick enough over there it might not be visible on that," he told her. "We might have to—" He stopped as her phone signaled a text. "I see what you mean," he said as she switched over to read the message that had gotten through.

Her breath caught as she read. And when she looked up at him, she knew the triumph had to be glowing in her eyes.

"I had my office call Molly Gilford." Daria gestured back toward the house they'd just left. "I thought the owner of that place might have tried the area out first, to see if he liked it enough to buy. She just called back. Mr. Nakamura was a guest at The Lodge several times before he bought this place."

Stefan's eyes widened. "And thus had multiple chances to encounter Shruggs."

"Yes."

He looked back the way they had come, although they could no longer see the house with the families. "That place looked fairly new."

She nodded. "Maybe when they bought the property, the cabin was the only thing on it. Then they built the house and let people rent or borrow the cabin. I know it's guesswork—"

"But it's good guesswork," Stefan said. "It makes sense, and it fits with everything we know."

"We could go back and ask him," she suggested. "Assuming he's the guy who's there now."

Stefan thought for a moment. "Let's not risk it yet. Just in case Shruggs is here and watching." He checked his own phone for texts. "Nothing," he muttered. "I want an ETA on backup."

"They'll get here when they do," she said, far too antsy to think about how long that might be. She knew she didn't have to remind him Shruggs had a new captive, who just might still have a fighting chance. "In the meantime, let's see if we can get the lay of the land around the cabin, and any sign that he's been here."

"We should wait. If he's there now—"

"We should at least be where we can see if he leaves."

She saw him take in a deep breath, then he nodded. "Point taken."

She thought she saw a flicker in his eyes, as if he were remembering what had become a private joke between them. She'd knit him that scarf, she thought, when this was over.

They made their way with as much stealth as they could manage in the general direction of the small cabin. And he'd been right—there were paths, of a sort. Just narrow tracks that meant walking single file, one foot directly in front of the other, and brushing branches both bare and evergreen as they passed.

"Animal paths," she murmured as they left the big house with the happy gathering behind them.

"And the city guy in me is a bit edgy about that," Stefan, who was ahead of her, muttered.

"I'll take these animals over city animals any day," Daria said.

It was a moment before she heard him say rather wryly, "Once again, point taken."

They fell into silence then as they got closer to where they were guessing the hidden cabin was. Stefan stopped in the same moment she spotted a straight, man-made angle through the trees, although the color was nearly the same brown as the winter-bare trees.

"Not quite as isolated as I expected," she said.

Stefan looked back toward the house where the families were playing. "No. I'd think someone down there could easily hear someone scream from here."

The possibility that they were completely wrong about this place shook her, threatened her with a burst of despair.

"It's still the best lead we've got," Stefan uttered firmly. "Let's go."

She nodded and they went forward even more carefully, until Stefan stopped again. Although this time he was looking down.

"The animal-track path dies out," he whispered.

"Odd," she murmured back. "I wonder why."

"Maybe they know."

If he'd been facing her, he would have seen her practically gaping at him. That was such a fanciful, if very dark, thing for this man in particular to say. He seemed utterly grounded in reality to her, and she wouldn't have guessed him capable of it. But were the circumstances different, she thought it would have charmed her. Not that he needed any help in that arena.

But the idea was now vivid in her mind—that even the wild creatures knew there was something abnormal here. Something to avoid. Something dangerous.

"They don't call us the apex predator for nothing," Stefan muttered, as if he felt the need to explain away what he'd said. Later, she thought, she would tell him how unnecessary that was.

"And we're the ones who take out the predators."

He looked back at her then. Gave her a quick, flashing smile that took her breath away and nearly blasted all sense of focus out of her.

"Yes, we are," he said.

And in that moment Daria knew he was as determined as she was, that they shared this goal, that it was why they were who—and where—they were. A sudden, crazy image shot through her mind, of her and Stefan sitting in her living room some unknown amount of time from now, discussing their respective current cases as Sam played his favorite game on the floor in front of the fire. And she was seized with a fierce ache inside to make that come true, to have that, for all three of them. Because they all needed it. And each other.

She felt the sudden need to say so, to say yes to the question he hadn't yet asked but had hinted at when he said he wanted more. And it seemed important to say it now, despite her common sense telling her this was hardly the place or the time. Then again, maybe that was what made it seem so important right now. Maybe it was the same sort of instinct that had stopped the animals from getting closer than they were now. She didn't know what might happen next, and—

Before she could even begin to find any words, a sound from the direction of the cabin snapped both their heads around. In an instant Stefan had the binoculars up to his eyes. Daria held her breath, waiting.

"Nothing moving," he whispered after a few tense moments. "Except there's a squirrel or something by that trash can out to the left from the building."

She leaned forward and spotted the large metal can. Even as she looked, the small creature vanished into the trees. She wondered if it had given up the task of trying to loosen the lid or if something had scared it off. Perhaps it had belatedly sensed whatever the other creatures who had gone no farther had sensed.

"I think we could get there," she said softly, gesturing through a gap in the trees.

"Want to go trash picking?"

"No, but yes."

That smile again. They should make him get a permit for that, because it was more lethal than any firearm.

"I suppose it wouldn't hurt," he said. "As long as we can do it without getting spotted."

It took them a little longer to get there than she'd expected, because of the effort to hold down the noise. Luckily for their purpose, the trash can was set against a row of trees that marked the end of the small clearing behind the cabin, masking anything—or anyone—behind them. Unluckily, the trees were so close together that it would be nearly impossible to get to the can without either making noise or visibly moving the branches. If no one happened to be looking this way at that moment they'd be fine, but…

"I'll try," she whispered. "I'm smaller." *And then some.*

Another of those flashes hit her, of just how much bigger and stronger he was. Cliché though it might be, it was true in his case. But then she veered into how he used that size and strength, that amazing body, when he'd been driving her mad with a sexual heat she'd never felt before—

Stop it!

He was looking at her, and she knew by the set of his jaw he wanted to say no. Was probably weighing what would happen if he did. His protection elsewhere might be needed, even welcomed, but if she couldn't do her job, there was no point in having it.

"Not on the job," she said to him, very quietly.

For an instant he looked surprised, but then rueful, as if he'd realized how well she'd read him. "Just—"

"Be careful. Got it."

"And if I touch you, freeze."

Not likely.

"Not a sound or a move," he went on.

"Copy," she said.

She got down on her hands and knees and crawled ever so slowly through the lower branches of the trees. Using the large trash can itself for cover, she reached up and released one of the latches that held the lid on, a frequently seen protection against bears and other animals that might be scavenging around. She fleetingly wondered if Shruggs was even aware of such things as she edged the lid partially off. Half afraid of what she'd find, she raised the lid slightly and straightened just enough to look into the can.

She had to move the lid a bit more to let in more light, for the contents were in the shadowy bottom of the can. But it only took her a quick look and a reading of a single torn wrapping to have her closing it back up and working her way backward. When she was clear of the low branches, and they had slipped back into place, masking them from the cabin, she rose into a crouch. Stefan came down to her level quickly, with that easy grace of his.

He didn't speak, just waited. She appreciated that, because the surge of adrenaline had her breathing quickly and it took her a moment.

"This is it," she whispered, letting her gut-deep certainty into her voice. "This is the place."

He didn't argue, just led the way back the same way they'd come, until they were safely far enough it was unlikely they'd be spotted or heard from the cabin. Then he glanced back toward where the trash can was. "What?"

"Wrappers." He looked back at her then. "From packages labeled…soundproofing."

She saw Stefan's jaw tighten. "That son of a bitch. He built himself another torture room."

"So the one in his house was just a…holding pen." She couldn't disguise the shudder in her voice. "Stefan, if that girl is still alive…"

"She might not be for long," he said grimly.

Chapter 28

"No texts?" Daria asked. Stefan shook his head. "So we don't know how far away they are."

"We need to know if he's here. We can't assume he's not just because it's so quiet."

"Agreed," she said. "But the girl…she could be in there, dying, right now." Tension echoed in her voice; she could hear it herself. But she went on. "If he's not there, this could be our only chance to save her."

"Daria, we have to wait for the breach team."

"I know, I know," she said. "I just hate this."

"So do I," Stefan told her. "But there are protocols for a reason."

"I know," she repeated. "Just tell that to my gut."

He gave her a commiserating grimace, and she knew he did understand. That underneath that cool, calm exterior he was probably as roiled as she was. But he was a professional to the core and wouldn't let it sway him.

"I didn't see a garage, or even a carport," Stefan said.

"Maybe it's down the hill, hidden on the other side of the cabin. For that matter, we might not be able to see a car out in the open from here, if it's on that side."

"It would help to know if his vehicle is there. Assuming he uses his. That bright yellow Italian sports job is pretty noticeable."

"Making up for his other shortcomings, no doubt," she quipped.

Stefan blinked. Then he grinned at her. As she had intended.

"Not," she said airily, "a problem you'd understand."

The shared moment of intimacy, achieved without even a touch, warmed her. But it was immediately back to business. They needed to know about a car, and there was only one way to do that.

"Up or down?" he asked, checking both directions in turn from where they stood.

"We could each take one way. Up means more cover but tougher terrain—it's pretty steep," she said, looking that way. "Down's easier, probably quicker, but more chance of getting spotted if he is in there."

"Kind of decides it, then."

She nodded. Then, decisively, he said, "Get back to where you can see the cabin, and I'll see how far I can get up there." She pondered that for a moment, wondering if he was pulling the protector card again. Before she could speak, he said quietly, "You're the sharpshooter—you need to be stationary."

He had a point. And his easy acknowledgment of her skill took any sting out of staying here while he risked the climb.

She heard him go, but once he was a dozen feet away

from her, she heard nothing except the faintest brush of branches that could have been from any light breeze. It was amazing that a man his size could move so quietly. That was, it would be amazing if you didn't know him, if you hadn't seen that tight-knit grace up close and personal. As she had.

She had to suppress a shiver, which was odd given the heat that had shot through her at the memories of that up close and personal. She almost gave herself an order to stop thinking about sex with him. Aloud. Which would have been picked up by Stefan's earpiece.

Now that would have been seriously embarrassing.

Then again...

Daria snapped out of it when something from the cabin caught the corner of her eye. She shifted the binoculars that direction, but nothing had changed. All she could discern was that a shaft of sunlight had broken through the November gloom, and it caught the upper corner of a window and sent back a flare of light. Yeah, that must be what she'd seen. She settled in to watch and wait. And listen. Most of all listen to that tiny unit in her ear.

It was several minutes before she heard anything, and then she couldn't be sure if it had been Stefan or some creature he'd disturbed.

"Okay?" she asked quietly; they'd decided on plain English because ten-codes varied between agencies.

"Proceeding," he said back, just as quietly. "And there's a pond in view on this side."

Lots of fish in the pond...

It seemed an endless stretch of time after that. She wondered idly how snipers did it, how they simply waited, ready, sometimes for hours. Sometimes even longer. Then she wondered about how some people were great shots with long guns, some with sidearms, a rare few with both, and what it was that made that difference.

Her mind kept racing in an endless loop. But it was the distraction she needed to keep from thinking about what could be going on in there, what that evil, repulsive psychopath could be doing to an innocent woman. Because if she started thinking about that, she wasn't sure she could just wait this out.

She'd thought, occasionally, about the hazards of the job. Known that the day could easily come when she'd be one of those uniforms that went down in the line of duty. But she'd set that fear aside most of the time. Besides, she had memories others didn't, memories of the biggest and best bodyguard service in the world, watching over her adoptive father like the predators they could become at the slightest hint of a threat. The people who could and did tell the president of the United States what to do, and he listened. Joe Colton had, anyway.

After all that, the peace of these mountains seemed endless.

Except you're sitting here waiting for a serial killer to stick his head out like a pumpkin in a shooting gallery. And praying his latest victim is still alive.

She told herself the girl must be, or Shruggs would be back home, his twisted, insane needs assuaged for the moment. Until they built and he struck again.

You will not!

Her mind nearly shouted it, as if he could hear her thoughts if he was indeed in the small cabin.

Stefan's voice came over her earpiece. "I've got movement—"

Crack!

Shot. Handgun. Large caliber. Probably a .45.

Daria's mind raced through the cataloging in a split second as she scanned the cabin again, but over it all hung one simple fact. Stefan carried the standard FBI-issue Glock 23 in .40 caliber. That was not what she'd heard fire.

Someone else had taken a shot.

"Stefan!"

When no answer came, her pulse kicked up another notch.

Daria started moving, trying to balance her haste with care, but as a second shot came, she abandoned any pretense at secrecy since it was obviously blown already. She simply ran, scrambling, glancing at the cabin when there was a break in the trees but otherwise focused only on getting to him.

"Window to the east of the back door."

Her breath came out in a rush at the sound of Stefan's voice in her ear. He sounded strained to her. But who wouldn't be with somebody capping off .45 rounds at you?

"Almost there. Status?" She allowed herself the question.

"Just get him. I'll keep his attention here."

His dodging the question in effect answered it, and her tension ratcheted up yet again. But he was conscious and coherent, at least. She kept moving. She had to veer right to go around a large rock, but as she did, she realized the spot had a clear view down to the cabin. To the back door, and the half-open window beside it.

And she could see Shruggs.

Even as she looked, another sunbeam broke through. It lit up this window as it had the other one, only this time it also caught the hand holding the large 1911-model pistol.

Again her mind raced through the calculations in a split second.

Right hand. Puts body mass to center or your right. Fifteen-degree downhill slope. Distance twelve yards. No wind.

Easy peasy.

Daria heard Stefan's shots from farther up the hill—he wasn't hurt badly if he was capable of shooting. But she stayed focused on the window. She saw the weapon fire, saw the recoil kicking that hand back as he tried to do it with one hand. Using the big rock for cover, she let out her breath slowly as she sighted in. Put everything, even Stefan, out of her mind. Her vision narrowed to her front sight, the window and her target, out of focus but there.

Three rounds as fast as she could pull. The hand and weapon in the window jerked upward.

Two more, one lower, one to the side, covering if he went down or dodged instinctively toward the solid door.

It was only then she hesitated. Their presence could drive Shruggs to kill his victim right now if he hadn't already. But if Stefan was hurt…

"Solid hits. He's down."

"Copy."

He sounded okay. Maybe she'd been wrong—maybe he hadn't been hit. But she couldn't let herself think about it now. She had a job to do, a life, please God, to save.

"What if he runs?" she whispered. His answer came back in her ear without hesitation.

"Let him. He's hurt—we'll find him. Let's get to her."

She felt a tug of some deep, heartfelt emotion as he put the victim over a capture.

Daria came out of the tree line, aware she was exposing herself completely. She dived, rolled, making herself as tough a target as she could. But Stefan fired again from up the hill. And she fired, too, only at the trash can, and her round made a loud, echoing pinging sound as it hit the metal.

Nothing.

She felt her tension ease when she saw Stefan emerge from the trees above, on his feet and moving fast. He was all right. They came at the cabin from opposite sides, reached the wall and started edging toward that back door.

Still nothing. She got closer, then close enough to get a darting glance through the half-open window.

Shruggs wasn't just down, he was out. She couldn't tell if he was still alive, didn't care. She reached through the window to the back door, had to flip a dead bolt but got it open. It jammed up against Shruggs, but she kept shoving. And then Stefan was there, adding his weight, and they were through.

She checked, found a faint pulse. "He's alive. Barely."

"There's a landline. I'll call it in—you find her. She'll trust a woman."

She nodded, shouted out an ID, hoping the victim would realize the good guys were here, and began a methodical search. She'd barely taken three steps when she heard a muffled cry from the right. Her gaze shot that direction, and she saw a closed door. She made her way over there, half listening to Stefan calling in the troops and medical help.

At the door she hesitated, then called out. "Are you

alone?" There was no indication Shruggs ever let anyone else in on his ugly games, but…

Again the muffled sound, definitely female. Daria turned the doorknob, shoved it open and jumped back out of a potential line of fire.

Silence.

She risked a look.

And saw a pair of terrified eyes, looking at her out of the badly bruised face of a naked young woman bound and gagged in the corner of the small, soundproofed closet.

"It's all right. It's over."

She knelt beside the woman, pulled out her pocketknife and quickly cut her free. The woman's sobbing was broken, and she sagged against Daria. On instinct she pulled off her own coat and slipped it around the woman, who pulled it tight with trembling fingers.

Daria drew in a deep breath and turned to give Stefan a smile. It died on her lips.

He'd slid down the wall next to the landline phone and was sitting on the floor, one hand pressed to his side.

A side that was bleeding. Profusely.

Her heart skipped a beat as her mind screamed a protest.

No. No!

Even as she looked, his eyes closed and there was a slight thump as his head went back against the wall.

"Stefan!"

She wanted to run to him, but the victim beside her had to be her priority, her job. But—

"He's yours?"

The tiny, tremulous question took her aback. She

looked at the young woman, who was looking at Stefan. Who had been shot coming to her rescue.

"Yes. He's mine." Never had she meant those words as she did now.

Even as she said them, she heard something in her earpiece, realized belatedly that the breach team would be on that same system.

"More help is here," she said to the woman, then gave the people outside the all clear and ordered up medical personnel.

Full of dread when she finally was able to get to Stefan, she knelt beside him. The moment she touched his cheek, his eyes opened. They were a little glassy, and she could see he was in some pain, but he still smiled at her.

"Nice shooting," he said softly.

She smiled back at him, realizing only when she felt the trickle down her cheek that she was crying.

It really was finally over.

Chapter 29

If one more person asked how she was doing, Daria thought she might just erupt. How did they think she was doing?

The ones that congratulated her were the worst. *Nice work, Bloom! Save the victim and take down the killer—can't ask for better!*

Well, yes, she could. She could ask that Stefan not be lying in the other room, hooked up to a blood bag as they replaced what he'd lost. Especially knowing if he'd stayed put after he'd been hit, if he hadn't run down to back her up, he wouldn't have lost nearly as much.

She sat in the waiting area clinging to the other, much more important words, from the young woman in the blue scrubs, that he would be all right. That in fact he'd been very lucky—the wound had done little damage as gunshots go, and it was the blood loss that had weakened him. Daria had thanked her even as she wondered what on earth the woman had seen that she could say any gunshot wound had done little damage. Especially after she'd peeked into the room and seen Stefan lying there, his beautiful mahogany skin a stark contrast to the sheets.

"Daria."

She looked up at her name being spoken softly. Trey. She rose quickly, even after he waved at her to stay seated. He was simply looking at her, and she couldn't read his expression. Her boss could be as inscrutable as he needed to be when it was called for.

"I won't say nice work, because I know you think anything that resulted in an injury to one of us didn't go well, but…you got him, Daria. I read both your preliminary statements, and that was some fine shooting."

She liked that he referred to Stefan as one of them. Some local and county officials got huffy over fed involvement, even when they'd asked for the help. But not Trey. The capture of the Avalanche Killer had always been his top priority.

"Thank you," she said, not certain what else to say.

"They're prepping Shruggs for surgery now. He's in bad shape but conscious. I thought you might want to see if you can get a statement out of him."

"You could do that," she said, thinking it might be that last bit to nail down a victory in the election tomorrow.

"You did the work," he told her. "You earned it."

Daria gave him the best smile she could manage just then. "As long as you talk to the media," she said and smiled at his grimace.

She walked in the direction he'd indicated, her thoughts practically glowing in neon in her head. This was why the people of this county had darn well better reelect this man. They'd never find a more honest, trustworthy and fair person to stand for them.

Shruggs was in much worse shape than Stefan; his skin looked like the underbelly of a dead fish. She felt no pity for him, not even hatred, for he was not worth so much emotion. She coolly opened the record function on her phone, just in case, although there were three other witnesses in the medical staff standing there, and none of them looked particularly sympathetic toward their patient.

When he looked at her as she stood by the gurney he was lying on, even the blue of his eyes—*Blue Eyes*—was faded.

She made her voice purposely nonchalant. "Anything you want to say now, in case you don't make it out of surgery?"

Even as weak as he was, his gaze narrowed. "What the hell are you doing here?"

"Me?" Daria gave him a dazzling smile then. "I'm the *woman* who shot you."

That one hit home, as she'd hoped. She thought he would have snarled if he'd had the strength. She pushed a little harder.

"And if you die in there, no one will ever know or care. You'll be forgotten as nothing but a sicko who got stupid and got caught." She saw something shift in his gaze at a particular word, so she repeated it. "You're nothing. Less than nothing."

"I'm the one who's gotten away with this under cops' noses for over a decade," he snapped.

"Not *this* cop," she said. "How does it feel to know a woman took you down? A woman just like April Thomas, Lucy Reese, aka Bianca, Sabrina Gilford—"

"She wasn't one of mine."

Daria sucked in a breath. Feigned surprise. "What?"

"That Gilford woman. She wasn't one of mine. She's not my type. Not my type at all—looked nothing like her."

They took him away then, leaving Daria staring at the swinging doors as they closed.

She'd been right.

Her mind was still spinning as she sat at Stefan's bedside. He looked much better already, and she silently thanked whoever the blood donors were. She knew his FBI brethren had lined up to donate when word had gotten out he'd been shot, and she was pleased when they'd told her several of her own department had been there for him, as well. And those who weren't a match for him would help others. A lot of others, it seemed, since his wound wasn't nearly as bad as she'd feared.

He appeared to be asleep, and she completely understood. She felt exhausted herself. They had both been running on adrenaline for so long that the crash couldn't help but be long and ugly. That was the one good thing that had come out of him being shot; he was resting whether he wanted to or not.

Now, if she could just turn off her own brain for a while…

She had told Trey what Shruggs had said about Sabrina Gilford and her not being his type. He'd told her not to worry about it right now, that she and Stefan had both earned a break and he expected them to take it. But she couldn't quite let go of it. Had Shruggs been telling the truth? It wasn't quite a deathbed confession—and almost sadly, it hadn't been his deathbed, he'd survived the surgery. But still, was he likely to lie knowing it could be the last chance he'd have? So many serial killers were proud of their work and almost gloried in bragging about it once they were caught. Was Shruggs one of those? She knew some of them were scrupulous about their kills, wanted credit for those they'd done and wouldn't take it for those they hadn't.

Problem was she didn't know enough about a serial killer's mind-set. She'd never expected to be entangled in a case like this, not here in Roaring Springs, where an out-of-control party or thefts from some upscale store were usually about the worst things they encountered. This was why Trey, no fool who refused to admit when something was outside his experience, had called in the FBI.

And Stefan.

She looked at him again, so relieved he was going to be all right. The depth and power of her relief was undeniable, and that in turn told her a great deal about what she'd come to feel about this man. He was—

"He's responding very well." Her head snapped around, and she saw the same doctor who had examined him initially, a petite brunette with a scattering of small freckles over her nose, standing there smiling. She rose to her feet as the woman finished with, "He won't be here long."

Daria smiled. "Thank you. So much."

"Thank him," the doctor said with a grin. "He's a very strong guy."

"Yes. He is."

"Taken?" she asked with an arched brow.

"Oh yes," Daria said fervently. "Very."

"I thought so. He was worried that you would worry," the doctor murmured, and winked at Daria as she added, "Hang on to that one, girl."

Daria was smiling as she turned to sit back down. And saw Stefan awake and looking at her. He was smiling, too.

"Very taken, huh?"

"Yes," she replied firmly. "And don't you forget it."

"Not likely," he said, and what she saw in his eyes warmed her down to her very soul.

"How do you feel?"

"Not sure," he admitted. "They give me something to put me out?"

"I'd think the last three months would have done that. And in case you forgot, you were shot."

He scoffed. "Barely more than a gouge. Only missed being a graze by a half inch."

She rolled her eyes. He grinned. And her world seemed to right itself. She gave him a quick update on things, purposely lowering her voice when she saw his eyelids start to close. He drifted off again soon after that, but Daria clung to what the doctor had said, that he wouldn't be here long. Of course what was long to the doc might not be what was long to Daria, which would be anything longer than him getting out right now. She wanted him out of here and where she could look after him. And Sam, he'd be worried—

Sam.

Her eyes widened as she looked at her watch.

Sam would be getting out of school in half an hour. Mrs. Crane would be there to pick him up as usual, but… Trey had gone to deal with the media. So it was already out there, no doubt.

She grabbed her phone and checked a couple of news feeds. Oh, it was out there, all right. Not that she was surprised. In a place as on edge as Roaring Springs had been, you didn't roll out vans and SUVs full of agents and deputies—and three ambulances—without it spreading like wildfire. And these days the theories were running amok on social media even before the people on scene had a full handle on what was happening.

She looked a little further, and there it was—the rumor that an agent had been shot at the scene. Would Mrs. Crane be aware enough to keep that from Sam until the boy knew his father was all right? She found Trey's initial brief statement, which said only that the victim had been rescued alive and an agent had been injured in the process but his injuries were not life-threatening. The suspect, he had ended with no small satisfaction, had been shot but was alive and in custody.

It hit her suddenly, really for the first time. Past tense. She'd been so worried about Stefan, and grimly focused on making sure Shruggs was wrapped up tight, she hadn't really let her mind run to the bigger picture. That the Avalanche Killer case was over. Oh, there was a quagmire of things yet to come—reports and eventually a huge, public trial—but the twisted, psychotic man who was Curtis Shruggs was finished.

With a burst of energy she stood, found a piece of paper in her bag and scribbled a quick note, and tucked it into Stefan's fingers. To make sure, she found the floor nurse and asked her to tell him, if he woke again before she got back, where she'd gone.

And then she left to pick up the child who had come to mean almost as much to her as his father.

Chapter 30

Stefan heard the nurse's quiet voice from just outside the room he was already tired of looking at. He glanced toward the door, glad he had convinced that nurse to raise the head of the bed so he could see. Okay, maybe he'd demanded. A *little*. But she had remained calm, only smiling and saying she was always glad to see fighting spirit in her patients. Especially those who had taken down a monster in their midst.

"That was Dar—Deputy Bloom," he'd said. "She did it."

That had earned him an even larger smile. "And I like even more those scrupulous enough to give credit where it's due."

The door was pulled back, and he smiled himself the instant he saw it was Daria. But it froze when he saw she wasn't alone.

Sam.

What the hell? Why had she brought him here? He

didn't want his son, his little boy, seeing him like this, wounded and in a hospital bed.

Sam was staring at him, wide-eyed. "See?" Daria bent to whisper to him. "I told you he was all right."

To his shock, Sam ran across the room toward him. Setting aside his anger, he held out a hand to the child. "Some people said you were dead."

He went very still, focused only on the feel of his son's small hand in his. Daria had been right. He hadn't thought that even at his age, Sam would have heard what had to be huge news all over town. "They were wrong."

"Daria told me they were. So I didn't worry anymore."

Sam had been worried? About him?

He lifted his gaze to her then. "I understand," she said softly. "But he needed to know. To see for himself." And as if she'd also understood his thoughts, she added, "He was very worried."

He wondered if the boy was actually worried about him or about what would happen to Sam himself if the worst had been true. Decided at the moment it didn't matter. Especially when Daria picked Sam up and sat him on the edge of the hospital bed, and the boy plopped down beside him. As if he felt that was where he should be, beside his father.

"You can't protect him from everything," Daria said. "However much you want to. He needs to know this kind of thing might happen."

Something in her voice made his brow furrow. "You say that as if from experience."

She nodded. "I—" She hesitated, then went ahead. "Yes. My father, my adoptive father, was a big believer in knowing what you were facing. He made sure we all did, and I think we were the better for it."

As he had before, when he helped her discover the sad fate of Ava Bloom, he wondered what it would be like not to know. His parents had been the rock of his life, the reason he was where he was instead of in trouble somewhere. He knew she loved her adoptive family, but it still had to make her wonder who the man was who had abandoned both her and her mother to their fates.

"They didn't give you any trouble at the school, did they?" he asked, glancing at Sam, who was now studying the IV pump with interest. "Picking him up, I mean?"

"No." Her expression was half smile, half grimace. "My face is apparently more known than I would prefer."

"You are…memorable."

"Only because I've had to talk to the media so much."

"No. Not only that. It's also because you're so beautiful."

He felt an inward burst of pleasure at the faint color he could see rising in her cheeks. Liked that he could see it, for it helped him know what she was thinking.

He looked back at his son, who was leaning over to look at where the tubes came out of the pump. "Wondering how it works?"

Sam nodded. "It puts blood in, right?"

"How'd you know that?" he asked.

"I saw it in a video. Only, it was about a hurt cat."

"Same principle."

Sam looked up then. "What's that mean?"

"It means it's the same idea as the cat one, just for people."

"Oh." Sam went back to studying the piece of equipment, leaving Stefan marveling at how much their relationship had changed. He shifted his gaze to the big reason for that change. Daria. "They told me just now you might get out of here tomorrow," she said.

"Yes."

"And how hard did you push to get them to say that?"

She, apparently, needed no help at all in knowing what he was thinking. "Maybe a little," he grudgingly admitted.

"If they do let you…escape, you'll need some help for a few days. At least until your folks get here."

He grimaced. Glanced at his boy. Knew she was right.

Suddenly Sam smiled at him. "Daria says we could go home with her tomorrow. Can we, Dad?"

His breath caught. "You'd like that?"

Sam nodded energetically. "I wanna see her house an' her yard an' her tree house."

His gaze shot to her face. She smiled. "It might be easier. And Sam would have…more room to run and play."

And get tired. He read it as clearly as if she'd said it. And he had to admit she had a point. And he also had to admit, the idea of being under the same roof as Daria was immensely appealing.

Unless, of course, she was looking at him as an invalid. His side might be hurting a bit more than he'd let on, but he wasn't about to let it slow him down. Much.

"You're not going to fuss over me, are you?" he asked warily.

She reached out and touched his cheek with the back of her fingers. And for that moment, he didn't feel anything except that jolt of warmth.

"Maybe just a little," she said softly.

And suddenly his entire outlook about it changed. Because, to his astonishment, he found himself *liking* the idea of Daria fussing over him. Taking care of him. Worrying about him. As his son had been worried, something he'd not dared hope for.

Once you've had that, son, that feeling of knowing you have someone who loves you enough to worry about you, to want to take care of you, and you her, then you'll know just how important it is.

His father's words, dismissed lightly in his know-it-all years, as his mother had called them, came back to him now with the fierce smack of truth. Because were it Daria who had been hurt, he would want to do exactly that. And how strongly pain and fear bubbled in him at the very thought of her hurt was like a flashing light in his mind. At one time, he might have wondered if that light was flashing green or red, but now he had no doubts. For him, it was full speed ahead.

"You're here for our star patient?" At Daria's nod, the nurse gave an amused rolling-eyes glance at the ceiling. "Good. He's been up pacing all morning. Night shift said he was up and down all night, too."

"He must be feeling better, then."

"He needs to get out of here."

Daria smiled. If Stefan was feeling as well as he had said he was when she spoke to him this morning, he was pretty restless. He was not a man to be kept caged for long.

"Driving you crazy?"

"Himself, mostly," the man admitted. "I'll check on the paperwork. Should be almost done. He is a VIP, after all."

With a grin she returned, he turned on his heel and headed toward the nursing station.

She turned to head for Stefan's room with the small bag she'd brought. He'd given her his keys—apparently without a second thought—and she'd gone to his place to pack some things for him and Sam. The boy had, excitedly, given her a list, which she had fulfilled, but for Stefan she hadn't asked; she simply made sure she'd brought things he'd be comfortable in, since she had every intention of keeping him inside for the duration. And had to remind herself he would be recuperating to quash the images that thought brought on.

She had felt a little qualm as she'd decided how much to pack for him, and ended up calculating the days until his parents arrived. She supposed his mother would want to take over—he'd called them last night, he'd told her, so they wouldn't see one of the more fallacious news reports and assume the worst—and she could hardly protest. Especially when she hadn't even met them.

Yet.

Maybe she wouldn't. Maybe by then Stefan would be back home, and her life would go back to normal. Normal being full of work, reading, knitting and gardening come spring. What had once been a much-longed-for peace and quiet suddenly seemed empty and endless.

She shook off the image of a rather dull future and headed for his room. She'd brought him the shaving items Sam had pointed out that he used every day, and clean clothes. Including a pair of knit boxers that she had to stuff hurriedly in the bag before her pulse kicked up too much as an image of him clad in them—and her peeling them off him—shot through her mind.

It was a new experience for her. She'd had relationships but too often she'd found out the man knew of her connection to the most famous Coltons and was after a connection of his own—but never, ever had she had to fight so hard to keep from thinking about a man every minute of the day. And while common sense might tell her that was because they'd been together so much and that it would change now, her heart—and apparently her body—felt differently.

When she stepped into Stefan's room, she saw he was already up and pacing. She'd told him she would bring fresh clothes, since his shirt was unsalvageable, and in her opinion the rest—except his shoes—was, too; she wanted none of those bloodstained items around as reminders that it could have been so much worse.

Normally the sight of someone in the usual floppy hospital gown was either sad or amusing. She was neither sad nor amused now, though, because nothing could detract from the sheer masculinity and power of this man.

Suddenly nervous, she set the bag down on the bed. "I brought your clothes and shaving gear if you want it."

"I might." He was looking at her intently.

"Sam told me what you used in the mornings, so that's what I brought."

That seemed to startle him. "Sam told you?"

She nodded. "I think he's watching you much more than you think. And that's good. He wants to know about his father, even if he hasn't realized it yet."

He looked a bit disconcerted at that, and her nerves eased a little. Doing something as personal as packing underwear for him had unsettled her, which was silly, considering.

"I'll just wait outside so you can get dressed," she said, groaning inwardly when she realized she sounded flustered.

He'd picked up the jeans she'd brought, but his gaze snapped back to her face.

"A bit late for modesty, wouldn't you say?"

She grabbed at the remnants of her poise. "Maybe I'm

just afraid I won't be able to resist your gorgeousness," she managed to say in a teasing tone.

That grin, that killer grin that had been so rare in the beginning that she'd savored every instance, flashed at her.

"Oh, I hope not," he rasped.

She felt heat flood her cheeks. "You're going to be convalescing."

"So you'll have to do all the work."

He was still grinning, damn him. The heat that had begun to recede rose anew. And flared when he nonchalantly dropped the hospital gown to get dressed. When he caught her watching him, that grin flashed yet again.

"Want to help me…tuck things in?"

"Not if you want to get out of here in time to pick Sam up from school," she managed, although the images his teasing brought on nearly derailed her self-control.

"Oh, well," he said in exaggerated disappointment. "I'd rather you untuck them anyway."

By the time he was dressed—without needing help, she noted, his innate strength and fitness helping him rebound more quickly than she would have ever guessed—she was grateful for the arrival of the nurse to tell them his discharge papers were ready.

"One thing I want to do on the way," he said as they headed out to deal with the paperwork.

"What?"

"Stop and vote for your boss."

She smiled widely. "I'll be more than happy to get you there."

She meant it. If there was any sense at all in this county, it would be a landslide.

Chapter 31

"Hard to believe this case is actually over except for the paperwork," Daria said as she slowed to go over the last speed bump in the hospital parking lot.

"Little matter of a trial," Stefan pointed out, stifling a wince as the bump, even as slowly as she was going, caused a tug on his wounded side. He knew they'd only let him out because he'd told them he was leaving today whether they discharged him or not. He had a small stack of papers stuffed into a pocket of the bag Daria had brought, including detailed instructions on how to care for the wound. He'd read them. Eventually. As soon as he could stop thinking about Daria truly wanting him—and his son—to come home with her.

"That, too," she agreed, "but that'll take a while."

"But Shruggs confessed to you. Not quite a deathbed confession, but still."

"Only because he survived." She halted at the driveway, scanning traffic. "But he couldn't resist the need to brag, just in case. Which reminds me…"

She checked her rearview mirror, he noticed, to make sure they weren't blocking anyone in the driveway. Then she pulled out her phone and called up what she wanted, explaining as she did, "Trey called me this morning. He said he mentioned what Shruggs said about Sabrina Gilford not being his type to his fiancée, Aisha—you met her, didn't you?"

"Yes. The clinical psychologist"

Daria nodded. "She's wicked smart. And an ace kickboxer, I might add."

He blinked; he hadn't expected that. "Kickboxer?"

"Yep. She's going to teach me."

He studied her for a moment, remembering with vivid clarity how her trim, strong body had felt in his arms, beneath him, atop him. "That," he said fervently, "I want to see. You'll be brilliant."

Daria flashed him a smile that told him he'd said exactly the right thing.

"Thank you," she said warmly. "Anyway, Aisha's the one who figured out his election opponent's brother was behind that attempt on his life."

"The one we thought was a hate crime at first?"

She nodded. "Anyway, she did a little research of her own and came up with this."

She held out her phone to him. He looked at the image on the screen. His brow furrowed. The woman looked familiar somehow, yet he was fairly sure he'd never seen her before. He'd seen a string of photos that resembled her, though, tacked to a crime board.

"Someone else missing?" he asked grimly. "Shruggs

has another victim buried somewhere we haven't found yet?"

Daria looked oddly satisfied at his question. "It's his mother."

Stefan looked up to meet her gaze. He nearly rolled his eyes. "So he's not only a vicious killer, he's a walking cliché?"

"So it seems."

"I guess things become clichés for a reason," he muttered, handing back her phone.

They found his polling place, and the voting itself didn't take too long, but he was still glad when he got back in the car. He had the niggling thought that maybe he'd pushed a little too hard too soon, but once he was sitting down again, he felt better.

"Lots of talk going on in there," he told her. "Most of it good, about your boss. Word that we got Shruggs spread fast."

"Good," she said. "Although they should have voted for him anyway."

"You're very…loyal."

"He's earned it."

He studied her as she pulled back out onto the street and they headed for Sam's school. Realized with a bone-deep certainty that Daria would be that loyal to anyone who earned it. Had he? If he hadn't, what did he need to do now to make sure? Maybe he'd ask his father, when they arrived. Winning the trust, loyalty and above all the love of a woman like his mother couldn't have been an easy thing. His mother was a force of nature, by turns as fierce as she was gentle. In fact, Daria reminded him a lot of her in many ways.

He found himself mulling over men and their mothers,

the thoughts about his own coming so soon on the heels of the discovery about their serial killer's seeming a bit ironic. But if nothing else, it reminded him how fortunate he'd been to have his mother, with her steady, unwavering devotion to her family. Daria would be like that, he was certain. Once she decided, she would never falter.

They reached Sam's school, and she pulled into the parking lot and to a stop where there were other vehicles with people waiting for children. She parked neatly, glanced at the clock—they were nearly half an hour early—then looked at him. Caught him avidly soaking in her presence. "I was wrong," he said softly.

"Wrong?"

"You're not just memorable. You're unforgettable."

She lowered her gaze almost shyly. He leaned toward her, wanting a kiss from that luscious mouth more than anything just now. He felt the sharp twinge from his side but hid it. A little pain was a small price to pay for this. And the moment he touched her lips, the pain seemed to vanish, swept aside by the heat he'd only ever felt with her. He deepened the kiss, tasted her, knowing with a strange sense of utter certainty that it would ever and always be like this, with her.

The honk of a car horn broke the moment. He straightened a little too quickly and winced.

"You shouldn't move like that."

"The day I can't lean over and kiss my woman," he began but stopped when he saw her eyes. She had that look that told him that mind he admired was working. Well, admired most of the time; at her expression he was a bit wary.

"There's something you need to know. And I should have told you before we..."

She gave a vague wave of her hand that irritated him.

"Spontaneously combusted?" he suggested, his own voice a little tight.

She nodded, and he saw the faint color in her cheeks again. "But more importantly, before I invited you both to stay at my place now."

"Retracting the invitation?" He didn't want to think about how that would hurt Sam. He didn't want to think about how it would hurt *him*.

"No!" She said it so fervently it soothed his annoyance. "I just mean…there's something you should know before we go any further."

He kept his tone mild. "I don't recall that the invitation was to move in permanently." That he almost wished it had been was something he kept to himself just now.

She lowered her gaze again, and something about the way her lips tightened slightly made him wonder if she did, too. But he knew full well he was no expert in reading the female mind, so he kept his mouth shut. Another wise lesson from his father.

After a long enough moment that he wondered if she'd changed her mind about telling him whatever it was, she said, "It's about…who I am. Really am, I mean."

His puzzlement cleared, and the annoyance vanished. In fact, he felt a jolt of relief that this was all it was. "A Colton, you mean?"

Her head snapped up and she stared at him. "You knew?"

"Well…yeah."

"Have you always known?"

He frowned. "Only since I ran the DNA for Fox and Kelsey."

Now she looked utterly flummoxed. "What?"

"You know, for the baby. You came up as a possible relative."

She was gaping at him now. "I...*what*?"

Puzzlement returned. "You're in the system, as law enforcement, right?"

"Of course. To be eliminated in case of evidence contamination."

"So that's why you came up when we did the genetic markers for the baby." She still looked bewildered, and he hastened to assure her, "It's confidential information, and since I knew you weren't the baby's mother, it was irrelevant to the case. I'd never say anything."

"I wasn't... I didn't think you..."

She seemed way too baffled for what was a fairly simple thing. He knew how smart she was, how together she was, so this made no sense.

"Daria?"

He saw a slight shudder go through her, had the feeling she'd given herself a sharp mental shake. When she spoke, she was enunciating so carefully it made his focus zero in on her like a case about to break open.

"Are you saying," she said, each word spoken with careful precision, "that I am a *biological* Colton?"

"Not me, the DNA," he said. "And not closely related to the baby, but..."

Her expression practically screamed the truth.

She hadn't known. She hadn't known she was genetically connected to the Coltons. But she'd been going to tell him she was a Colton? Now he was confused.

"Daria..."

The moment he said her name out loud, it belatedly hit him. Daria. *Daria Colton.*

He swore, low and harsh. He felt as if the entire world

had tilted on its axis. Her words came back to him vividly. *I've had enough of living with a lot of people around all the time.* He'd just bet she had, because she'd once lived in the biggest goldfish bowl in the world.

No wonder she had seemed familiar from the first time he'd seen her. Because she was. He'd even seen her photograph years ago, in FBI informational reports put out when the Secret Service was in town, although she was always in the background.

Daria Bloom…or was it Colton?

Of the California Coltons. Headed up by Joe Colton.

The former president of the United States.

Chapter 32

Stefan was on his phone. She had no idea to whom—she couldn't focus on a single thing beyond the internal turmoil that had erupted the instant she'd realized what he'd meant. That the DNA tests he'd pushed through for Fox Colton had turned up an unexpected connection. A possible relative to that tiny baby that he and Kelsey were adopting.

Her.

She was a biological Colton.

She felt a hand on her arm. Slowly, as if moving underwater, she looked over at Stefan. "Maybe there was a mistake," he said quietly. "Maybe because of…of your adoptive name something got crossed."

"My adoptive name," she said, very slowly. And for the first time thought of a very unpleasant possibility. "Did they know?" she asked, barely aware of saying it out loud. "Dear God, did they know and never tell me? Did my father—the freaking president—lie to me all these years?"

"Whoa, now, don't jump the gun here. Let's make sure of this. I'm no expert on reading DNA reports, and there could have been a glitch somewhere."

She thought, as if from a distance, that it was nice he was so worried. And that he'd set aside what she'd told him—or rather, what she'd meant to tell him—in favor of addressing her more pressing concern, touched her to the core.

"Here's the plan," he said briskly. "We head for the Crooked C. Now, because Fox and Kelsey are both there, but they have to leave soon. They've got the reports. Can you access yours?"

She nodded, rather vaguely. She'd filed a copy in a cloud storage service, just in case, during her long search for her mother.

"Sam," she said, not even sure why.

"We'll pick him up first. He'll have fun—he's never been to anything like a working ranch. He'll have plenty of distraction while we find out what we need. I don't think he's ever even seen a cow up close."

"Duck pond…there's a duck pond behind the main house." Somewhere in the back of her mind, a faint alarm bell was ringing. It took her a moment to find the words for it. "Can he swim?"

She heard an odd sound, as if Stefan's breath had caught in his throat. Then she felt his big, warm hand over hers, which was cold for reasons that had nothing to do with the temperature outside.

"I can't tell you what it means to me that you're

worried about that now, in the middle of what you just learned."

"Of course I am. He doesn't need any more trauma in his life."

"You've just had a bit in yours."

She tried a smile, managed only a brief, slightly lopsided one. "Here I thought I'd be shocking you."

"Oh, you did." He gave her a rather wondering look. "I can't believe I didn't recognize you."

"That was years ago." *I'm older now. Too old for you.*

She tried to quash the thought, because he was right; if it were reversed, no one would think a thing of it. She had the feeling that would be one of the last inequities to fall in this world. If it ever did.

"I saw you once. When President Colton made a stop at the capitol in Springfield. I remember thinking how amazing it was that someone who looked like you lived in the White House."

"You mean because I'm Black?"

"No. Because even then I thought you were beautiful. I thought you should be modeling, or maybe out in Hollywood."

She made a face. "Please," she muttered.

"But now I know better. You wouldn't settle for doing anything you didn't think was important."

"I got that from Dad," she said. "He told me he didn't care what I did as long as it was something that made me eager to get up and get at it every morning."

"Sounds like my dad."

She realized suddenly that she was calmer. Much calmer. She'd even managed to speak of her adoptive father with the admiration she'd always felt for him. And on the heels of that, she realized that had been Stefan's intention all along, he who rarely indulged in small talk but just had. To get her through the sudden chaos of this unexpected discovery.

She met his gaze, held it. "Thank you," she said softly.

He lifted a brow at her as if he had no idea what she meant. But she knew better.

"Is this the way to Daria's house?"

"No," Stefan said. "We have to make a stop first."

"Oh."

His son sounded so downcast it almost made Daria smile. Or rather, smile again, because she had smiled broadly and happily when Sam had first emerged from the school and worriedly asked his father if he was all right now.

"I'll be okay, buddy, but I have to take it easy for a while," Stefan had said. "Rest a lot."

"You mean stay in bed?" Sam asked innocently.

Daria had had to look away then, and she felt her cheeks heat yet again when Stefan said with all seriousness, "I think that's an excellent, excellent prescription, Dr. Roberts."

She had had the feeling Sam had no idea what a prescription was, but being addressed as Dr. Roberts set off a gale of laughter. The boy had come a very long way in a short time. And if she'd had some little bit to do with that, she was both happy and proud.

"We're going someplace very cool, though," she said as she made a turn.

"Where?" Sam asked, wide-eyed.

"It's a ranch," Stefan answered.

"You mean with horses and cows and stuff?"

"Exactly that."

"Cool!" the boy exclaimed.

She knew too well where the Crooked C was, because it was where all this had started for her, when Wyatt Colton had found the first body. It had also been the first direct experience she'd had with the kind of pressure the Colton name could bring to bear.

The Colton name.

She felt a little stab of the guilt she'd been carrying since Trey had turned this case over to her. He'd done it to avoid any appearance of favoritism, given he was a Colton himself. She'd rationalized it with the fact—she'd thought—that she wasn't really a Colton, it was only by adoption.

But now…

She was going to have to tell him. And she had no idea how he would react. She had no idea how she herself would react, once she knew exactly what the connection was.

She made herself focus on her driving. She noticed the last bits of snow were disappearing, with the occasional trickle of water from the melt crossing the roadway. It was a near-balmy sixty-one degrees today, and Sam had already shed his jacket. She hoped the good weather made people get out and vote. And hoped the news of Shruggs's capture reassured any who had doubts about their current sheriff.

The Crooked C was a sprawling ranch of hundreds of acres, and Daria smiled anew as Stefan pointed out to Sam the weather vane on the roof of the main house, which was a rearing horse made of copper. But they kept going, past the promised duck pond, southward until they reached a large red barn that looked a bit weather-beaten on the outside. But when she'd first been here—when they'd found the first body—Daria had noticed there were several features that didn't fit, including glass windows that looked fairly new and double paned, both on the upper level and below.

"Fox is really dedicated to breeding healthy, long-lived horses. So he took this barn over and converted it to living quarters upstairs, with his office and work space below. Guess which is bigger," Stefan added to Sam with a grin.

Daria smiled. She liked seeing anyone with a passion following it.

Sam was looking around wide-eyed. He immediately fixated on the corral beside the barn, where a couple of horses that looked young to her inexperienced eye were watching them in turn.

"Can I go see 'em?" Sam asked, practically dancing with eagerness.

Fox Colton and his new wife, Kelsey, a petite woman with lively hazel eyes and strawberry blond hair, had come out the door in time to hear this.

"I'll get somebody to show him around while we talk, if that's okay with you," the tall, lean man with bright blue eyes and rather shaggy brown hair said.

"Please, Dad?" The boy was practically dancing with excitement.

"That would be great," Stefan said. "If it's not too much trouble."

"After what you did for us?" Kelsey said. "Not a chance."

Once Sam was set up, they went inside. The newlywed couple's first words were congratulations—and thanks—that they'd cracked the Avalanche Killer case.

"Word gets around fast," Stefan mused.

"For all the glamour, underneath Roaring Springs is still a small town," Fox said with a smile.

"And that *is* huge news," Kelsey added, with a wide smile.

Daria had been a little surprised at first, at the woman's immediate and enthusiastic offer of any and all help, but then she recalled Stefan had used his connections at the FBI to rush through the DNA testing that had proven the paternity of the baby that had been abandoned literally on Fox's doorstep.

Besides, Fox had gone through a shock of his own recently, discovering his dead father had not really been his father after all. So he understood how she was feeling and was thoroughly empathetic to her plight.

As it turned out, Kelsey, who was an equine geneticist, was of the most help. She was much more used to deciphering genetic reports, had gotten out the one that had proven who Fox's real father was, and had already started sorting through what they had and begun comparing it to the report Daria had accessed for her.

"Things settle down for you at all?" Stefan asked Fox.

The man shrugged. "My parents—or rather, my father and my aunt—said this morning that they've separated. I think… Dad needs some processing time."

The correction, and the way he'd hesitated over the word *Dad* told Daria he was still adjusting to the idea that his father wasn't just alive, but was Russ Colton… the man who'd actually raised him. She wondered how long it would take her. She supposed it would depend on what she learned in the next few minutes. Assuming there was enough here to tell her that.

She didn't pace while Kelsey continued to pore over the papers spread out on what she guessed was Fox's desk, but it was an effort. When she finally straightened up, she gave her a sympathetic look.

"It's there," she said. "The number of markers is undeniable."

"So," Fox said, turning to look at her. "It's official. You're a Colton."

Chapter 33

"How close?" Stefan asked since Daria couldn't seem to find her voice.

"I can't be sure. I can only extrapolate from what I've got here," Kelsey said. She glanced at her husband. "This looks close to Russ, but she's not your half sister. That much I can say."

Fox let out a relieved breath, then looked rather guiltily at Daria. "Not that I'd mind if you were, I mean, but—"

"It would mean your father made it a habit," Stefan said gently.

"Exactly."

"Maybe your uncle Whit?" Kelsey asked.

"He's got the track record for it," Fox agreed. "But could it be?" he asked, gesturing at the reports.

"I don't know. If there was one more marker either

way… I'd need a genetic test from him to be sure. And one from Earl wouldn't hurt."

"At this point, I want everybody in the damned family tested," Fox muttered. "As if life as a Colton wasn't already complicated enough."

Stefan was quite aware Daria still hadn't uttered a word. He turned to face her, reached out and gently grasped her shoulders. "What do *you* want?"

She looked up at him. He saw the rapid-fire emotions in her expression, guessed she was feeling pretty tangled up right now. Probably even wishing, with some part of her, that she'd never found this out. But he also knew what was at the core of her and knew what her answer would be. And after a long, silent moment, it came.

"I want the truth."

He'd known she would. And the fact that he'd known, that he'd been so certain she would want exactly that, proved to him that this woman was exactly who he thought she was. That he knew who she was to the core.

"Then we'll find it," he said softly, in that moment meaning it more than he had ever meant any vow in his life.

Fox looked back at Stefan and Daria. "We were already set to make a trip to the Manor. I think we should go now, and you'd better come with us."

Stefan blinked, felt Daria draw back slightly. "The Colton Manor?" she asked.

"Yes. Speaking of my uncle Whit, his son Remy's half brother, Seth, called a meeting. He's got some sort of announcement to make. We should make it just in time."

Daria's brow furrowed. "Seth Harris? I've talked to him. He works at The Lodge, right?"

Fox nodded. "He manages the whole guest operation. He's really good with the high-end clients."

Stefan remembered the slim, sandy-haired man who looked like he'd be more at home in New York City than the slopes of the Colorado mountains. He could see where the guy would make those high-profile sorts feel at home. Personally, he'd found him a bit over-the-top unctuous, while Daria's conclusion had been a bit more forgiving, given the rough start he'd apparently had in life before his half brother had stepped in.

"Why don't you round up your boy and we'll get ready to go," Kelsey suggested. "There's a playroom at the Manor with every video game known to man. Will that keep him occupied while we deal with all this?"

"He'll be in heaven," Stefan replied.

"What, exactly," Daria said, rather carefully, "is the plan?"

"Beard the lions in their den, as it were," Fox told them cheerfully, and headed upstairs after his wife.

Daria seemed to hesitate when Stefan turned to do as Kelsey had suggested and find Sam.

"Second thoughts?" he asked.

"They're the power around here. Anybody would have second thoughts."

"This, from the woman who calls a former president Dad?"

She looked startled, as if she hadn't thought of it in just that way. "Point taken."

"And I see now why you like your place so much—partly, anyway. Got pretty tired of all the fuss and bother of the White House and a protection detail?"

"I declined the detail, but it was still…a lot of pressure."

"Then this should be nothing. Besides," Stefan added, "you're returning the victor. The one who probably salvaged their entire year's business by taking out the Avalanche Killer. They should bow down."

As he'd hoped, that got a low chuckle from her. "Right. Their savior."

He grinned at her. "Exactly."

She reached up and brushed her fingers over his jaw. His pulse kicked up instantly. "Thank you. For being here for me, through this. And making me feel so much better."

He leaned over and kissed her, then whispered a rather potent suggestion for how he could make her feel even better.

"You're supposed to be taking it easy, remember?" she said, but she was smiling now. Widely.

"Yeah. In bed, like Sam said."

She laughed then and shook her head. "I'll deal with you later."

"Promise?" he said archly.

"Fervently," she said, with a smile that sent a shiver of anticipation through him. "But now, let's go find Sam."

Colton Manor was as huge and sprawling as one might expect from this rich and influential family. Although from what Daria had gathered, the Colton children didn't have much connection to it. She could understand that; the place wasn't exactly a warm, cozy home.

Essentially it was a massive, eighteen-thousand-square-foot showplace for the senior Coltons, including the now rarely seen patriarch, and a staff she couldn't even guess at the size of. She supposed the size of it had a benefit, however; Russ and Mara Colton could live completely separate lives under the same roof until they decided what their future would or wouldn't be.

"Ten bathrooms, I heard," Stefan muttered as they went inside.

"Eleven," Fox corrected with a grin.

"Obnoxious, isn't it?" Kelsey said, also grinning.

And Daria realized she quite liked both of them.

The gathering was in the living room—one of them, anyway—with its high, vaulted ceiling and the view of the gondolas going upslope out the expansive windows.

"Ever been on that thing?" Stefan whispered.

She shook her head. "And after Molly Gilford's experience, not likely to."

"Copy that," Stefan said rather fervently.

Thinking of the sweet, good-natured woman reminded her rather forcefully that while Roaring Springs no longer had a serial killer haunting its environs, there was still a murderer on the loose—the one who had killed Molly's sister. She had made a brief call to the woman, who had just had the baby now named after that sister, and in view of that had broken the news as gently as possible that Shruggs had not killed Sabrina Gilford. Molly had been understandably upset, but at Daria's vow it was not over and Sabrina would not be forgotten in the hubbub about Shruggs, she had calmed a little.

Daria had suggested to Fox that they wait with Sam in the game room, since whatever Seth's announcement was, it appeared to be a family affair, but Russ Colton spotted them first. His voice boomed out in the room, congratulating them for finally catching the killer. The buzz through the gathered group, many of whom she recognized, but some she did not, was loud and exuberant. Mara was there, Daria noted, but carefully on the opposite side of the room from her husband.

Daria was more interested in observing the rather intense look shared by Fox and the man who'd raised him and who had turned out to also be his biological father. And she was honest enough to admit that she was watching because she was wondering how she would feel if somehow this new discovery led her to her own father.

"He looks a bit miffed," Stefan whispered again.

She looked up, realized he meant the man who'd called this gathering. Seth was indeed frowning a bit, as if they'd stolen his thunder. But when he saw them looking at him, he managed a creditable smile. And proceeded with his announcement, which turned out to be his engagement to Vanessa Fisher, the tall, dark-haired woman who stood rather shyly beside him. She noticed the woman was slouching slightly, wondered if it was because she was taller than the man beside her. Daria knew Vanessa was the daughter of a wealthy investment banker, but not much more.

Some of the people gathered looked surprised, some not, but the most loudly congratulatory was Russ Colton himself.

"A great match," he exclaimed. "Just wonderful. A wonderful addition to the Colton family," he added, smiling widely at Vanessa, who looked as if she were a bit uncomfortable in the spotlight. Then he turned to Seth. "I see a very bright future for you with The Colton Empire."

Seth fairly beamed, while Daria was inwardly rolling her eyes at the grandiose name, although she supposed it fit what the man had built here.

"I wonder where Remy is?" Fox muttered. Daria knew he meant Remy Colton, the director of PR at The Chateau.

"Maybe getting his first sleep in months," Kelsey suggested. "He's had his hands more than full trying to cope with the ton of bad press from the Avalanche Killer."

"Or working, glad to not be spinning for a change," Daria said.

Stefan nodded in agreement. "I'd guess now's the time to trumpet the return to normalcy, and get reservations back up."

Fox smiled at them. "You two ever want to change jobs…" His smile faded. "I still can hardly believe Shruggs pulled this off right under our noses. All those women…it's horrific."

Daria liked him even more for that. The Lodge.

Kelsey said something quietly to Fox, who then looked at Daria. "I'll go get… Russ," he said, clearly still having trouble adjusting to the change in their connection. "I think we're going to need his cooperation on this."

"Will you get it?" Stefan asked.

Fox's mouth twisted into a wry smile. "He wants a relationship with me, so yeah, we'll get it."

When he'd headed across the room toward Russ Colton, Daria looked at Kelsey. "Your husband is quite a guy," she said quietly. "Going to this length to help someone who's practically a stranger."

"Yes," Kelsey agreed as she watched him go, the love clear in her expression. "Yes, he is." Then she looked back at Daria. "But I hope you don't stay practically a stranger, whatever we find out. All of you," she added with a glance at Stefan. "Especially that adorable kid of yours."

Stefan smiled. "Speaking of kids, how's little John doing?"

That sent Kelsey off into new parental joy, and she

happily told them about the baby who would be theirs as soon as the paperwork was done with Fox's cousin Mason.

And then Fox was back with his father. Russ Colton was still an impressive figure and an obvious power broker.

"So what's this all about?" he asked briskly.

"Not something I think you want to discuss out here," Fox said.

Russ looked at the young man he'd raised but had never known he'd fathered and quickly stated, "All right, let's go up to my study."

They started up the curved staircase, and Daria saw the edge of what appeared to be an indoor pool on the level below. She wondered what other extravagance the place held and guessed it could be just about anything. Even the hallways were spacious, with niches here and there where artworks worth probably more than she made in a year were hung and seen only by those invited to the inner sanctum.

Russ stopped at a set of carved wooden double doors and reached for the door handle. There was a sound a few feet farther down the hall—a set of footsteps and an odd sort of whooshing noise. Daria's reaction was automatic; she turned to look. She saw a very elderly man in a wheelchair, pushed by a woman in a nurse's uniform.

Earl Colton, she thought. Even now, fragile and frail, he resembled the pictures she'd seen from the days when as a dynamic and clever young man he'd built what was now The Colton Empire, thanks to his penchant for slapping his name on everything he bought. She had heard he suffered from dementia now, and often talked to the wife who had been dead for fifteen years. She herself found that understandable; if he took comfort in that, he'd earned it, if only by surviving this long. Although she had to say he looked quite alert and aware now, and she heard him call the nurse by the name on her name tag, so he appeared to be coherent at the moment.

He'd noticed them now, and his rather shaggy white eyebrows lowered as he stared at them.

No, her. He was staring at *her*.

His eyes widened, and his jaw went a little slack. And then, in a tone of shock, the old man spoke.

"Ava."

Chapter 34

He had pushed, Stefan had to admit, nearly as far as he could. He could feel collapse hovering, much as he hated to admit it. And no amount of telling himself his wound was minor was helping.

But Daria had just received the shock of her life, and she needed support. And he wasn't going to do her much good if he passed out on his feet. So he summoned up what reserves he had left and kept going.

It was at that moment he realized just how far he would go for this woman he'd come to so admire. To respect.

To love.

He hadn't really admitted it before, had shied away from the possibility even to himself, but now that he had, the truth of it rang like a clarion bell. He had to resist the urge to tell her, right then. Even if she had recovered enough from the earlier shock, he doubted she would want to hear it just now, in front of this handful of strangers who she had just discovered were actually family.

His brain was too weary at the moment to figure out the intricacies of her connection to each one, but only one really mattered. And that was that the old man in the wheelchair, Earl Colton, was her father. Because once the obvious shock in his lined face and weary eyes had faded, everything had come pouring out as the old man faced the woman he obviously thought was Ava Bloom.

He swore he hadn't known she was ill, and for a Colton fairly groveled for abandoning her and their child when he'd found out she was pregnant. He should have manned up, Earl had said brokenly. Alice would have understood. Stefan had his doubts about that, but there was no doubt that the Colton patriarch meant what he said.

Lot of good that does Daria now.

He was silently grateful when they finally made it into Russ Colton's office and sat down to begin to sort it all out. It took some time for the chaos to settle, but in the end cautious welcomes were extended from some, happy and amazed welcomes from others. Russ Colton, Stefan suspected rather strongly, was calculating the worth of having the deputy who had broken the Avalanche Killer case in the family. Although, to his credit, he seemed as concerned as the rest of the Coltons that their cousin Sabrina's case was still unsolved, and her murderer still out there.

But most of them seemed cordial enough to the idea of Daria being one of them, and he got the feeling she would have a place here if she wanted it. For some reason Sam's angry face flashed through his mind. An anger he hadn't seen…well, practically since the boy had met Daria. He wondered idly how much of a difference it made to be an adult and have your whole world shift on you. It belatedly occurred to him that she might want some time alone with her newfound family, and he stood up, feeling stronger now that he'd been off his feet for a bit.

"I need to go see my son," he said when everyone looked at him. Nobody seemed to question that, and Daria smiled when he looked at her and added, "Take your time."

It had been a rather tight smile, however, and he knew she was still processing. Driven by an urge he didn't even try to resist, and despite the twinge in his side, he bent down and rather blatantly planted a kiss on her cheek. In front of all of them. As if he were staking his claim in front of the family she had just gained. As, perhaps, he was.

He lingered there for a moment and whispered, "I'll stay if you need me, but some alone time might be good."

"Go to Sam," she whispered back. "I won't be long."

So she wasn't going to linger, let them throw a party for her since everyone was already here. No, his Daria would want time to process this revelation, and he would see to it that she got it.

Even if he had to enlist the help of someone who knew quite well what it was like to have your entire life turned upside down.

He found the game room, and Sam engrossed in driving a race car over some very unlikely terrain. Having learned by now, he waited until the inevitable crash, then sat down beside the boy.

"Can you pause for a minute? I need your help. For Daria."

That startled Sam enough that he immediately put down the controller. "What?" he asked, sounding anxious. "Is she all right?"

"She will be, I think. But do you remember how you felt when your whole life got blasted apart and you had to come here?"

"Yeah," Sam said, watching him warily. Then, with a frown, he added, "You're not sending me back now, are you?"

He reached out and gripped the boy's shoulder. "Not a chance. You're mine for good, buddy, and even if your mother wanted you back, I'd fight her."

The shy smile that curved his son's mouth made the dull ache in his side recede.

"What about Daria?" Sam asked, sounding anxious.

"Well, her whole life just got upended, like yours did. So we need to take extra-special care of her for a while. Can you help me with that?"

"We're still gonna stay with her while you get better?"

"Yes. It's just now…she and I both need to heal a bit. So we'll need your help."

This seemed to intrigue the boy, and he drew himself up straight. "I can do it," he announced.

For a moment Stefan felt a surge of wonder that Leah hadn't managed to cripple the boy's generous heart. And a bigger surge of gratitude that Daria had come into their lives and shone a light on the path to where they were now. That his relationship with Sam had improved so much so fast was, he knew, entirely due to her.

"I know you can," he said softly, this time running a hand over Sam's close-cropped curls. The boy ducked his head but didn't pull away.

It was approaching dark by the time the three of them left the Manor. Stefan had offered to drive, but Daria said the distraction of having to focus on driving would help her. She didn't talk, so Stefan instead sat and savored the image of Sam immediately going to her and taking her hand and assuring her everything would be all right. He didn't think he'd mistaken the sheen of moisture in her eyes. That those eyes had stayed calm and assessing while her entire life changed before them, yet teared up at soft words from his son, made him ache inside in a way he could barely fathom.

When they got to her place, there was just enough light for Sam to excitedly explore a little bit. And it had been all Stefan could do not to laugh when his son had solemnly broached the idea that maybe he should skip school tomorrow. "To take care of you and Daria."

And he wondered how bad a father it made him when he gave in and agreed the boy could stay home. And if he was crazy for, when he said the word *home*, thinking of this place, not his own.

"They won't be surprised when he doesn't come to school," Daria said as Sam ran off to unpack the bag she'd brought for him in the bedroom she'd shown him to, the one with the view of the backyard and tree platform, which Stefan knew he wanted to climb up to the first chance he got. "I'm sure it's all over the news that we broke the case."

"And that I managed to get myself shot in the process?" he suggested dryly.

Her brow furrowed. "If I could only have gotten him—"

"Stop. Right there." He'd been about to sit down but instead turned and grabbed her before she could finish the sentence. "You did great. Spectacular, in fact. I'm the one who pushed my luck and risked being spotted for a glimpse inside the place."

He was glad when her arms came around him, didn't even care when she brushed his wound and he felt a twinge. They'd done it, at last. Solved that damned case. The relief was staggering.

Then a small gasp escaped her. "Your parents! What if they heard? It's probably national headlines by now."

"I called them on my way to get Sam."

"Oh. Good."

Her worry about them nearly sent his emotions spiraling out of control; she'd hadn't even met them yet, but they were connected to him and so she cared. The enormity of what he'd found with her was truly beginning to sink in.

"Daria."

She tilted her head back. And for a moment, as those stunning golden-brown eyes looked up at him, he completely lost the power of speech. So he kissed her instead, trying to put the words he couldn't find into it. He poured everything he was feeling into that lip-lock and ended up setting them both on fire.

"Wow," she said, sounding a bit wobbly when at last he broke the kiss. "That was…"

"That," he said carefully, "was because for a moment I couldn't find the words."

"I'm not sure mere words could match that. But what words?"

"I love you."

Her eyes widened. "Stefan," she began.

He shook his head. "I don't expect it back, not now, not when your whole life's been upended. But… I needed you to know."

She said his name again, softly, and hugged him. Hung on as if he were the only thing holding her in place.

"Do you really know somebody with that cabin with no cell or internet?" he asked after a moment.

"Yes."

"Does it have a bed?"

He heard the smile in her voice as she again said, "Yes."

"Can we borrow it?"

"I'm sure we could." But then she pulled back sharply. Looked down at his side. "You're bleeding!"

He'd been vaguely aware of the dampness for a bit now but hadn't let it stop him, since that's all it was. "Seeping, I think. They said it would happen."

"We need to clean that up right now. And get you into something more comfortable."

"Naked's comfortable," he said in mock thoughtfulness.

She gave him an arch look. "You're in no condition—"

He pulled her back close. "I'd have to be dead not to want you."

This time she stayed there, and he thought in that moment, with her in his arms and his son down the hall, life was as close to perfect as it had ever been.

Chapter 35

Three days. They'd had three days of peace and perfection, and Daria couldn't seem to stop smiling. The house that she had at first hesitated to buy because it was bigger than she alone needed was suddenly the perfect size. The weather outside was perfect, chilly but crystal clear. The warmth inside was perfect, with Stefan and Sam sitting at her table on this Saturday morning, the boy chattering excitedly about going outside as soon as he finished the French toast she'd fixed especially for him, because he'd once told her it was his favorite.

Even the ache inside her was perfect, because it was only there because of how full her heart was.

The day after Stefan had been released from the hospital had been a marvel of being together for all three of them. Sam had delighted in his explorations of her vast yard while she and Stefan, still taking it easy, had watched, arm in arm, both smiling so broadly it almost hurt. Waking up to the news that not only had Trey won his election, he'd won it handily, had been the icing on the cake.

"Thank you," her boss had said in a call just after the seasonally late sunrise. "It could easily have gone the other way if you hadn't wrapped up Shruggs when you did."

Daria had laughed. "I think you underestimate the respect you've built. But you're welcome anyway, if it did help."

"You always have had great timing," Trey had joked, and it had done her heart good to hear the lightness in his voice. "Now take a few days for yourself. You've earned it."

Normally she would have declined the offer, preferring to work. But not now. Now, she wanted to savor every second of together with the two men in her life.

"I will," she told him. "And when I come back, I'll need a few minutes with you for...something else."

"You can have my whole day," Trey had said, and she could almost see him grinning.

And when she'd hung up, it was to find Stefan grinning at her. "Gonna tell him you're his aunt?"

She rolled her eyes at him, then sighed. She had realized that particular connection somewhat belatedly, and while she had felt very strange about it, Stefan had only laughed.

"I hope that doesn't overly complicate things," she said.

"You broke the Avalanche Killer case. I think nobody's going to care."

"We."

His grin had widened at that. And he'd kissed her rather urgently; he'd clearly been feeling much better already.

Sam had only very reluctantly gone back to school the

next day, although the excitement of his grandparents arriving this weekend was a distraction. And she decided she would sort out the tangle of actually being a Colton by blood—albeit a very different branch than her adoptive one—eventually. She didn't need or want the rich connections, but maybe she would take the name back. Eventually.

And come Sunday—God help her, tomorrow—she would meet the parents. Stefan's mother and father had already assumed epic proportions in her mind, and she was having to make an effort not to be intimidated.

Chastising herself for her nerves, given that it had to be a lot more momentous for Sam, she put that aside and tried to savor the day. She had hours of peace and quiet coming to her, and she was going to take them. She had the two people she had come to treasure under her roof, and she was going to enjoy that. She wanted to savor this perfection and didn't want anything to change the way she felt at this moment in time.

All brought on by three little words. *I love you.*

That night Stefan steamrollered her protests about his injury as if intent on proving the truth of those words—and that he was physically fine, more than fine—driving her body to new heights with a fierce intensity that she supposed was born of having escaped an injury that could have been much worse. If this was what getting shot and surviving did to you, no wonder some people became danger junkies.

And in the quiet aftermath she returned the words, although she had to work up to it.

"I hope your parents like me," she said quietly into the dark.

"They will."

"That's good. Because otherwise it's going to be awkward when I tell them how much I love their son."

Stefan went very still beside her. She heard him swallow, as if his throat was tight. "You think maybe you could tell him first?"

She lifted up on one elbow. Reached out to cup his cheek. "I suppose I could. I love you, Stefan Roberts. For so many, many reasons."

"Even as a…package deal?"

He sounded slightly hesitant, and it took her a moment to understand. "You mean Sam?" He nodded. "I wouldn't have it any other way," she assured him. "I'm quite enamored of the little charmer he's become."

"That's good, since it's thanks to you. He's crazy about you, too."

She smiled, widely, at the admission in that *too*. But she answered the just now more important part. "Don't discount yourself in that process. You've made great strides together."

"Only because you showed me the path," he insisted gruffly.

That night, when they both went to tuck Sam in, it was clear the boy was nervous about the imminent arrival of the grandparents he'd never met.

"They're going to spoil you rotten," Stefan told his son.

"What's that mean?"

"It means that, unlike me, they'll find you very hard to say no to. Use that power carefully."

Sam blinked. "You're funny, Dad."

Daria saw Stefan blink a couple of times, rapidly. It hadn't been so long ago that Sam never called him Dad—now he always did.

"He is," Daria confirmed, saving him from trying to speak just then.

But then the boy had sighed sadly.

"I thought you were looking forward to meeting them," Stefan said, his voice steady enough now.

"I am. I just… I don't wanna go back to the other house." He gave Daria a sideways, shy look. "I wish we could stay here. F'rever."

Daria thought her heart would melt at the longing in the boy's deep brown eyes. "Me, too, Sam," she whispered.

She sensed rather than saw Stefan go very still beside her. But he waited until they were back in the living room before he spoke.

"Did you mean that?" His voice sounded oddly strained, as if he were having to try and keep his emotions in check.

She didn't pretend not to understand; they were way past that. She had been happy here, in the nest she'd built. But it had begun to seem much too empty. Until now. "Yes," she said simply.

"Daria—" He stopped, swallowed. "Are you sure?"

"Very. I could give you a string of reasons why it only makes sense," she said. "I have more room, especially outside for Sam to play. He wouldn't have to change schools, and you would actually be closer to your office."

"All true." He said it, then stopped, as if he knew there was more. There was, and she said it.

"But the most important reason is I love both of you, in a way I was afraid I never could. Until now this place has been a…cozy nest for me, but it's been an empty one. Now it finally feels right."

For a moment he just stared at her. But then she was in his arms, and he kissed her until her blood was singing in her ears and her pulse was hammering with all the swirling emotions only this man had ever roused in her.

"Can I take that as a yes?" she asked when she could breathe again.

"Daria." He said her name as if it were the only thing he could get out.

"I know there'll be details, and changes—I was thinking we could turn the den into a game room, and I've been thinking about moving my office into the sunroom in the back, so if you need an office of your own—"

He put a finger to her lips to hush her. "I'll share. I just want to be with you."

"Your parents—"

"Will be fine with it. Once they see us together, they'll know."

"Know?"

He gave her a slightly crooked smile that made her stomach do a little flip. "That I finally figured it out. And found what they have." His expression changed slightly. "Fair warning, they're very traditional. They're going to ask when we're getting married."

"And what will your answer be?"

He reached out and ran the back of his fingers lightly over her cheek, as if she were some precious, fragile thing. "I'll tell them as soon as I can convince you."

"I can hardly wait. You do some pretty impressive convincing."

He laughed. Daria let the sound wash over her. There was still much to do professionally, first and foremost the still-unsolved murder of Sabrina Gilford. But her personal life had never looked better. And she knew with Stefan's solid, clearheaded help, she would find her way through the complications of the changes in her self-identity.

With this man beside her, and with Sam to bring her the kind of delight she'd never dreamed possible, her future was suddenly as bright as the sun on new snow.

* * * * *

Don't miss the previous volumes in the Coltons of Roaring Springs miniseries:

Colton Cowboy Standoff *by Marie Ferrarella*
Colton Under Fire *by Cindy Dees*
Colton's Convenient Bride *by Jennifer Morey*
Colton's Secret Bodyguard *by Jane Godman*
A Colton Target *by Beverly Long*
Colton's Covert Baby *by Lara Lacombe*
Colton's Mistaken Identity *by Geri Krotow*
The Colton Sheriff *by Addison Fox*
Colton on the Run *by Anna J. Stewart*
Colton Family Showdown *by Regan Black*

Available now from Harlequin Romantic Suspense.

And don't miss the thrilling finale to the Coltons of Roaring Springs,
Colton's Rescue Mission
by Karen Whiddon,
Available in December 2019!

COMING NEXT MONTH FROM

HARLEQUIN®

ROMANTIC suspense

Available December 3, 2019

#2067 COLTON'S RESCUE MISSION

The Coltons of Roaring Springs • by Karen Whiddon

The sudden spark of attraction toward his brother's former fiancée, Vanessa Fisher, takes Remy Colton by surprise. Seth's addictions and emotional distress have gotten out of control. Will Remy's desire to protect Vanessa from his brother be his own downfall?

#2068 COLTON 911: FAMILY UNDER FIRE

Colton 911 • by Jane Godman

Four years ago, Alyssa Bartholomew left Everett Colton rather than see him in danger. Now, when their unexpected baby is threatened, the FBI agent is the only person who can keep her safe.

#2069 DETECTIVE ON THE HUNT

by Marilyn Pappano

Detective JJ Logan only came to Cedar Creek to figure out what happened to socialite Maura Evans, but as the mystery surrounding her deepens, local police officer Quint Foster finds himself hoping she'll stay a little longer—if they get out of the case alive!

#2070 EVIDENCE OF ATTRACTION

Bachelor Bodyguards • by Lisa Childs

To get CSI Wendy Thompson to destroy evidence, a killer threatens her and her parents' lives—forcing her to accept the protection of her crush, former vice cop turned bodyguard Hart Fisher.

To get CSI Wendy Thompson to destroy evidence, a killer threatens her and her parents' lives—forcing her to accept the protection of her crush, former vice cop turned bodyguard Hart Fisher.

Read on for a sneak preview of
Evidence of Attraction,
the next book in the Bachelor Bodyguards miniseries by Lisa Childs!

"What the hell are you doing?" she asked as she glanced nervously around.

The curtains swished at the front window of her parents' house. Someone was watching them.

"I'm trying to do my damn job," Hart said through gritted teeth as he very obviously faked a grin.

She'd refused to let him inside the house last night. From the dark circles beneath his eyes, he must not have slept at all. Too bad his daughter's babysitter had arrived at the agency before they'd left. He wouldn't have been able to take Wendy home if he'd had to take care of Felicity.

But even though his babysitter had shown up, the little girl still needed her father—especially since he had full custody. Where was her mother?

"You need a safer job," she told him.

"I'm fine," he said, but his voice lowered even more to a growl of frustration. "It's my assignment that's a pain in the ass."

She smiled—just as artificially as he had. "Then you need another assignment."

He shook his head. "This is the one I have," he said. "So I'm going to make the best of it."

Then he did something she hadn't expected. He lowered his head until his mouth brushed across hers.

Her pulse began to race and she gasped.

And he kissed her again, lingering this time—his lips clinging to hers before he deepened the kiss even more. When he finally lifted his head, she gasped again—this time for breath.

"What the hell was that?" she asked.

He arched his head toward the front window of the house. "For our audience…"

"You're overacting," she said—because she had to remind herself that was all he was doing. Acting…

He wasn't really her boyfriend. He wasn't really attracted to her. He was only pretending.

HRSEXP1119

ROMANTIC suspense

Heart-racing romance, breathless suspense

Can't get enough of Coltons?

Don't miss any of the exhilarating stories from

COLTON 911

Available now

Available December 2019

Harlequin.com

HRSBPA66226

HARLEQUIN®